eighteen
seconds

eighteen
seconds

LOUISE BEECH

First published in 2023 by Mardle Books
15 Church Road
London, SW13 9HE
www.mardlebooks.com

Paperback ISBN 9781837700202
eBook ISBN 9781837700271

A CIP catalogue record for this book is available from the British Library.

Every reasonable effort has been made to trace copyright-holders of
material reproduced in this book, but if any have been inadvertently
overlooked the publishers would be glad to hear from them.

Printed in the UK

10 9 8 7 6 5 4 3 2 1

All names – aside from those of my close family – have been changed.

To protect the innocent.

Note from the author

When I started this book, it was just for me. Just an exploration of my past; of buried trauma; of the shocking violent act that defined 2019; of surviving it all. I wasn't sure I would submit it for publication. I began before everything changed. Before Covid-19 put us into lockdown. Halfway through, I was not only chronicling my childhood and how it created the adult and writer I became, my mother's suicide attempts and alcoholism, and its impact on the family, but also the pandemic that brought the world to a halt. That inspired me to share my story. I realised that I was writing the most universal tale of all; one of survival, of remembering, and of forgiveness. A story of stories that happen as you write them. Mine. And maybe a little bit of yours.

The wound is the place
where the light gets in – Rumi

PREFACE

Once upon an 'around that time'

A BBC radio presenter once asked me when I started writing. The answer was easy enough; it was one I'd given many times, in varying ways, during my career as an author. The next question surprised me though.

'And what was happening around that time?'

I'd never thought about that.

What *had* been happening around that time? I tried to think. It felt like seconds ticked by too fast, the radio silence getting fatter and louder, the gap between his question mark and my answer stretching endlessly

'We had to go and live somewhere else,' I said eventually, knowing how vague my words were, and that the listeners wouldn't know the *we* was supposed to mean my three siblings and I. When we tell our own stories – because they are so familiar to us – we presume everyone knows these characters as intimately as we do, and forget to explain. In short, our own truths make us lazy writers.

'I mean my sisters, brother, and me,' I said, trying harder. *Claire, Grace, Colin,* I could have added, but the editor in me kept their privacy. 'We didn't have much time – not even the chance to grab a favourite toy – before we went with this strange woman in a yellow car.'

The realisation haunted me long after I left the radio station; I had started writing – *properly* writing, not just in my head but on scraps of paper – after my mother's first suicide attempt, when we were separated from her, suddenly and without explanation, for six months. Then, when I later had notepads, I'd record stories in lavish detail there.

Looking back, most of the necessary skills were already in place.

I loved to read, and I'd been making stories up in my head since I was tiny. I inherited my mother's fluency with language and was fascinated with how the arrangement of musical notes on my father's sheet music became a melody. I could walk into a room and get a sense of who was happy, who was sad, who was a threat, who was trustworthy, and what people were trying to hide. I was invisible because I often felt too shy to speak. I would smile with concealed teeth (something I got berated for) and put my words away, the way we do special biscuits for a worthy guest. I liked my own company, and I had a ridiculously vivid and wild imagination.

These skills are perfectly suited to writing.

Of course, I didn't know that then. I only knew how absolutely right and absolutely natural it felt to open a notepad and put down words. I could trust in it. It gave back what I put into it. It listened to me. No one told me I was good at it, but that didn't matter because something unfurled in me when I wrote.

I had a voice.

It felt like a gift.

But a gift can't be used until the wrapping is torn away and my mother's first suicide attempt was that rip. I was nine years old.

1

Not Wordsworth's daffodils

I wandered lonely as a cloud
That floats on high o'er vales and hills,
When all at once I saw a crowd,
A host, of golden daffodils. – **William Wordsworth**

I was never supposed to see the daffodils.

It was dawn. Earlier than when I usually arrived at the river. And I was the lonely Wordsworth cloud that happened upon a crowd of daffodils. Mine didn't dance or flutter though; mine were still; dazzling but inert against the dull curls of February mist.

I wasn't supposed to be there, pausing by the river, pulling my headphones from my ears for a moment, wanting all my senses present. I wasn't supposed to have been captivated by four flowers huddled close, protecting one another from something I couldn't see. I eternalised them with a photo at 8.38am on 28th February 2019, intending to Instagram it, perhaps later, but never doing so.

I was supposed to be at home, doing laundry, responding to emails, trying to write.

I saw them because of a parcel.

Half an hour earlier, my husband Joe and I had been arguing about it.

'Are you home all day today?' he called from the bathroom.

'Nope,' I said.

He came downstairs, dressed for work. 'I thought you were writing.'

'I am.'

It was a fib. I was in that strange place between books; like a foster child awaiting a new family. I wasn't sure what I wanted to write next and felt lost. I had this flickering idea of a ghost story set in a theatre, but I hadn't yet written a word.

'I've got a parcel coming,' Joe said, 'and they haven't specified a time. Can you stay in all day for it?'

'I have to go for my walk,' I said.

'You don't *have* to.'

'I do. It's good for my sanity.'

I'd been to a mental health wellbeing day at work the previous afternoon where it had been discussed how important physical exercise is in enhancing our emotional mood. I was a theatre usher. I loved that the job fit around being an author and the front of house staff were such great friends.

'Your sanity.' Joe smiled, quite rightly mocking me.

'I have to cling to what bit I have.'

After the wellbeing day, I'd gone as a guest on Fiona Mills' BBC Radio Humberside Unheard and Uncensored show. She is a dear friend, and we go back many years to when we volunteered at a community radio station. Her star was now on the ascent and her show was breaking rules and livening up the airwaves with its weekly discussion of taboo topics rarely heard on radio. She's a bit of a witch is Fiona. She *knows* things. She looks past my always-in-place smile and says in her glorious Irish accent, 'You're worried about something, aren't you, sweetheart?' Or 'Something good is coming, I can feel it.'

She's always right.

That night she studied me and simply said, 'You're sad.'

I was. I didn't know if it was the wellbeing course that had affected my mood. Is it irony that a wellbeing day had made me feel worse?

'Surely one day won't matter,' said Joe, bringing me back into the present.

'One day what?'

'Not doing your walk.'

I did one every day. My routine was to set off at 9.30am and walk along the River Humber. It was the only hour when I truly switched off, when my anxieties floated away on the water. Then, invigorated, I'd write for a few hours, before going to work in the evening.

'I'm *not* missing it,' I insisted.

He was obviously thinking of a way around this challenge as he got his keys and coat. I was being stubborn, the way you are after almost twenty years of marriage. It's a game you play. I love Joe to bits. He's patient and kind and we laugh like schoolkids together, but that doesn't mean I give him an easy time.

'Would you go now?'

'Go where now?' I asked, thinking he wanted me to leave.

I'm always prepared to leave. Always have half of me ready to be moved along; to detach quickly from whatever I have become attached to and reattach elsewhere. I am constantly testing Joe, because I have to know he'll stay. I guess I want to make sure he can deal with the ugliest, rawest, realest me. In case one day I remember every part of her; in case the shameful secrets she shares with me are too much for him.

'For your walk,' said Joe.

Oh. Yes. My walk.

'*Now*?' I was still in my dressing gown. I had hair like Brian May on a wild morning. No make-up on. It was 8:15am.

'If you go now, I'll wait for the parcel and go to work when you get back.'

I considered it. I get nervous at sudden changes of routine. I have to mentally assess how it will affect everything else. How the dominos will fall. Joe's request was perfectly reasonable, and I suddenly felt great affection for him, this man who never lets me down.

'Okay, I'll go now,' I said.

'Thank you,' he said.

And so, there I was, standing with the shivering, hopeful-yellow daffodils at the crack of dawn, still no make-up and hair like a Queen guitarist after eight gigs. I felt like I was the only person in the world who could see them. Like maybe I'd imagined them. Made them up, as I do stories. Not Wordsworth's daffodils; *mine*. I'm not sure how long they kept me, but for the next five minutes of my walk along the chalky beach and under the Humber Bridge, I couldn't get them out of my head.

And then I forgot them.

The way you do when so much else is on your mind.

That afternoon I pottered about. I wanted desperately to write – to calm a niggling sense of unease I couldn't explain – but the flickering idea of a theatre ghost story remained hidden, a shy actress offstage and afraid to walk on. I listened to music, shared some reviews of my latest novel, responded to emails and started writing lists for my trip the following week to London; but I don't know exactly what I was doing when my sister Claire's name lit up my phone.

I do know that I didn't want to answer. I do know that – much like those dreaded middle-of-the-night-phone-calls – it filled me with unease. I do know that it was 1.07pm and I thought, *but she's at work, it must be important.*

As Claire spoke, I saw the deer Grace and I had seen two days ago. I saw us laughing on one of our long walks in the country, climbing stiles, crossing fields. I saw us as two children for a moment, being silly, recording ourselves having one of our random conversations about words of the week or witchcraft in the woods, planning to share it on social media and make people laugh. I saw us stop dead in our tracks. Saw me look down. Saw Grace recoil. Saw the huge deer, broken, cold, eyes wide open and milky with absence of life. I often have signs in my novels. Coincidences. Some readers have said they are far-fetched. But they're inspired by what I've experienced. It's all there if you look for it. The deer was stone-cold dead. I had said to Grace, 'I have *such* a bad feeling about this.'

Then I was back in my living room.

I heard Claire's voice.

I wanted her to tell me that she'd had a good day, that her health was on the up.

What she said instead was: 'Mother jumped off the Humber Bridge.'

2

There's power in patience

*Giving a single daffodil
as a gift predicts misfortune.*

Don't look back yet. Wait a bit longer.

I had a scene in my head, just now. Three girls, in a window, waiting for a yellow car. Two small ones, excited and bouncy; one older, more cautious, knowing and hating knowing. Fingers on the pane, net curtains in disarray, a voice from the kitchen telling them not to get the glass dirty.

But I'm not ready for it in full.

Not yet.

In many of my novels I waited several chapters before sweeping readers back to a time that was most painful.

There's power in patience.

Let the reader live in the present for longer. Let them get comfortable. Let them get settled in this *now* place, look around, see and hear and feel it, before you whisk them back to previous times relevant to the story. If we get to know a person – as they are, here and now – we're all the more curious about their background. Hungry for history. Desperate for deeper delving. This kind of delay can make for a stronger opening to a novel. I learnt this the hard way, with lots of editing and revisions.

But this is different.

It isn't a novel.

This is my story. No fiction to hide behind.

My novels have been commented upon for being character led. The truth is that I listen carefully to my characters' voices and try to give them equal airtime. I want those who whisper to be heard as much as those who push through more roughly and shout. Some of these individuals are people often not listened to by the world. There is ten-year-old Conor, a boy in care trying to find his true place in the world. There is nine-year-old Rose, struggling with a cruel condition that turns her world upside down. There is twenty-year-old Sebastian, autistic and looking for love. I let them tell their stories through me.

But they've gone quiet now.

And I know why.

I can almost hear them softly stepping aside, nudging me to get typing. This time though, I can't write everyone's story; I can only tell mine. I'll listen to my uncle and my brother and my sisters too; their words are scattered throughout. It's taken a long time to write this story because when I was a child, my voice was silenced.

I have another scene in my head. A woman in a daffodil-yellow dressing gown with a zip all the way up the front, face red with tears. A girl of six kneeling at her feet, trying hard to make her laugh, feeling the weight of responsibility for her happiness.

Soon I'm going to have to sweep back – not to the fictional histories of made-up characters, but to my own childhood. I'm not thinking of you the reader here; not trying to delay in the name of setting up a great story. I'm just nervous. I can hear the past whispering to me, now I'm thinking about it, and I'm afraid to listen. Because one of those whisperers is the child inside me.

And I'm terrified she knows everything I can't remember.

3

But for that parcel...

We have short time to stay, as you, we have as short a spring. **– To Daffodils by Robert Herrick**

I realised Claire had said first, 'She's OK,' like she was trying to reassure me before she said, 'Mother jumped off the Humber Bridge,' but the heart hears what it hears. The heart wants what it wants. I would say that to our mother, in a future I didn't yet know, in a thoughtful moment, and – high as a kite – she would say, 'Don't be so fucking ridiculous.'

I don't know if Claire said it again.

Mother jumped off the Humber Bridge.

Maybe I just heard an echo. The gap after her words felt like the one on the radio where I had to recall what had been happening when I was nine and started writing. Everything tried to fill the void. A kaleidoscope of images. I saw us as children, being whisked away to our grandma's house. I saw my mother the last time I'd seen her, days ago, from a car, crossing the road, looking gaunt and sad. It felt like everything that had ever happened had led to this single moment at 1.07pm on 28th February 2019.

Then came my questions.

'She's OK then?' I asked. 'When did it happen? How is she? *Where* is she? Who told you?'

'Colin just rang me,' explained Claire. 'The police rang him.'

'The police?'

'Yes. I think they went to the scene and then in the ambulance with her.'

The scene. I didn't want to picture that.

Claire's voice was flat – clearly the numbness of shock – as she relayed answers to my barrage of questions. Someone had found our mother, perhaps one of those people who patrol the bridge. She hadn't been there long. She had jumped onto a path, not into the water. Was this better, worse? Did it matter? She was alive. I waited for the feelings to bombard me like the questions were my head.

Then Claire said it had likely happened mid-morning.

And I thought about the parcel. The parcel that hadn't arrived yet, that I was supposed to stay in all day for. The one I now realised had kept me from walking under the bridge at my usual time. My usual time that might have been the moment when my mother walked up to the bridge. Stood on the bridge. Jumped from the bridge.

Hit the ground.

'How is she, do we know?' I asked.

'They said she has life-changing injuries.'

I didn't even know what that meant. It didn't sound good.

'Where is she?' I asked.

'Hull Royal Infirmary. I don't know where exactly. Which ward. I guess she'll be at the Emergency department. Colin is on his way there now.'

Poor Colin, I thought. *He can't be there on his own. It's too horrible.* Claire lives in Grantham, a good hour and a half from my hometown of Hessle, just outside Hull. She has two children, was at work. I knew that even if she could leave there and then, she wouldn't be here fast.

'Does Grace know?' I asked, suddenly thinking of our other sister.

'I rang and rang her mobile, but there's no answer. She won't have it with her at work, will she?'

Grace worked at a medical centre as a nurse practitioner, so likely could only look at her phone occasionally through the day. She hadn't worked there long and had been so excited when she got the job.

'I'll try calling her now,' I said. 'We should go to the hospital.'

'Yes. Depending how Mother is, I'll see if I can come later today.' I felt for Claire being far away from us. Having to take this in but unable to do anything.

I hung up. Paced the room, not wanting to tell Grace. Wanting to keep her safe from this horrible, violent, shocking news. But I couldn't. Like Claire had, I rang Grace's mobile, only for it to keep going to the message service. Eventually I called the medical centre she worked at. The receptionist went and found Grace. My heart was in my mouth. An overused cliché, but it really was. When I heard her voice, I felt as Claire must have done – distraught that I was the bearer of such news.

'She's OK,' I prefaced as Claire had, 'but Mother jumped off the Humber Bridge.'

'Oh my God.' Grace's voice was soft. I remember that. 'I saw all your missed calls when the receptionist said you were on the phone. I knew it couldn't be good. Where is she, Hull Royal?'

I passed on everything Claire had told me.

'We should go to the hospital,' Grace said. 'I'll come for you now.'

I rang Joe while I waited for her, if only to stop myself thinking too much. I told him the horrible news. Still I felt numb. He sounded more distressed than either of my sisters had; and more than I felt. Perhaps his biological distance from the woman who was his mother-in-law permitted that ability to feel it immediately, full on. He was kind, the way he always is; calm, no nonsense, no drama. As soon as I'd hung up, I realised I'd meant to ask him not to tell our kids yet. Conor lived in Mansfield with his girlfriend Ieva, and Katy was in her first year at Lincoln University. There was no need to distress them yet. My instinct to protect them from harm hadn't faded because they were grown up and gone.

I was still wearing my scruffy walking clothes, my hair wild, my face bare of foundation. Should I tidy myself up? Which shade of lipstick and which outfit was suitable for a trip to the hospital to see whatever was left of my mother? Make-up has always been my armour. If the exterior is presentable, nerves and anxieties are not as apparent. But I didn't have time.

Grace arrived half an hour later.

She has since said that she remembers little about the moments after I told her. Only that she must have looked stunned because a co-worker's kind hand landed on her shoulder, and guided her into their boss's office, where people offered to drive her to where she needed to be. Seeing her waiting outside my house brought up many emotions. I saw our trips; joyful adventures. The times we had laughed uproariously as we headed off on a long country walk. Yet this bleak journey felt like it had been a long time coming. I braced myself. Fastened my coat. And joined her.

Our humour never fails us.

It didn't then.

'This is an inconvenience,' said Grace. 'I'd just microwaved me dinner.'

'I know. They could have called us *after* we'd eaten. And I hope there's food at the hozzo if it gets to teatime or I'll savage someone.'

When someone undertook her on the dual carriageway, Grace yelled, 'Where do you think you're going? Did *your* mum jump off a bridge?'

When our laughter dried up and we fell silent, she said, 'I knew Mother was depressed. But I didn't think it was this bad. What possessed her? To go up and there… and *jump*. It's awful.'

How could any of us have known?

'She must have really wanted to die,' I said. 'No one jumps from that height and expects to live. How the fuck is she still alive?' I couldn't get my head around it. It was an actual miracle. The stuff of angels or God. 'That woman is made of titanium. She'll outlive us all.'

I can't remember where we left the car. I can't remember walking into the hospital. The next thing I do remember is being met by two police officers at the secure entrance to the emergency department's temporary cubicles. It came to me that we had been here before, for Grace. If I had started to think about her emotional breakdown that night, I might have turned around and walked away.

Grace recalls now that one of the police officers was tall, fair-haired and more naïve-looking, and the other was dark, well-built and seemed authoritative in attitude. Apparently, he took it upon himself to do more of the talking – in a forthright manner, my brother recalls. We could see through the glass doors that Colin was inside, in a cubicle, presumably with our mother. After a while he came out.

Colin: *I was at work when the call came in, I think at about midday. It was a Hull number, but not one I recognised. Funnily enough, as I picked it up, I did think there was something odd or wrong about it. When a male voice asked if that was Colin, I knew something was up. He said it was Humberside Police, that my mother was in hospital, that she'd jumped from the Humber Bridge. I think I remember asking, is she alive, and he said yes, yes, she is. I walked around the office aimlessly, which is strange because I knew I had to leave. I knew I'd have to ask my boss if I could go and wasn't sure whether to just say, my mum jumped off the bridge, or I have a family emergency. In the end, I just left and messaged someone. There were two police officers outside the emergency room. I got a sense that they were shocked by my reaction, because me being me, I just asked straightforward questions: is she dead, what kind of state is she in, can we* *see her? I think they expected me to be running around, wailing, with my hands in the air, which – to be fair – would have been much funnier. They warned me that she had some serious injuries. And then I went in.*

'How is she?' I asked Colin.

'OK. They're still doing things to her. We might have to wait a bit to go back in.' I realised he was holding a Catherine Cookson novel – *The Tide of Life* – and a dark green Parka jacket that I recognised as our mother's. 'Someone gave them to me,' he explained. 'Mother was wearing this, and she took the book up to the bridge with her.'

We found out at some point – perhaps then, from the police officers, perhaps later – that she had left them at the top by the railing, with her brown shoes, before jumping. I could see them as clearly as if I had been there; the jacket neatly folded, shoes side by side, book on top. It was a cold day. I wondered why she had taken them off. I wondered why that book in particular. Was she reading it?

No. She had said she was too anxious to read.

I realised again that I'd almost been there to see it happen. I wondered absentmindedly if Joe's parcel had arrived, since my departure from the house, and with no one to sign for it. Where would they put it?

'What do we know?' Grace asked the police.

'She left a letter,' the darker-haired one said. 'On the kitchen table.'

They had been to her house. Already. *With* her? No, that didn't make sense.

'Where is it?' one of us asked, I can't be sure who.

'We have to keep it for now. If she survives, it will be returned to her, and she can decide whether she shares it with you or not. If not...' He paused. 'Well, then it will be given to you.'

I wanted to see it. I wanted to know what she wanted her last words to be. What did I hope they were? An acknowledgement of the things she had done? An admission of her part in our neglect? An apology? Perhaps just *I love you* would be enough.

'When did it happen?' I asked.

'We think this morning,' said the dark officer. 'Maybe around ten-thirty.'

I could have been there, I thought again.

The officer said that it was only because she had left her things at the top that someone found her. It probably saved her because it's quite deserted where she fell. That person – one of the workers on the bridge – went down to where she was, covered her in his coat, and comforted her. Then he called an ambulance. She was fully conscious. The officer insisted that she wasn't like that for long, as though to reassure us, but we'd never know if it was true. She could have been there hours.

Then, more gently, he said, 'It happens a lot. People going up there. That's why they patrol the bridge. But people rarely do it.'

'What do they mean by life-changing injuries?' I asked.

Apparently her leg was shattered. Her back too. There were probably internal injuries. I tried to picture it. How high had it been? How had she jumped? Looking down. Looking up. Backwards. Facing the ground. Did she scream?

As though hearing my thoughts, he said, 'She went feet first. That may be why she survived.'

'I can't imagine what possessed her,' I said. 'She hates heights. She clings on like a bloody maniac on an escalator.'

'Was she very depressed?' the fairer police officer asked.

Colin explained that Mother was under the care of the mental health team, though they had been unable to get her into a mental health unit because there were no beds; Grace said that she had made a suicide attempt with pills two weeks ago; I added that she had been ill since Christmas, that she'd suffered with depression on and off all her adult life but hadn't had it this bad for a long time.

'You couldn't have known,' said the fair-haired officer.

'Known what?' I asked, dumbly.

'That she would do something like this.'

I knew he was trying to make us feel better. But I still felt numb. I definitely didn't feel guilty. With a certainty that only comes with experience, I knew this wasn't our fault. My mother was on her own path.

Then, finally, we could go in to where she was. It's often two to a bed (visitors not patients!) on a ward, but I imagine that due to the situation – the fact that she still might die – they overlooked protocol. Thankfully, she was covered with a plain sheet, but awake. When the sheet moved, I saw her leg was bandaged. Her neck was in a brace. I remember her nose and forehead were crimson and that I wanted to wipe the blood away. Some of her teeth were missing, so when she spoke it sounded like she was drunk. An IV drip snaked from a bag of fluid into her arm, replacing fluids lost due to shock and blood loss. She had a tube up her nose too, oxygen, Grace said, and a probe attached to her finger to measure vitals, which kept coming off.

In one hand she held rosary beads.

They were broken.

Grace was kind, and went into her natural nurse mode, voice soothing and manner practical. Finally, for me, some emotions arrived, like late mourners sneaking in at the back of the church twenty minutes after the ceremony has begun. I cried, quietly, not to make a scene. I don't even think anyone noticed.* I didn't want them to. Didn't want to draw attention to myself. I wiped the tears away with my sleeve. I could identify my feelings now – pity, sadness, and anger – but I wouldn't let them overwhelm me. I still felt disconnected from them.

I suddenly had a vivid memory; me, aged fifteen, telling my mother I felt depressed. Her, angry. Telling me I'd no idea what depression was, no right to use that word, and to never again use it to describe how I felt.

When your feelings are dismissed, ignored or belittled as a child you end up burying them so deeply that in adulthood you can't access them easily. There's then a fear that they'll overwhelm you. Destroy you. Now I asked myself questions to access them. Did I love my mother as she lay on that hospital bed? Yes. Was I heartbroken that she'd felt so desperate that she had walked up to the bridge and jumped off? Yes. Was it awful to see her broken like that? Yes. Did I want her to feel better? Yes.

Was I angry?

Fuck, yes.

My mother was in great danger. But she had put me in great danger too. She had done that to me, *and* to my siblings, many times over. And when the one person who's supposed to make sure you are safe – supposed to put you before everything else – does that, it's difficult to forget it, even if you can forgive it.

Even when she might still die.

*My brother read this and messaged to say, 'I noticed,' which touched me deeply.

4

Looking at the wolf

A house with daffodils in it is a house lit up, whether or not the sun be shining outside. – **AA Milne.**

Every story we tell is a version.

For many years, I viewed my entire childhood as a *version*. The one I was given, by my mother, by my father. When I was small, I felt I existed quietly as a character in the story they created.

My mother, with a glorious flair for language, told her tale in an eloquent and descript way, shining so brightly that I believed every word; she was the perfect mother, she loved us dearly, and we were the most adored and cared for children in the world.

My father told his tale the way he saw it, sparsely, practical, with less detail. I've also read myself as a version written down in detached documents by social workers. I've heard stories from the mouths of my grandparents and other relatives.

Which tale is true?

They all are, to the people telling them.

My story, of course, is only *my* version.

Novels are a version too. I've been asked many times how I write them – do I plot carefully or do I fly by the seat of my pants? I fly. I've seen some incredible author pictures on social media;

17

rows of daffodil-yellow Post-it notes on walls, notepads filled with hundreds of careful bullet points, large sheets of paper covered in words. And I've thought, should I be doing this? It looks like the right way to do it. But I've learnt that there is no right or wrong way. Only what works for you. And with each of my own books I simply set off – characters clearly visible but no map in my hand, no guide, few notes – and I found the story by writing it.

In a way, I'll have to do that this time too.

It's time to listen to the child I've ignored; the child who was voiceless; the child who was sad and had to hide it; who was hurt physically, mentally, emotionally, and sexually but never spoke out; who was angry and had to suppress that too. Some of it I'm going to have to remember first.

I know the general story. There's no need to plot. I know me. I know the basic facts: my name, where I was born, where I lived, what food I like. But I don't know all of it. My sisters hold the key to some parts; my brother can open the door on others. As I go further back in time – delve deeper – I may have to refer to photographs, to the care records we got years ago when seeking answers, to medical records.

The most difficult part is the buried memories.

Am I ready to go there?

I don't know.

It's like looking at the wolf in the woods.

I think the reason it can take until our forties, fifties, or even beyond to look back at abuse is because we need distance. When a wolf chases you – snarling, drooling and evil – your first instinct is to run. To run and run and run. Escape. Not look back. Find a safe place. A safe house. Once inside that house, you lock the door and shut the curtains. You don't look outside. You're too afraid. You can still hear the wolf so you stay inside your house until you think it's gone. Even then, you daren't look out of the window to make sure. You pretend it's gone; make yourself *believe* it's gone. But it never has. It circles the house until you feel strong enough to open the door and face it.

This is my version.

It's finally time to open the door and look at the wolf.

5

Dancing on the ceiling

Tradition holds that if a daffodil is forced to bloom for the Chinese New Year, it will bring luck to the whole household.

We were in that tiny hospital cubicle with our mother for endless hours: my brother, my sister, and me. At least it felt that way but looking back it's hard to remember exactly how long it was. Such places are timeless; a void. There were no windows onto the outside world. We didn't see it grow dark, didn't see if the clouds dispersed, didn't see the rush-hour traffic build. That room was our world. It was our mother lying flat, awake, and surprisingly coherent. It was a beeping machine. Bags of fluids dangling from a hook. Wires and tubes that led to her body. It was cupboards full of blue gloves and sharps bins and vials and other medical regalia. It was a frail old man in a bed opposite, clearly injured and groaning at inopportune moments. It was staff rushing along corridors, alarms going off.

Grace took Mother's hand in hers and said kindly, 'You'll be OK now. You're in a safe place. They'll take care of you. There's no need to worry.'

Our mother seemed high, which is understandable with the painkillers pumping through her shattered body. She didn't have the dull expression and vacant eyes of recent weeks. Since

Christmas — so for two months — she had looked frail. Depression is often visible in every move; in a slower walk, in speech that takes effort, in lack of appetite, in restlessness that prevents sleep.

'I've done a terrible thing,' she said reverently. 'I'm a wicked person. I'm going to hell, aren't I?' A Catholic upbringing sticks.

'No,' said Colin, a resolute atheist. 'You're not going anywhere. Except maybe home once they fix you up again.'

I'm not sure what I believe. I'm not an atheist. I think there must be… *something*. I can't imagine that this is it. Just us. Just the physical. Too many curious things beyond any logical explanation have happened in my life. What are we made of beyond flesh and bone? Where does our soul go when we die? Is it all just a random mess or is there some meaning to it all?

'If there is a God,' I added, 'he surely won't be so cruel as to condemn someone in abject misery to the horrors of hell. Anyway, you're not dead yet.'

'But it's a sin,' she insisted, and I almost started singing the Pet Shop Boys anthem. 'The greatest of all the sins.'

'No, there are worse,' Colin pointed out. 'Murder is probably worse.'

'But I haven't killed anyone,' she said, confused.

'No, you haven't,' said Grace. Pause. 'As far as we know anyway.'

'Only myself,' Mother said.

'No, you failed,' said Grace. 'And I don't think God can do you for that.'

'I'm not dead now, am I?'

'No. You survived,' I said simply.

It was still hard to believe. Our mother must have jumped more than forty feet; maybe fifty. Onto concrete. I knew from my research for my fifth book that falls from higher than forty feet have a 50 percent chance of death; that the average lethal distance is forty-eight feet; that landing on your side is the best way to survive; headfirst, the least good.

I was a fall specialist.

Having gone feet first, Mother could have landed on her side. But why feetfirst? Had she not actually wanted to die? Was it a cry for help? No. It couldn't be. Who would do something so extreme for that? I needed to see the exact spot. I needed to see where she had stood, thinking of doing it. Where she had put down her shoes and book and coat and climbed over railings and jumped.

But not yet.

Sometimes I think I write my life before it happens; that I can remember what *will* happen more than what *has* happened. In that fifth novel, I'd described a character contemplating what would happen if she fell from her window. Those words haunted me in the cubicle with my mother that day.

The doctor who regularly came in and out of our mother's cubicle – checking her leg and reading her vitals – looked about fifteen. He spoke so softly that we had to ask him to repeat what he had said a few times. It got embarrassing, so we just guessed what we were all agreeing too, and then tried to piece together the syllables after he had gone. We understood that she needed a full scan to assess for internal injuries. Then they would know what needed to be done. For now, they were keeping her alive; keeping her comfortable.

'Why are you all standing sideways like that,' she said suddenly. 'It looks like you're all on the ceiling.'

Another song came to me – Lionel Ritchie's 'Dancing on the Ceiling'.

'It's because you're lying down,' explained Colin, 'and that might be making you disorientated.'

'Why am I lying down? When can I get up?'

The frail old man in the bed opposite groaned.

'Not right now,' said Grace.

'And I'm definitely not dead?'

'If you are,' I said, 'we all must be too.'

'Including him,' said Grace of the old man opposite.

I had so many questions. Why had she chosen the bridge? What time had it been? Why that Catherine Cookson book in particular? What had she written in that final note left on the kitchen table? But now was not the time.

'What are we still waiting here for?' asked Mother casually, like we were in the queue for a hair appointment.

'They're going to get you scanned,' explained Grace.

'But I'm thirsty,' Mother said.

'There are fluids going directly into you.'

'My throat hurts. I need a drink.'

'It's probably shock,' said Grace. 'I don't think you can drink in case they have to operate.'

This made me sad. More than the whole situation. More than the dark reason we were there. That she was thirsty. Sometimes I think when a trauma is this huge, we can't take it all in. Instead, the system reacts to something small.

'Speaking of thirsty,' said Colin. 'Does anyone want anything? I'll go to the machine, make a few phone calls.'

He disappeared for a while. Probably needed it. Understandable.

We had tried to get Mother committed. Tried to get her a bed on a mental health ward. But there were none. The country was in dire shortage. Mental health teams were stretched to breaking point through lack of funding. It was a different world to the one eighteen years earlier when Mother had last been depressed and was admitted to a hospital straight away. This time she had gone to casualty late one night, begging for help. There was none. She then stayed with a friend, and with me. Even a suicide attempt with pills two weeks ago hadn't meant a bed.

It had been a Sunday night. I was watching *The Voice UK*, tired after a lovely day visiting my daughter Katy in Lincoln and meeting her boyfriend for the first time. When Colin rang, my heart sank. Not my usual reaction to him, but I knew that at this time of night it wouldn't be something good.

'Just got off the phone to Mother,' he informed me. 'She sounds odd.'

'Odder than usual, I take it?'

'Yeah, not drunk. Just... *odd*. I'm a bit concerned to be honest. I feel I should go and check her.'

'Pick me up,' I had said. 'I'll come too.'

When we got there, I realised that Colin's assessment of odd was an accurate one. She definitely wasn't drunk – something we'd have known after forty years of her drinking – but neither was she sober, for want of a better word. She was vacant. Calm. Seemingly OK, the evidence of a meal there, and the TV on: *The Voice UK*, which I knew she hated. We spoke with her for a while, and came away, not entirely satisfied but sure she was safe. I looked in the window as we left, and she was staring at the TV like a zombie, which upset me; it made me feel as helpless as I had when I was a child.

It turned out that that afternoon she had taken enough medication to kill a horse. But then woken up. Alive. Still. Her oddness had presumably been the lingering effects of that. We hoped that relaying this to the mental health team would mean she got more help. It didn't.

Now Colin came back to the cubicle with bottles of Coke, which we hid from Mother, feeling bad for her thirst. We moved around the small space, taking turns to sit, taking turns to rummage through cupboards, to play with the gloves, to make the usual jokes. I imagined what it would look like if someone filmed us from above and time-lapsed the whole thing. I tried to think who else needed to know she was here, what else I should be doing.

After a while she slept and the three of us went to the hospital café. Nice food, not much atmosphere. Wouldn't give it more than three stars on Tripadvisor. We ate out of necessity. I was on a low carb regime, so for me the choices were limited.

'If I get even fatter,' I said, choosing a cookie, 'I'm blaming her.'

Colin tapped away on his phone.

'Are you going to work tomorrow?' I asked Grace.

'Probably not. Do you think it's OK to ring in sick for something like this?'

'I'm not sure.' I genuinely wasn't. Should I just pile on the make-up, smile as always, and march on? Sometimes I'm so worried about doing what makes everyone else happy that I forget what I want; forget what is normal.

'I won't be,' said Colin, practical as ever. I could measure my what-you're-supposed-to-do by him.

'Me neither then,' said Grace.

I was supposed to be working the *Walk Like A Man* show the following night – it was a musical journey through the career of Frankie Valli and The Four Seasons. For all the many things I forget, this I remember, strangely enough. I was anxious because I knew it would have sold out, and that every single usher would be needed.

I hate letting people down. Even sitting in a hospital café, with my mother desperately ill, I felt I should go in. But I couldn't. I paused over how to word the message to my boss. What do you say in these circumstances? Pussyfoot around it? Pretty it up with silly euphemisms? In the end I sent:

I'm so sorry, but I won't be able to work the 6.45pm shift tomorrow night as my mother jumped off the Humber Bridge. She's been depressed. She's alive but not good. Just waiting for surgery. So sorry. Letting you know well in advance. Can you tell A or J in case they need to know? I don't mind you telling them why.

His kind reply brought tears to my eyes and validated that it was acceptable to take a night off for this. I still had my big awards event in London next week, and then a book tour, but I couldn't think about that yet.

'Do you think she still might die?' I asked Grace.

'Who?'

I smiled.

'Yes.' Grace paused. 'And then we can get more time off.'

Nothing is off-limits with our humour. People have occasionally been shocked at it. But without it the four of us would likely be in a variety of asylums across the country.

We headed back to Mother's temporary bed, using the toilets on the way. In the harsh glare, I looked like I hadn't slept for a year.

'Why do they insist on this awful blue lighting?' I asked Grace.

'To make it more difficult for drug users to inject into their veins,' she said.

'Bet they don't have it in the staff toilets.'

Mother's bed was empty. I thought about my question earlier. *Do you think she still might die?* I tend to plan the practicalities before I think about how I feel. I imagined taking our mother's shoes and book and jacket home. Putting them on the table in my back room. Finding them there in the morning. Telling everyone she had gone. That on her third serious attempt, she had succeeded.

We looked at one another. The frail old man in the bed opposite moaned. I was sure he was purposefully making it sound sexual.

Turns out Mother had just gone for a scan.

6

A ruined jumper

Daffodil bulbs contain poisonous crystals
and can make your pets sick.

Here we are at chapter six.

Around the point where in my novels I previously swept readers back to a wartime South Atlantic Sea and to teenagers playing a dark game. Am I ready to look back? Have I let you get settled in the now enough? I think so.

My earliest memory is of almost drowning.

It's 1974. There's a field. A river. In Wales. It's summer. There's a girl. Me, aged three-and-a-half, wearing a yellow jumper that my grandma had knitted, with blonde curls and a red plastic handbag across my chest. We were on holiday. My mum, my father and me.

I was an only child, though my mum was five months pregnant, and I was excited about having a little brother or sister. We were staying in a cottage with the family who lived in the house opposite ours; I remember wooden stairs, and my bedroom being at the top, and a new flowery nightie that had an itchy lace collar, and a daddy-long-legs on the wall as I ate beans on toast alone at a table.

But that day, we were in a field.

It can't have been hot, or else why was I wearing such a thick jumper. I was a quiet child who did as she was told, so I doubt I had demanded to wear it because of the pretty colour or it being a favourite.

My parents and the other two adults were far across the field, sitting, enjoying a picnic. Distance is different to a child. It could have been a small field; it could have been vast. My perception was that they were miles away. I was playing with our neighbours' son along the tree-lined, muddy banks of a large stream. He was about eight, which seemed old to me. We had sticks and were playing some sort of game that involved finding what we could on the ground.

I don't quite know how I ended up in the water.

The banks sloped gently down, and I must have lost my footing. The next I knew I was in the stream. I don't remember panicking at first. I remember seeing leaves and twigs and bubbles floating in the brown before my eyes. I sank down on my back, looking up, the bottom sucking at me like someone had pulled a plug out. That was when I began to panic. I don't know how deep it was. Maybe only a few feet, which would be deep to me. I remember knowing – without a scrap of self-pity – that I must save myself. No one was coming for me.

Now, this makes me sad.

Now I'm an adult who looks back on that small kid and sees how at risk she was in that moment; how she could have drowned.

The rest is a blur. Did I surface? I think so. Somehow. Gasping and scared. Did I sink again? I'm sure I did. I'd not had swimming lessons so I have no idea how I managed to get back to the river-bank, but the next thing I recall clearly is that I climbed up the slime, clawing at it, panicking when there was nothing to grip onto, terrified I would fall back into the water.

And then I was out.

I expected the world to be in shock as I stood there on the banks, dripping wet and shivering now. But my parents were still at the other side of the field. The boy was staring at me, saying, 'Where did you go?' Then he laughed.

I went across the field to my mum. She fussed and tried to dry me.

'Your lovely jumper is ruined,' she said.

Finally, I cried. Because it was.

And my red bag too.

Later I remember being in the back of our car – before seatbelts and booster seats were law – only being able to see the tops of trees and the sky out of the window, and making stories up like I always did, naming the clouds and the branches, lost in my own safe world.

Edwin (my mum's brother): *There was a time when you, your mother, your father and my mother came up to visit me in Glasgow. I was living in Gibson Street at the time, I was a student then, and you all stayed the night with me. I remember having harsh words with your father. I felt he wasn't being nice to you. I don't recall the exact thing, but I faced off with him. And Grandma told me to settle down. Then we were driving up north towards Loch Lomond and we were tired, and we wanted to stop for ice-cream for you. Your father wouldn't stop. I remember saying that I'd stop the car if he didn't. Eventually we did stop, but he wouldn't pay so Grandma did. I remember pleasant things from that era too, like going to watch your father having a jam session with his band in someone's attic. Ginger Baker was one of their favourites. Your father was a very good guitar player.*

Another early memory I have is of my father trying to show me how to play the guitar. He's a gifted musician. He can pick one up and play anything. His sheet music had fascinated me from a young age; how those little symbols became the haunting music he played. I was maybe three and keen to please when he offered to show me. He sat cross-legged and I sat in his lap, the instrument in my hands, with his fingers guiding mine. But the strings hurt my fingertips. I was surprised; why was it so painful to try and make the music he so effortlessly played? Eventually he gave up. Even now, if I hear anything by The Shadows, particularly 'Apache', I'm there, in that house, his music swirling around me.

He gave me a love a of music, but he didn't try to teach me again.

I've often thought that you can't teach talent. You can either sing or you can't. You can improve the voice you have with practice, but nothing will give you the ability to hit those high notes in tune. I wonder if the knack for playing certain instruments – the piano, the violin, the guitar – is there at birth too. Anyone can learn to go through the motions and play a song; but only some have that indefinable magic when they play, that ability to transcend the chords, to make them into something more.

I had no interest in the guitar.

My love was creating stories. Lying in bed, whispering them aloud in the dark to drown out arguments I could hear downstairs. Having my teddy bears and dolls act the stories out before I had siblings to play with. No one showed me how to do that.

It was all mine.

When I was small, I was fed and warm. There was routine. There were always meals. Birthdays were remembered and there were presents at Christmas. The house we lived in until I was eight was nice; a traditional three-bed-semi, with a long back garden that had trees at the end, and a paved front garden with spiky rose bushes. My father's guitars lined the walls of the chilly front room where I was only allowed to go in the evening for an hour of TV and where I knew I had to be very quiet and very good. There was a bookshelf in the hallway between the back room and the kitchen that I was fascinated by. I longed to be able to read so I could find out what the one with a picture of a strange metal creature on legs was about; it was *The War of the Worlds* by HG Wells.

Yes, it was a nice house. But there was little compassion in it. Few hugs or kisses. No encouragement of boisterous, fun games, no affectionate nicknames.

My father often felt as distant to me as the top of the bookshelf I loved; I couldn't reach him. He fascinated me but I didn't quite understand him. He's always said that he believes children need a roof and food, and that they will find you if they need more. In recent years, we've come to believe he has ASD (autism spectrum disorder). He agrees with the possibility, but due to his mistrust of doctors, and the nature of this condition, he'd never look into being assessed, not that there is an established procedure for diagnosing it in adults.

When he was small, in the 1940s and 1950s, it would never have been something that got picked up because only those with severe symptoms were diagnosed. He is high functioning, with a high IQ, but has always preferred his own company, living a hermit-like life for the last forty years or so, and being absent from our lives for twenty-six years, departing when I was sixteen and returning when I was forty-two.

He met my mum at university; grief bonded them. My mum's dad had just died and my father, who lost his at three, was sympathetic to her pain. They were both intelligent, my father academically, my mum more creative. He worked as an engineer and also played guitar in some big bands in the 1970s; she was a French and English teacher.

She often looked sad to me.

She was also beautiful.

Not just in my adoring child's eyes. I loved my mum the way all small children do; with absolute faith and complete trust. But she was entrancing to others too – the kind of woman people noticed in a full room with her olive skin, dark eyes, and lustrous black hair down her back. When she's happy, she's a captivating talker. When she read stories to me – something that declined with time – I loved hearing *Goodnight Moon* and *Snow White and Rose Red*. She also has a rich sense of humour, one I have her to thank for, for passing on to me and my siblings. Pictures of her back then – and younger – show the truth, that she glowed with vibrancy.

I longed to be like that.

'Unfortunately, you look like your father,' she often told me.

It was true. I inherited his fairer skin, blue eyes and unruly hair. I was a plain child, thin, my curls cut very short, so I looked like a boy. Quiet then too, which many find hard to believe. I brought a school photo home once where I had smiled with my lips together, not showing my teeth. My mum said I looked gormless, grinning like that, and she didn't buy it. It was probably just too expensive but after that I tried to smile properly. To be pretty like she was.

Now, I question why my mum – who knew she was beautiful, who has told us many times – would not see that prettiness in her own child? I believed it was because I was ugly. A few months ago, a friend sent me an article about narcissist mothers. It explained how they see their daughters as both a threat and as a part of themselves, so they criticise and shame them, creating insecurity, while also praising any skills that make them stand out. When I read it, I thought of my mum back then; of how she often made me feel ugly, with her words and actions. But she could also be warm, and she made me laugh.

Narcissistic personality disorder (NPD) is characterised by exaggerated feelings of importance, an intense need for attention and admiration, and a lack of empathy for others. I dismissed the idea; she couldn't possibly be such a thing. But my friend's article had planted a seed.

Another of my earliest memories is trying to cheer her up.

It was often in the back room. She sat on one of the white Formica chairs and I sat at her feet. Her dressing gown was daffo-dil-yellow. A long zip cut the front in half – like if I had pulled on it, she would fall out. Tassels dangled in rows, some threadbare, some entwined. Sometimes she didn't speak but I was an expert in reading her body language. Sadness oozed from her; how she moved, how she sighed, how her eyes were dead. She was often like this, her face pale, her mouth downwards. I chattered away, trying desperately to make her smile. My inability to light her face up made my stomach hurt.

It made me unable to eat, which caused my parents grief.

I sat at the table for hours – a plate of casserole or fish in front of me – and couldn't consume a single mouthful. I was afraid I'd choke but didn't understand why. My father told me I couldn't leave the table until I had eaten. Sometimes it was dark when my parents were finally satisfied that I had done as I was told. But they didn't know I'd hidden most of the food in a pocket of my striped apron. I'd then sneak upstairs and flush the food away in the toilet.

Food seemed to be quite the issue, and this is perhaps why I've had eating disorders over the years. My father liked his food to be 'just right' – a male Goldilocks looking for perfection in his nourishment. He was a perfectionist in all manners, expecting the same of himself as he did others. But it was hard to meet those standards, especially as a small child.

Edwin: *I was visiting Hillcrest Avenue* (the house we lived in) *for a time. We were having something for lunch and your father came home from work. Your mother had prepared, I think, vegetables and lamb. And unfortunately, it wasn't the best cut of lamb apparently, and your father made some reference to 'this is scrag end', which I believe is neck. Your mother protested a little. Your father got shirty and said he wouldn't eat it. Then he bogged off in a huff. I ate mine of course. I probably ate his too. I thought, 'Fuck this, I never get lamb, I'll have it.'*

My mum's happiness was the core of my security.

Her sadness was the core of my turmoil.

She had postnatal depression after giving birth to me. It left its mark. She wasn't drinking. Not yet. But she was struggling. There was a stigma to the illness back then. She never got the medication she needed, so it lingered. She had a husband who worked long hours, her dad had passed away three years earlier, her only sibling was studying in Glasgow, and her mum lived too far to come more than a few times a year.

She just had me then.

And I didn't know how to make her better.

It's difficult to be a feeling child in a house where your emotions must be supressed; where they swirl around you in the adults' behaviour, confusing and out of control and scary, wild monsters in the dark; where you feel simmering, unspoken things in the house, and no one comforts you or explains it to you. I heard arguments at night, ones that were obviously loud enough to drift up the stairs. I sensed things that had happened that we hadn't witnessed – they lingered in the air. We always knew we should behave. It was unsaid. It was expected.

I experienced what my mum did; I felt *her* feelings more than my own. In focusing on her emotional needs, and in her exposing me so violently to this so young, she taught me that unless she was happy, I might never be either.

I tried hard to make sure she was OK in my own small, inept way.

But if I tripped over, no one picked me up. If I cut my finger, no one kissed it. If I was ill, it was a nuisance.

I fell down the stairs one day, so hard I was winded, but I still had to go to Sunday school, even though I could hardly speak. After a while, I stopped crying. I learnt that it was pointless. I poured affection into my toys, into caring for my dolls the way I felt a mother should, feeding them, rocking them in my arms, and making sure they were swaddled for bed. And as soon as I could write – which was early, along with reading – I created a safe world for me to live in.

I still turn to my stories to escape reality. Fiction has been like a filter. A way to let in difficult feelings, gently, bit by bit, in small paragraph-sized lumps so they are easier for me to digest.

My mum was the centre of my real world then.

I would have done anything for her.

But then, when I had just turned four, six days before Christmas, two people arrived in the house who would forever change me. Two people who I'm told by my father I came alive for. Two people who fit neatly and perfectly into my life. Two people I could help look after, who brought me a lot of joy.

My twin sisters. Claire and Grace.

My soulmates.

7

Smiling brightly with teeth

March: This month is synonymous with the onset of spring. With hope. Accordingly, the flower associated with this month is the daffodil, also known as Jonquil or Narcissus.

The day after our mother jumped from the Humber Bridge – Friday the 1st of March – I bought two thin bunches of daffodils in the Co-op because they were only a pound each and put them in a jar in the back room.

That morning, Grace, Colin and I went over to Mother's house. I'm not sure why. Perhaps to pick up a few things in case she needed them at the hospital, which I'm sure we did. Perhaps we *needed* to. It was the house we moved into when I was nine. The house where so many things have happened. A house I don't like now.

It was reasonably tidy, though there were dirty pots in the sink.

'Bloody hell,' I said. 'She could have washed them before she pranced up to the bridge.'

We sorted them out. Her little ornaments and treasures on the windowsill choked me; miniature cows and dust-frosted picture frames. On the sofa arm, a TV mag was open at her planned viewing for the 28th of February – programmes she would never watch. And on the kitchen table was an exercise pad, one page torn out. The imprint of words she had written on that missing page were etched into the remaining one. I touched the lines. It must have been her final note. One we would never see. I tried to decode the words, but I couldn't. Maybe it was a good thing.

Claire arrived mid-afternoon at Grace's house where we were all waiting, in limbo, pending news of Mother's surgery. That day, the incredible, tireless, underfunded NHS did their best to begin fixing her. She had heart surgery first, this being the most critical. In the subsequent days and weeks, she had many further surgeries. It's hard to recall the exact order and dates, but we believe it was heart first, followed by back surgery, then leg surgery, and finally shoulder surgery, with tests and scans in between.

Colin and Joe were there when the surgeon explained what he would do to her leg, and they saw the scan. He told them it was one of the worst breaks he had ever seen. That it looked like she had stepped on a grenade. Joe told me afterwards that in the black-and-white picture it looked like someone had emptied a bag of crisps and smashed them with a fist. Bones – because they break so absolutely and obviously to the eye – are easier to repair than the mind; the physical heart is the same.

The emotional one, not so much.

While we waited for news that Friday of Mother's heart surgery, we watched our favourite clips from *The Office* and *Extras* to cheer ourselves up. We watched the clock too, the hands dragging slowly around. It reminded me of days waiting for someone to have a baby; or when staying in for a parcel that never comes, like the one which arrived late that awful day and was received, eventually, by Joe. Endless cups of tea were made that afternoon, and sandwiches were eaten, while we tried to guess what was happening, knowing a phone call might bring bad news. It got late. It had been dark when I arrived at Grace's and now it was again.

Eventually we got the call – surgery had gone well, and Mother was in recovery.

It was so late that we agreed Claire should just go to the hospital, with Colin, since she hadn't been yet.

Claire: *I went into ICU, and I remember thinking she was very small and frail and obviously she had all the tubes breathing for her. She wasn't really with it at all, so I just talked to her because they believe patients can still hear you, even when they're out of it. She didn't do a lot. She was still dirty from the jump – on her face and beneath her fingernails. She was covered in dried blood. I remember thinking, 'I wish they could wash her up a bit.' I remember trying to clean her a little bit and someone telling me her nose was broken, and I felt bad that I might have hurt her. The next day, the Saturday, was much worse as then she was trying to pull the tubes out and clearly very distressed.*

I came home that night shattered; emotionally, mentally, physically. I caught up with Joe. He had told Katy and Conor. They were concerned and sent their love. With them living in other towns I tried to underplay it so they wouldn't worry, but how do you minimise such a violent act? They might have been almost nineteen and twenty-eight, but to me they were still children. Katy was doing a mental health nursing degree and had enough on with that and her type 1 diabetes; Conor had just met a lovely girl. So, I insisted that their grandma was doing well. I was the buffer between tragedy and their wellbeing; I turned the horror into a gentler fiction for them.

I still had to make a decision about the upcoming week.

In just three days, it was my award ceremony in London followed by a book tour of Manchester, Birmingham and Hungerford with a host of other authors. I was torn; it was the biggest achievement of my career that far, with my fourth novel shortlisting for an award. The glittering ceremony was on Monday night at The Royal Horseguards Hotel in London; some of the biggest writers were going. I'd been excited about it for months, in abject disbelief that I'd been considered for such an esteemed prize.

As my career soared, my private world plummeted.

I couldn't go now, could I, with my mother so ill?

'Yes, you can,' my siblings had said earlier when I brought it up. 'And you should. You can't put your life on hold. The books are your *world*. It's not like it's another country. You're never farther away than four hours and you can come home if… well, if you need to.'

I supposed I could.

But then there was the guilt.

How could I be so heartless as to go away to such a joyful event when my mother could still die?

I didn't know if I could do it. Put on the smile. Act like everything was fine for an audience. Yet hadn't my entire childhood prepared me for this? Equipped me for putting my feelings aside, for smiling brightly with teeth, for making sure those around me were OK first. Wasn't I the master of putting my feelings away like unwanted food into a striped apron and pretending they were gone?

I tussled with the decision all night.

I had heated nightmares about smashed up limbs and bloody bodies. But when I woke in the morning, I knew what I should do. It took me over ten years, hundreds of short stories, four novels, and a million rejections to finally get a book deal. When I was fourteen, I wrote my first full-length book and told anyone who would listen that one day I was going to be a world-famous novelist. I owed it to that teenage girl to go to London.

I owed it to me.

8

This is it

*Four yellow daffodils; their beauty shatters toxic past;
their luminance dispels the shadows.* – **Grace Wilkinson**

Edwin: *My recollection of receiving the news about your mother is this. It was
early morning here in Tasmania, and I took the call outside because I didn't
want to wake up the people in the house. My initial reaction was shock. Not so
much that my sister had made another attempt but at the method; because after
the previous drug overdose, I was talking with her and we joked about people
who opted to use the bridge as a means of ending it all. And we had a laugh
about it, saying, well, there's an option. So when I got the news, my initial
reaction was no surprise. But when Claire mentioned the bridge, I thought,
Holy fuck, did I plant the seed? After that, it was disbelief that it had failed
because I'm familiar with that bridge.*

On Saturday morning – back at Grace's house – the four of us
spoke with our uncle Edwin, in a group chat via WhatsApp,
with one of our phones on the coffee table and all of us crowded
around it, multiple tea-stained cups an attending audience.
Edwin said he would wait longer before coming to England
because – on the practical side of things – he knew there might
still be a funeral.

'I don't fancy jetting halfway across the world,' he said, 'and then returning home, putting my feet up and making a nice cup of coffee, only to be called up again for a funeral.'

It was understandable.

We still couldn't believe it; she had jumped off the Humber Bridge. And survived. It's almost a year on as I write this, and I still can't believe it. I'm on a train, on my laptop. Each time we pass a bridge I assess it for suicide success. I mentally work out the height and what kind of damage it might do if someone jumped there. I wonder how many people have stood at the edge, looking over, thinking about letting go.

We updated Edwin on the heart surgery's success and assured him we would keep him updated on further operations. If there was one positive in our mother's suicide attempt it was that it brought us closer to our uncle; he might have been 10,000 miles away, but we felt his presence acutely during those difficult early days.

That Saturday, two days after the jump, was the worst.

Mother was seriously ill in the ICU, on life support. Tubes went into every part of her – veins, nose, mouth. She slept most of the time but when she woke, she gagged and gagged, trying to speak around these hindrances. When she opened them, her eyes were wild with pain and fear and confusion. Looking back, this was the day I think she came the closest to dying. The day where she seemed to be suffering so much that I *wanted* her to let go and die. It may sound cruel, but I wanted her to have the oblivion she had so often sought. To be at peace.

During a moment straight out of *Fawlty Towers*, Colin and Claire were at her bedside at one point, and after their tender words of encouragement she started croaking, 'I'm trying, I'm trying, I'm *trying*.'

They urged her on with, 'Yes, good, *great*, you keep doing that, Mother.'

She repeated it over and over; they insisted 'yes, do'.

It turned out she had been saying, 'I'm dying, I'm dying, I'm *dying.*'

Naturally, we had a chuckle at that.

The four of us spent all day and evening on that ward, taking turns going in because it was two to a bed. Many of Mother's long-time friends came, and we all gathered in a stuffy, nearby room, making small talk, squeezing into the few chairs, and waiting to take our turn on the endless carousel of handholding and soothing words at her bedside. There was a small TV in the waiting room, but I couldn't tell you what was on. Joe joined us and took his turn at Mother's bedside, his face sad when he came out. In that halfway place, we made calls to those we could think of who didn't yet know but needed to.

One of the most tiring aspects of that already difficult time was updating people who lived out of town. Our mother had lots of friends, and there were relatives up north we had to inform. I understood that people wanted to know how she was, but it hurt to repeat it over and over. Some expected us to give them every single update, every day. This aspect left me exhausted. I'm thankful I had my siblings to share this task with.

I remembered being at the hospital twelve years earlier – and nine floors higher up – when Katy was diagnosed with type 1 diabetes and we almost lost her. When she broke her arm aged five. Unless you've only been there to give birth, hospitals evoke sad memories. Each time you visit, you think of the times before. I remembered the extreme reaction I had three weeks earlier when working there with my theatre. We ushered a special screening of a play for elderly ward residents. When I arrived in the foyer for the shift, I was overwhelmed with dread. I wanted to run away.

Was it a violent version of the gentle foreshadowing I use in novels?

Throughout that Saturday, the staff dealing with our mother wanted her background – details about the depression, previous suicide attempts, her general health. We told them she had been a heavy drinker for forty years. We might have used the word *alcoholic*, and if we did, I would have most certainly imagined my mother's heated denial of this in my ear, words I'd heard many times for real. They obviously had her full name, but checked what she liked to be called – Trish, we told them, not Patricia.

At one point, it was just Colin and I with Mother. We were exhausted. One of the machines kept stopping, and I thought, *This is it.* And then it wasn't. Then again, they went off. But still, it wasn't the end. I couldn't take it. I was sure Mother must have just wanted peace. I noticed the tears on Colin's face but knew he wouldn't want to make a fuss, so I just squeezed his arm across the bed.

We went and spoke to a nurse.

'If it's possible, we want to request a Do Not Resuscitate,' said Colin softly. 'We hate the idea of someone pounding her chest or doing things that might further hurt her. We think it would be kind to just let her go if the time comes.'

The nurse looked aghast. 'You can't request a thing like that.'

I felt like a criminal, and I'm sure Colin did.

Like we had asked them to pull the plug on her machines.

'We thought it was something that *could* be requested,' I said, coldly, not liking how brusquely she had responded to Colin's sensitive request.

'No, not at all.' And she disappeared with folders.

Grace: *Me and Colin were at either side of Mother's bed at one point. She was attached to an obs machine that alarmed when she had insufficient oxygen. We were both sitting there, and her oxygen levels kept dipping. I pressed the nursing buzzer. Then there was a new noise – the alarm for the nurse and the oxygen buzzer. Colin turned off the nursing buzzer thinking it was an alarm that wasn't needed, and I was saying, 'Oh God, the alarm keeps going off.'*

Meanwhile I'm pressing it trying to call for the nurse. All the while, Mother's oxygen is going down. We discovered when Colin stood up that he had been sitting on the oxygen, so she'd not been getting any! Once we had rectified the matter – and brought her back to life – we obviously cancelled the nursing call.

At the end of one of the most exhausting days of my life, Claire slept at my house.

'The daffodils are nice,' she said of the jar on the table.

'I know. Only two quid. From Co-op.'

I made pizza for supper and we sat in the front room. I switched the TV on to distract us. It was 80s sci-fi show *Buck Rogers in the 25th Century*. It was so random and unexpected that we laughed hysterically. Then I finally cried. I wasn't sure if I had the night she jumped, but this night I did.

'I didn't know if I loved her anymore,' admitted Claire. 'But I've realised that I do. Whatever she is, I *do*.'

'Me too,' I said softly. 'I hate seeing her in that kind of pain. It's cruel. She wanted to die, and I think it would be more merciful if she had.'

I had seen our mother in all kinds of states. So drunk she couldn't walk; so hungover I'd had to ring in sick for her from as young as ten; so angry I'd had to protect Grace from her onslaught; so sad it had broken me; so neglectful I'd endured physical assault from her boyfriends; so funny I'd laughed until I couldn't speak. I'd loved her and I'd hated her. I'd longed for her praise and I'd wanted to kill her.

Now I wanted her to be out of pain.

Claire nodded. 'What kind of life will she have now?'

'I hope we get a phone call tonight.' I looked pointedly at Claire. 'I'll sleep if we do. And I won't go to London on Monday.' I paused. 'Kathleen,' I whispered, speaking of our grandma, 'come and get her.'

The night was quiet. No phone calls punctured the dark. In bed I kept thinking of a mouse called Lucky that my son Conor had when he was small. It had been rescued from a snake. Not a wild snake – a pet snake, a Mexican black king. My brother's, and then my sister's. It was a lovely creature. It had to be fed dead mice or insects. For some reason – perhaps lack of knowledge – my sister tried feeding it a live mouse that it wouldn't touch. We thought it was the luckiest mouse in the world to survive a snake. Hence the name. Conor begged to keep it for a pet. He was eight. We let him. One morning I came downstairs and he was crying, Lucky in his hands. He had died. I realised it had likely been ill and that was why the snake had rejected it.

Our mother was like the mouse.

She was lucky to have survived.

To have got through yet another night.

But she was very ill.

Sunday came and it was a little better. We didn't know if it was the drugs, or that she felt calmer, but Mother settled down. Whatever she had been fighting for the previous day – whether it was to live or to die – she surrendered now. Claire was relieved because she had to return to Grantham.

I was, because I had to go away too.

9

Sheep and wolves

Charming and very fragrant, Narcissus 'Baby Moon' is a
sweetly scented miniature daffodil boasting up to three
to five small, soft, golden-yellow flowers per stem.

My first memory of my twin sisters' arrival was of one of them,
wrapped tightly in a white blanket, being held up at a window in
a door. I didn't know then which one of them it was, but I now
think it was likely Claire. I know we were about to go into the
hospital, though I can only vaguely recall the actual visit. I seem to
think I only saw Claire; Grace had to go into a separate incubator
straight after the birth because she wouldn't feed. She was there for
a while. Even then, aged just four, I wondered how she must feel
being separated from her womb-mate.

It must have been difficult for my mum; finding out late on in
pregnancy that she was having twins; then one of them needing
extra care after the birth. She had struggled with postnatal depression after me, but didn't seek help, which is understandable as
mental health was a taboo subject back then.

She was young when she had me, just twenty-two.

The story went – according to her – that she lost her virginity
on Valentine's Day and I was the surprise nine months later. This
version has changed over the years to include her tending to my

then flu-ridden father in his sick room, taking him chicken soup and ending up in the bed. I like the idea that I was conceived on the Day of Love. It certainly fits with my due date. My mum has a wonderful way with words. She is a storyteller even if she's never written a book, so I can never be sure how much of my conception story is fantasy and how much really happened.

Our middle names were inspired by steam trains because our father was a devoted trainspotter. The 6223 maroon Princess Alice was a Coronation Class train that gave Claire her middle name of Alice. The 6201 Princess Elizabeth, also maroon, gave Grace her middle name of Elizabeth. The red 6204 Princess Louise, also a Princess Royal class, inspired my middle name.

You may be confused, knowing Louise is my first name. I was actually christened Jane-Louise, and everyone called me that until I went to school. A teacher thought it was a mouthful to say and asked which name my parents wanted me to be called by. They picked Louise, and it stuck. I changed it legally as an adult, tiring of people seeing my official name on documents and calling me Jane.

I decided to have a little fun with this name change. I added a few extras. In honour of my heroine, Marilyn Monroe, I added Lady M. And also, the cute nickname Joe calls me: Puffbrains. So, if you ever read my name in full on a document, you'll get quite the eye-full – Louise Jane Lady M Puffbrains Beech.

If my mum suffered with postnatal depression after I was born, it must have been doubly so after the twins. I remember helping a lot. I loved it. It felt natural to me. I'd hold a bottle to one of the propped-up-on-a-cushion babies while my mum held and fed the other one.

'Which one is which?' I asked often, fascinated by how similar they looked to me. They weren't identical though – Claire had brown eyes and was covered in dark hair, while Grace was blue-eyed and fair.

And my mum, obviously knowing, would tell me. As they grew, they were often dressed in the same outfit in a different colour, which helped me identify them.

'Do they know who I am?' I wanted to know.

'Yes,' she would say, which was sweet.

'Do they know who *they* are though?' I remember asking once. 'Do *they* ever get muddled about who is who?'

I'm not sure what answer I got to that.

There are lots of things I'm not sure about. At times, it's hard to distinguish between simple memory loss because time has passed and the events I've actively buried because they were too painful to face.

I can't remember the moment my mum went away. Perhaps this was when I began burying things too traumatic to understand, let alone deal with. But she did. She left. It happened.

Edwin: *I remember staying at Hillcrest Avenue after the twins were born. I was living in Glasgow as I'd graduated in the May of 1974 and was likely working at Glasgow Royal Infirmary. One morning I was still in bed and your mother was downstairs with the twins, and probably you. Your father was down there too. I could hear them talking. I got a bit disturbed because the talking got louder, and it was obviously a confrontation of some kind. Then I distinctly heard your father say, 'Put the baby down.' That raised alarm bells with me – I thought, 'Something's not right here, I'd better go downstairs.' By the time I got down there, your father was holding one twin and the other was in a receptacle. It got less heated when I appeared. Then I recall your father being on the phone and cups of tea being made. A rather well-dressed, older man came. I believe he was some sort of psychiatrist. I was no longer in the room then, and he had a long chat with your mother and father. Very shortly after, an ambulance arrived. Your mother was led out of the house and off she went. After that, I don't have very clear recollections. I stayed for a while. I bottle-fed the twins. My mother came down, and I remember Grandma Armitage coming at one point and putting a wash on.*

I do remember Grandma Roberts being there.

She was my mum's mum. A devout Catholic, she was strong, kind and strict, and she always made me feel safe. Though she was not affectionate or demonstrative, I knew absolutely that she loved me. Her mother died when she was just sixteen and she had brought up her young siblings. She gave all her energy and time to other people, volunteering at church and going on long trips to Lourdes with groups of disabled or needy people.

During those weeks, I got up early with my grandma and helped warm the bottles and feed my sisters. I might have only been four, but it felt as easy as if they were my own babies. I loved the smell of their heads and how warm they were to hold. Perhaps it gave me comfort in the absence of my mum.

She was in the hospital for three months.

And yet I can't remember the moment she left or came back.

As an adult, I am always ready for someone to leave me. My sisters tell me they are too, which is understandable because as those tiny babies, once upon a time, they must have had some awareness of the absence of their mother. It's a very practical preparation; I think, *I'll take these few things and I'll go there, and I'll find a way.* I'm barely even sad about it. Every day, I'm in disbelief that I've been happily married for over twenty years because my natural inclination is to be alone.

For me, the house filled with joy when my sisters arrived. As soon as they were old enough to play, I loved it. Our games were like theatre shows. We didn't play games where there were set rules, or we competed. We made up stories and then acted them out. Some were less complex. Running Girls simply involved fighting over this thick, long, black wig – I have no recollection of where it came from – and then running back and forth, swishing our 'hair' like models. Perhaps it was because we always had short hair that we longed for such luscious locks, but the two without the wig used a scarf or whatever else was available. We also re-enacted TV shows, fighting over who played the best character.

I remember playing Tarzan – being the oldest, it was my lot – and falling from a top bunk bed, naked, onto a brown wicker chair. My stomach was cut to shreds. But I knew there was no point in crying. I'd only get in trouble.

Grace always had a scar or two on her arm. It was around this time that she began biting herself, a habit that lingered until she was fifteen. Now it would be recognised as self-harm, due to trauma, and not being allowed to vent powerful emotions. But back then, no one noticed. She bit the same place, often drawing blood. It must have been a release. I remember it, and just thinking it was one of her quirks.

Claire: *I've very little memory of the time at Hillcrest Avenue, which was until I was four. I remember a bonfire at the end of the garden. I remember toys in a cupboard behind a curtain. I remember not being allowed to go in the front room where father's guitars were, how it was his room. I remember losing a blue shoe behind the radiator in our bedroom; being in the chilly downstairs toilet, seeing the window cleaner and being afraid; sneaking into Dad's bedroom and peeling his eyes back while he slept. There's a sense of us always having to be quiet and well-behaved. We played a game called Sheep and Wolves where we would crawl, and Louise chased us. When we played it, we got told off – Father would say we were too old for such games. I rarely cried. I just knew not to. I was an inconvenience. All of these memories are like seeing a film. I don't have any feelings about them.*

I remember the hot summer of 1976. Playing on the street. Learning to ride a bike. Watching *Thunderbirds* on a Saturday morning in a boy's house up the street. Sitting in the paddling pool with the twins in a scorched back garden. I remember Christmas 1977 when I went to the toilet in the night and saw my mum carrying a blue bike from a cupboard into the back room. Realising there was no Santa. Only seven and knowing the best thing I believed in was a lie. Then continuing the pretence for my sisters, my storytelling abilities coming to the fore.

I also remember the issue of food again.

We were sitting at the white Formica table in the back room, Mum, Claire, Grace and me, eating tea. The meal itself, I can't recall, but I know that – as usual – I could barely eat it. My father must have been late from work, or maybe my mum had made it too early, but whatever the reason, when he came into the room, he pulled the cloth roughly from the table and the food flew everywhere.

Claire, Grace and I then sat on the floor with three of the Formica chairs as our mini tables, and tried to eat what was left, while the fight went on around us. None of us dared to look at the adults, and I felt protective of my sisters. Grace, adoring her food, probably ate what was left of everyone's, including our father's. But I was glad I had less to eat now. It was one blessing. This moment, years later, inspired a scene in my first published short story and gave me the confidence to send out my novels for publication.

There was one type of food I did enjoy: Mum's baking. It seemed she was always doing it. Perhaps it gave her joy. Was an escape. She had a Mickey Mouse-shaped cutter for biscuits, and she made Swiss Tarts with jam on, and large sponges, and Maid of Honours. I can still see these treats cooling on the kitchen work surface. We once took bits of a sponge cake before we were allowed to. I was the only one who could reach so I burrowed into the side of it and shared it with my sisters. Then I turned the cake around so that the gaping hole was at the back. Of course, we got found out, and were sent to bed early, but we giggled for a long time under the covers.

Grace: *I remember getting my hair cut and going to bed and not wanting to put my head down because I thought all my remaining hair would fall out. I tried to sleep with my head off the pillow so I must have had a stiff neck the next day. I used to sing* 'London Bridge Is Falling Down' *at night, looking at the top of the Humber Bridge from our window.* (The bridge towers were built at this stage, but it didn't open until 1981.) *We played with a boy up the street who was our age. My favourite toy was a tractor that you pedalled.*

In the house, there was a Spanish doll ornament on a windowsill, and I was fascinated by it. We had these huge, naked dolls that for some reason we never got clothes for. I had a lot of problems with my bowels (we called it constip!) and Mum always gave me plums. I'd go and shit behind the curtains. Once on the drive. My dreams were always vivid back then. One involved Claire and me trying to escape from a helicopter.

My dreams were vivid too; I'd tremble in the dark for ages after. The worst was when the radiator in my bedroom came to life. It didn't even feel like a dream. It was breathing and pulsating and breathing and pulsating. It moved across the bedroom towards me, a lumbering, terrifying, hungry creature. Though I never went downstairs once I was in bed – we weren't allowed to – now I was so afraid, I did.

And that was when I saw what I thought was a game.

One I didn't understand.

Halfway down the stairs I stopped. The backroom door was ajar. My mum wore her yellow dressing gown with the dangling threads and a zip up the front. She was on the floor. Cowering. My father was standing over her with his belt in his hand. She looked as scared as I had been of the radiator.

I was confused.

Was it a game of Sheep and Wolves?

I had no idea what to do. My mum looked afraid. I wanted to wrap my body around her to protect her but was also afraid. I'd be in trouble if they knew I was up. I went back to bed and pretended I'd never seen it. And after that, no matter how bad my dreams, I never again went downstairs during the night.

Colin was born a week before my eighth birthday. I remember it was at teatime and my father answered the phone in the hallway and told us with a big smile that we had a baby brother. I was as excited as when my sisters had arrived. My mum was so terrified of the debilitating postnatal depression that she got prescribed something before the birth and this time she didn't suffer and could enjoy her new baby.

There seemed to be a brief time of joy.

Colin was a gorgeous, placid baby with big brown eyes, and dark eyelashes and hair with the kind of fullness that people would say is 'wasted on a boy'. He wasn't named after a steam train; he was named after everyone. Colin for our Grandad Colin, then James after our father, and Edwin after our uncle. I watched him for hours, even though he didn't do much except burp and spit up milk. One morning, I lit a candle for him in a school assembly where we were sharing and celebrating happy things in our life.

On my eighth birthday, Mum told me Uncle Edwin was coming to visit. I was excited all day. As kids, we loved his boisterous sense of humour and silliness. But it got to bedtime and no Uncle Edwin yet; so up the stairs I had to go. There was no deviating from routine, even on a special day. In bed, still awake, I heard him arrive, his booming voice impossible to ignore. Desperate to see him, I dared to creep onto the landing, hoping he would see me and tell my parents to let me come back down.

He did.

And he had a gift for me.

My father suggested I wait until morning, but I begged to open it then, risking being told off. Edwin insisted I should have it. It was a Tiny Tears doll. I'd wanted one forever. I called her Lucy and I played with her until she literally fell apart.

That was my last birthday in Hillcrest Avenue.

Living there, before my parents were divorced, was actually the least difficult part of my childhood. If there was occasional violence, it was at least only between family members in the house. If there were times my mum was absent, it was only for a few months. If there was a lack of affection, there was at least sobriety. If there were days I couldn't make my mum happy, I at least loved her absolutely and without condition. If I had nightmares, they were at least still only in my head.

10

We may need a bigger suitcase

Four yellow promises, their soil hard and dry,
weathered by the wicked storm. Four yellow
promises, heads held high. – **Grace Wilkinson.**

I remember my mum telling me we were moving. She wore her yellow dressing gown and sat, as always, on the white Formica chair in the back room, me at her feet. I was eight, and I wasn't surprised. I sometimes knew things before anyone told me. It's hard to explain. Like remembering something not yet happened. Maybe it's because I learnt early on to tune in to my parents' moods so I'd know what kind of day it would be, an awareness that lingered and now informs my prose.

She said, 'But your father isn't coming with us.'

That part surprised me but didn't particularly upset me. I had friends at school whose parents had got divorced, so I knew the word, and I guessed this was that. I hoped my siblings were coming with us but didn't dare ask this in case not. What would I have done? I have no idea. Thankfully, they did.

We moved into the upstairs apartment of a grand house where my mum had got a job as a teacher. A woman she knew had bought the place – a pre-Victorian house built in the 1800s – a year earlier and opened it as a school in April 1979. Serendipitous timing for us.

Of our departure, my father said he was 'abandoned'. That he came home one day, and we had all gone, leaving him 'nothing'. My mum said simply that she couldn't stay with him. I have always known how it affected her because she told me it was the beginning of her darkest breakdown. I've never thought about how it might have marked me, or my siblings, this separation; back then my mum never asked how I felt so I guess I've never really looked back since that day.

We lived in the school during the summer of 1979. Despite the fact that my parents had just got divorced – something that's a trauma for many children – I enjoyed the freedom we had in the beautiful grounds on a weekend and during the school holidays. After the quiet oppression of our last house, this one seemed like a fairytale castle. There was an expanse of sloping lawn to the front, overlooking all of Hessle and Hull, a small wood you went through as you drove to the main doors, a rose garden with crazy paving and, to the rear, a courtyard and some old stables.

We ran wild in this new play area. After having learnt to be silent, this was heaven. Perfect for someone with an imagination like mine. Colin was still a baby, so he stayed inside with our mum. But Claire and Grace – then four – joined me in adventure. We explored for hours. We bathed our dolls in a washing-up bowl on the grass. We found an old piano in a stable behind the house and clumsily pounded the keys, Grace and Claire pretending to be Richard Clayderman. They later learnt to play, and Grace excelled at it. They – like Colin, and some of our children – have the musical flair my father had hoped was in me, aged three, holding that guitar.

Inside, the house was huge. Downstairs, there were classrooms off a square hallway where fish swam in a bubbling tank. I told Grace they were baby sharks. We sneaked into those airy school rooms when they were empty, pretending to be teachers and drawing on the board, borrowing *Beano* magazines and returning them when we were done. I loved having so many books at my disposal. That summer was when I fell in love with reading. I devoured CS Lewis, consumed *Jane Eyre*, and adored the *What Katy Did* series.

Our bedroom was like something out of the books I read. Two tall, curtain-less, sash windows; wooden floor; high ceilings; a little balcony with a brick floor that cooked in the sun. Claire, Grace and I shared it, our beds forming a triangle, while Colin slept in his cot in the smaller room next door. We made 'dog food' out of coloured tissue soaked in water and pretended to eat it on all fours. We had pink cots for our dolls and Lucy, my beloved Tiny Tears, slept at my side. I loved that there were no curtains. At night, I fought sleep and waited for the stars to come out. I would lie in bed, looking at the dying light, happy that my sisters were safely with me, my brother close by.

No one argued downstairs.

No one threw food around.

My nightmares died like the sun did before my sleep-heavy eyes.

But I now learn that it was not quite so idyllic for my sisters.

Claire: *I remember being frightened a lot in the school. Our bedroom to me was huge and old with high ceilings. There was a balcony, and I was scared it would fall off and collapse down to the ground. Also, outside there was a hole under some paving slabs and a caretaker told us it was bottomless, so I was petrified. He was probably just trying to keep us away from it. I was scared of the long passage leading to the toilets. I got my head trapped in the banister upstairs. I was leaning down, looking at the school children below, and I remember them all looking up at me when I was stuck. I also got stuck in the toilet upstairs. There was a dragonfly in there with me and I was frightened. Louise used to tell us ghost stories, mainly about Jenny Brough (a woman the street was named after) who apparently committed suicide by hanging herself from a tree. Louise used to put her head around the bedroom door and say she was Jenny Brough.*

It always amazes me how moments spent together mean such different things for each person concerned. This is why all truth is only a version: our version. That while I was happy we'd left Hillcrest Avenue, Claire was still anxious. We laugh now about how I scared them to death with my stories. I feel bad that I traumatised them. I was a born storyteller – at times the darker the better – but I never knew how much it upset them. I watched them sleeping at night, glad they were OK, and yet I'd probably given them nightmares!

Grace: *I remember putting my hand in the fish tank and getting hold of one of the fish. I remember it all dingly-dangly in my hand and Louise telling me there was a shark in there that would bite me. I remember the huge classroom on the left with a side door that led to the rose gardens. I remember my friend coming on her bike, a three-wheeler type, and the plastic seat had a crack in it, so it hurt your leg. I went upstairs to get some trousers and I was scared to be alone, so I ran really fast.*

I don't remember much of my mum during this time. Perhaps because it was such a glorious summer, and I loved being outside so much. Perhaps I felt she was OK now she had left my father and so I was free to have some fun. Perhaps she no longer seemed sad and I no longer felt I had to make her happy.

We dined in a large kitchen where French doors opened onto the gravel drive and lawn, and a sagging red sofa squeezed like an overweight woman into a box-shaped corner. Even though it was the white Formica table, I could enjoy food again. I could eat without worrying it would choke me. I loved that Colin sat in his highchair too, messily eating rusk, the August sun on his back.

Our father took us out on Sundays. He didn't come into the house. He parked on the gravel drive and we went to him. I don't recall missing him too much. Sad, but I guess you don't miss what you're not overly attached to. But, in some ways, I enjoyed his company more when we didn't live with him. He could be fun, repeating jokes he knew, and taking us to the local woods where he enjoyed taking photographs.

Sometimes he took us back to Hillcrest Avenue. Our old house was a different place; emptier, colder, with bare walls and barren surfaces. Our toys were still in the cupboard behind the striped curtains. I felt sad for my father, there alone, with a few ghostly remnants of us. We found a striped baby shoe behind our bedroom radiator and tried to retrieve it but couldn't. One day when we went, all our toys had gone. He had got rid of them. Perhaps they upset him, who knows?

Our parents eventually sold that house, and he bought a flat.

Recently, on a walk, Grace and I sneaked into the grounds of the school where we lived to have a look. It seemed smaller. I could have sworn that the main doors were a grand *Gone With The Wind*-esque affair. In other ways, it was exactly the same and I could see us in the upstairs window, looking out, faces sunburnt, dolls in arms.

Time makes no difference and yet every difference. Everything goes with us. Gets packed up and follows us. I think we may need a bigger suitcase.

Back then it seemed like the sun shone every day: a glorious, endless summer. That school was a refuge, nourishing us for a while, letting our daffodil petals grow. But it was the last genuinely happy time of my childhood.

11

Lashings of Cod Liver Oil

*Rijnveld's Early Sensation – this lovely trumpet
daffodil can flower as early as January, so is
ideal if you're looking for winter colour.*

We moved next into a gloomy and damp house called The Cliff, which sat like a grumpy old man on the edge of the River Humber. The council had bought the mansion in the 1970s and renovated it into flats for homeless families; *renovated* is a generous word since it was not fit for human habitation. Originally it was probably beautiful, with sweeping views of the river before hungry trees swallowed the brick and pebble-dash walls, with seven bedrooms and a gently sloping lawn to the front. It was owned by the sailor and accomplished artist, George Holmes.

We moved into The Cliff in the winter of 1979 because we could no longer stay at the school. Living upstairs when we needed a home had never been official, and the council said we had to move on. If that house was an endless summer, then The Cliff was a Narnia-like winter. It was a place of shadows, whistling winds, ice cold, perpetual dark, and surrounded – we were sure – by wolves. Nothing filled or warmed the cavernous rooms. Draughts invaded every gap. Windows rattled. The only source of heating were coal fires in two of the bigger rooms.

I shared a bedroom with my sisters again, and Colin slept with our mum. It was a vast room, and my bed was near the door, as though I had been assigned protection of Claire and Grace from the howling we heard at night. It was likely just the wind, but it sounded like the wolves we had pretended to be in our Sheep and Wolves game. The river foghorn only added to the spookiness.

I didn't help our fears with my customary bedtime ghost stories, shared when we were supposed to be sleeping. This time it was one about a skeleton with red eyes that someone at school had terrified me with. It involved this hideous creature of death clacking up the stairs, bloody eyes aglow. My poor sisters. If I caused nightmares, I did at least look out for them as they slept.

Late one night, like a mini-mum, I checked on the twins. On the wall next to Grace – who was hugging Panda close to her chest – sat an enormous spider. I'm petrified of them, but I couldn't let it crawl on her. I had never sought out my parents for such dilemmas, and this was no different. I squashed it with a cushion, proud I had saved my slumbering sister from imminent attack.

Grace: *In the Cliff I remember it always being dark. I remember being sick all over my favourite orange-flecked cardigan that Grandma Roberts had made me. I remember being in the kitchen at the Formica table with all of us and putting the stones we had collected on the foreshore onto it, pretending they were treasures. I remember being fed cod liver oil. I can still taste it now. I remember boxes in the middle room – and I remember vividly losing Panda, my favourite toy in the world, being upset and looking for him in those boxes. I never found him. Grandma Roberts visited. Behind her back, she had two surprises and we had to pick. They were toy watches. We were so excited about them. We played on the foreshore all the time, collecting stones, literally under the bridge where Mum would one day jump.*

Much like in the school, I have little recollection of spending close time with my mum. I knew she was sad, but I was afraid of it. Of its weight. Of it sucking me in too. I wanted to be happy; to be free to play. Children have a right to be children – to be playful, spontaneous, free from adult concerns. But I felt guilty about wanting this. My mum has since said that her most serious depression began here.

I can understand why.

She wore her yellow dressing gown a lot that winter. It must have been hard having four children under nine, living in such an inhospitable residence, solely responsible. As Grace recalls, she gave us lashings of cod liver oil with our porridge, and other vitamins too, but still we caught every bug going. We were always coughing or sneezing or throwing up. I remember trying to keep warm by running up and down the long corridor between the main door and the kitchen.

Running girls, but with no black wig.

I celebrated my ninth birthday in The Cliff, though I have no memory of it other than that someone bought me a Basil Brush purse that you wore around your neck on a red string. Like most kids my age then, I loved watching *Tiswas* on a Saturday and making up games with my sisters, and reading. The house was isolated, a good walk from the main town, and not visible from the foreshore road, so it felt like the only time we left was to go to school. Our mum didn't drive then, and though I know he took us out occasionally, I don't really recall time with my father. A little girl lived with her single mum in the flat adjacent to ours, but we never spoke to her. I just remember seeing her behind their glass door, with a pram, looking sad. I don't think our schoolfriends came over often; and we never went to their homes either.

But, every weekend, we sisters spent hours exploring the overgrown, wild grounds of the house. We wandered into a nearby cottage and a vicious dog chased us away. We played on the foreshore, collecting stones and glass. It occurs to me now that we were very young – just five and nine – to be playing alone near one of the most dangerous rivers in the world, in the shadow of the not-yet-completed Humber Bridge, but they were different times. And our mum had a baby to care for. I missed Colin when we had played out for hours. I loved when we went back inside – our cheeks pink with cold – and he was there, grinning no matter what, crawling around and trying to follow us wherever we went. The love I felt for him, all chubby hands and face, brought me great joy.

Claire: *In The Cliff I remember being frightened a lot. I thought there were wolves outside coming to get us. I was very scared in bed at night. It was always very cold and dark and seemed so big. I remember baths there, us all sharing, and being cold. I was often ill. I remember Uncle Edwin coming because I was on the sofa in front of a coal fire – not feeling very warm, maybe there was only one lump of coal on it! – and watching* Bonanza.

Like Claire, I was anxious here. I wondered where else we were going to live. I worried about my mum again because the light had gone out of her eyes. I worried that we would leave suddenly. I worried endlessly, for some reason, that we'd be split up. That my siblings would be taken from me. I wished someone would assure me that it was all going to be OK. This anxiety manifested in an inability to eat again. Food had no appeal for me and could be why I was often sick that winter.

I saw a ghost one night.

I was woken by a draught. The bedroom door had blown open. Claire and Grace were sleeping. I still never liked to disturb my mum at night, so I crept into the corridor. The main door to our flat – rippled glass with a dirty net curtain at it – had blown open too. On the stairs, carrying a lamp, was an old woman in a long white gown. She smiled at me and continued down the stairs, until she was swallowed by the dark.

There was no one who looked like her living in the building at the time.

Edwin: *I have a vague recollection of visiting the Cliff place. I remember it as tall ceilinged, cold, and sparsely furnished. I recall a coal fire with not a lot of coal, reminding me of the fire in Mr Scrooge's office. Very Dickensian misery. Your mother was very stressed.*

I started going to the Brownies that winter. I loved it, though I was never very good at getting the badges as I never had the materials or encouragement. I remember the Halloween party and telling spooky stories in the dark while boxes of things were passed around – jelly sweets that felt like worms, and liquid that I guessed was supposed to be blood. My group was in the Methodist church and opposite it was a row of old, white cottages. I used to look at the end one with its black wooden entrance, tiny garden in front, and cosy windows, and imagine living in such a safe-looking place.

'We've got a proper council house,' my mum told me one morning, happy for a moment.

And I knew. I don't know how.

'It's not on the council estate,' she explained. 'It's lovely – this little cottage on Tower Hill.'

'The white one?' I said. 'Opposite Brownies?'

'Yes. How do you know that?'

Had I wished for it, or simply heard her talking to someone else about it?

'I just knew,' I said.

I was so excited about moving into what I called The Cottage in my head. I don't call it The Cottage today. I haven't thought of it that way for many years. It isn't the same house now. My mum bought it from the council more than twenty years ago and continued to live there alone after her second husband Andrew died. She sold it recently to move into a flat, and the people who bought it have gutted and renovated it.

I wonder if they ever see ghosts.

The ghosts there would not be smiling old women with lamps though. They would be women who stagger, and men who smash things and wander in and out of bedrooms. The last time I was in that house, the air was stagnant, and the walls whispered all sorts of things I didn't want to hear, and I never wanted to go back.

12

A good time to talk about Ted Baker

*Daffodils are beautiful but potentially toxic. Eating
any part of the plant can cause low blood pressure,
abdominal pain, vomiting, and damage to the liver.
Keep them out of the reach of small children.*

Memory is such a curious thing. I read somewhere that the mind forgets trauma so you can stay sane, recalling it only when you're strong enough to process the things you supressed. The things I do remember are graphic; the things I don't, nothing.

I remember little about the train journey to London that Monday, just four days after my mother had hurled herself off the Humber Bridge. I know I ignored the metal expanse of cable and fence as I travelled beneath it. For a long time after her suicide attempt, I couldn't look at it. Most of my life I've been able to see it from a bedroom window, hear traffic going over in the night, watched my kids ride bikes across it, walked it with my sister while training for a charity walk.

Now, my affection for it had been destroyed.

I do remember trying to distract myself by thinking about previous journeys, as we often do when we travel. They flashed through my mind the way passenger-filled windows whizz by when a train passes on the opposite track. I saw Joe and I heading to an award ceremony four years earlier. The prize was publication.

Everything depended on winning. All of my first four novels, over the previous seven years, had been rejected by every publisher, a tidal wave of rebuffs.

I'd had a premonition that the winner would be wearing a crimson dress, so I bought the brightest of red frocks to wear. When I arrived at the venue with Joe, desperately hopeful, I scanned the room. A beautiful, dark-haired woman caught my eye. She was dressed in red. She won the prize. I was delighted for her because I knew how happy she must be. But when Joe and I walked back to the hotel, I cried inconsolably. I felt like my career was over before it had begun.

I know now that this loss hurt so acutely because my writing is personal; it's where I escaped as a child. I've always believed that writing is what I'm supposed to be doing, who I am. Rejection of my work was a rejection of that little girl's dream. And acceptance would be like having a parent figure say, 'Louise, you are loved.'

On the train home, Joe was honest. 'I hate seeing you this upset. Why don't you stop? Accept that it isn't going to happen. I can't see you go through it again if you write another book and that's rejected too.'

He was being kind. Just as I'd prayed for my mother's oblivion, so she didn't suffer, Joe had wanted to protect me from more pain.

'I can't stop,' I told him. 'If I do, it'll definitely never happen. If I continue, it might.'

Thankfully, I didn't take his advice. And eventually, in 2015, I got a book deal. I finally had the longed-for parent figure pat my head and tell me I was a clever girl. Dreams could come true, if you didn't give up.

Now, on my way to London again, one of my books had been shortlisted for a big prize. I was where I'd always longed to be. My fifth novel had just come out in eBook; the previous four had charted on Amazon and Kobo, been selected as a *Guardian* Readers' Pick and a Book of the Year at LoveReading, longlisted for the Polari Prize, and garnered reviews in a variety of newspapers and magazines. I'd received messages from people all over the world who had enjoyed them. I'd done panels at Crimefest, Aye Write and Newcastle Noir, been a guest on Arvon courses and at book clubs, had launches in London, and done talks for literary groups. But despite what people often think about writers, I wasn't rich, because mine was an indie publisher. I still needed my other job as theatre usher.

I felt numb.

I hadn't packed a red dress this time; I took a black one bedecked with tiny silver stars. I didn't feel sparkly though. Despite my never-give-up attitude, I often feel I don't deserve good things; that there will be some sort of price to pay for happiness. If that's true, I sure as hell hope they take credit.

At the hotel, I was upgraded to an executive suite for no reason other than that it was available. Was it a good omen? Was the universe compensating me for previous rejections – or for the fact that my mother was fighting for her life in the hospital? Could I have both – my mother's recovery *and* a big win? In the lift, the wallpaper was rows of paperbacks. I couldn't help but think of the Las Vegas episode of *Friends* where Monica and Chandler look for signs that they should get married, and they're all positive. Although they decide to live together instead.

In my super-big room with panoramic views of the London skyline, I caught up on messages from home, even though I dreaded it. We had created a WhatsApp group so that Claire, Grace, Colin, Edwin and I could speak easily about the situation. It had a variety of humorous titles over the months; using my mother's name we created Trishtopher Reeves, RoboTrish, Oscar Trishtorius.

They said Mother was still in the Major Trauma Unit; still stable. Grace said she had requested a full investigation into her care because we felt the suicide attempt could have been prevented.

In response, Edwin pointed out that it was Lent tomorrow, and we should ask Mother what she was giving up.

Humour. Always the humour.

I knew my family weren't sharing the full story to keep me from worrying. They wished me luck for the ceremony, joking that they'd even crossed our unconscious mother's fingers.

And then I had to leave.

The taxi driver asked where I was going and was excited for me. 'I'll Google you,' he said.

When I got to the Royal Horseguards Hotel, I wasn't quite sure where the entrance to the huge building was and felt stupid, wandering gormlessly about, dressed up to the nines while it was still light. Eventually I found it, and a sweeping staircase – think Scarlett O'Hara – took me up to the Gladstone Library, where guests were milling about with drinks.

We were photographed by a professional. I liked that my shoes were pinching my toes because it kept me present. I needed it; the whole thing was surreal, like I was watching it after it had happened. I smiled as the camera flash went off. I also took a photo on my phone. Despite how I felt, it's one of my favourite pictures, with the pink banner and the London Eye lit up behind me. I look at it now, proud I went that night, alone, just four days after an event that even a year later I can't think about without wanting to go upstairs, climb into bed, and never emerge.

It was time to take our seats for the announcements.

I took off my shoes, but without that toe-pinching pain, I couldn't focus, so I put them back on again. I can hardly remember when they announced the winner in my category, and it wasn't my name. I hadn't won. I wanted to go home. Except I wasn't at home; I was two hundred miles away from it. I had a lovely but empty hotel room waiting for me. I left shortly after that because it hurt to smile and make small talk.

Back at the hotel, I rang Joe to tell him. He asked if I was OK, perhaps remembering the last time. I assured him that it was fine. How could I get upset about a book prize when my mother was still in the trauma unit? It was no tragedy in comparison.

I then messaged our family WhatsApp chat.

I wrote: *I didn't win. Which probably sums up this week.*

Colin wrote: *You won in getting there. And that ain't some pick-me-up shit.*

Edwin wrote: *Everyone's a winner!*

Grace and Claire asked how I felt. Then after a beat, Grace wrote: *Is now a good time to talk about Ted Baker?*

I had promised I would buy her a Ted Baker bag if I won.

Edwin wrote: *Who is Ted Baker? Excuse my ignorance.*

I wrote: *Handbag designer.*

Edwin wrote: *Oh, like Jimmy Shoe.*

I had never loved them more. Or missed them more. Or felt more alone. I was still travelling up to Manchester for the book tour in the morning, but I couldn't sleep for a long time.

Maybe I should have worn a red dress.

Maybe I should have stayed at home.

Maybe everything was just happening exactly how it was supposed to, and it's never meant to be easy, and what the hell, maybe I'd get a book out of it.

13

Waiting for the shrapnel

While daffodils in the UK are synonymous with the colour yellow, daffodil species are often white, with breeders trying to develop deeper, richer and clearer colours like orange or pink.

The morning after the awards ceremony, I woke early, having barely slept, and got ready to leave for Manchester. I was excited but also felt overwhelmed by the events I'd have to do, three nights on the trot. I love meeting readers, signing pages. But that day, as the light woke gently over London, I longed to be at home.

I caught up on messages in our family WhatsApp chat.

Grace wrote: *I've started experiencing a heavy feeling of guilt.*

I wrote: *We could never have known Mother would do this.*

Claire wrote: *She hid her plan to jump very well, lying about where she was in the days leading up to it.*

Colin wrote: *Only the illness was to blame, with a slim chance it could've been avoided if they had sectioned her, as she'd wanted.*

Edwin wrote: *It's been a long day. No one needs to feel guilty. If there is any guilt, then your mother must own it.*

Claire wrote: *My good psychologist friend told me that in her vast experience, there's nothing you can do to help someone who's suicidal, aside from sectioning and suicide watch. We need to look after ourselves now. We are experiencing trauma and unfortunately it is repetitive of our childhood experiences, so particularly severe. Of course, we help Mother, but we must look after ourselves.*

She was right. Had I made a big mistake coming away, spending lonely nights in a variety of hotels when I needed my family? Tough. I had to leave and head out to Euston station.

On the train I wrote in our chat: *Hello Suicide Squad. Just catching up on messages. It's hard to be away from you. Plus, I'm travelling so it's hard to focus on it all, so apologies. Taking in your thoughts and processing mine still.*

Claire wrote: *Thinking of you, Louise.*

I wrote: *If I don't respond, it's only cos I'm working/travelling.*

Claire wrote: *So not because you don't give a shit.*

I wrote: *You're all cunts and I'm never coming back!*

Grace wrote: *Remember that* A Star is Born *didn't win that award because* Bohemian Rhapsody *won it.*

I wrote: *Are you saying that the winner last night had big teeth and was the lead singer of a rock band?*

Grace wrote: *That's exactly what I'm saying.*

I spoke with Joe and he told me how proud he was of me for going ahead with the tour. The journey passed in a blur and before I knew it, I was in Manchester Piccadilly station and the other authors descended on me. Our publisher had told them what happened with my mother. I needed them to know, in case I got upset or had to escape. They squashed me in a huge hug. Johana, a French author, grabbed my hand and said in her glorious accent, 'You come to me if you need anything.' Her beloved grandmother died while we were at Crimefest two years earlier and I felt so sad for her that I'd not left her side. Now she returned that love.

That evening, at the hotel, I caught up on further messages from the family.

Colin wrote: *With Mother now. She's quite alert and significantly less confused than yesterday when she came around. She keeps asking for bloody yoghurt but it's nil by mouth as she has surgery on her back and knee tomorrow.*

Grace wrote: *She's singing opera to Andrea Bocelli, which is a good sign, though not so much for everyone else in the hospital.*

This was just five days after the jump, so quite the miracle.

But I had to close these messages, cover my tired lines, draw on the smile people expected from me, and go to the Waterstones event. It took every ounce of my energy – quite literally a huge inhalation of breath – to walk out of the door. We sat in a row, fifteen writers, and their company buoyed me.

But as I did a reading from my new novel, I felt detached. Like I was watching from above. I had recently taken part in a workshop that taught me to look down at the line on the page and then look up to actually say it, so that you connect with the audience. I'd enjoyed the effect of doing this when I had read an emotional scene aloud a year earlier and looked up to see a renowned blogger and dear friend crying openly.

But now, I couldn't do it. I stumbled through the words.

My friend was in the audience again. She hugged me afterwards and said quietly in my ear, 'Louise, I feel like you've lost your sparkle tonight.'

I told her why, and she held me tighter.

I was scared then that I had lost it for good.

That I was changed forever; sparkle-less.

We went to a bar after the event. I was flagging. I felt ignorant checking my phone, but I had to, in case there was news. The gin made me lightheaded; made me feel again like I was watching our group from above, there but yet not there.

My phone buzzed. The dread at opening the message made me feel sick, but it was Joe saying I'd been sent flowers. He sent a picture. The card read – *We're thinking of you, Louise. With much love, John, John & Oscar xxx.* John is a dear writer friend of mine.

I was so touched by the gesture that I had to excuse myself and go to the toilets because I knew I was going to cry. My mother had received showers of flowers and cards, rightly so. But these were the only ones I got during that time. And I wasn't even at home to enjoy them.

That night in bed, I thought endlessly about what it must feel like to walk up to a bridge and jump; putting one foot in front of another, getting there, taking your shoes and coat off, climbing over the railings, and *jumping*. Did my mother pause to think? Was she scared? Did she almost change her mind?

I've had some dark moments – and I've certainly been through things that would push anyone over the edge – but I feel lucky or blessed (or whatever you want to call it) that I've never once wanted to die. Is it in our DNA to feel so inclined? If so, I *should* have felt that way. Is it due to external circumstances rather than DNA? If so, again, I *should* perhaps have felt this way, at some point. Is it a mix of the two? Mother never helped herself with drinking and other behaviours, but I'm not perfect either, by any stretch. Why have I embraced life so much with this darkness around me and in me? I feel sadness deeply, overwhelmingly, but I love life.

I love living.

Depression is an illness. As much as any other. And just like with any other – with cancer, with a cold, with type 2 diabetes – you can do things that help. We told my mother for years and years to stop drinking. To get help. Not just because she destroyed relationships and our childhood, but because she was prone to depression, and drinking could bring it back. She was in denial about it for almost forty years. She paid for that, I believe, on 28th February 2019, when she jumped.

But we did too.

I thought about this over and over, all night, and realised that along with my siblings, it is my creativity that has saved me. The gift my mother gave me – in part – helped me deal with the things she did to us.

In the morning I opened our family chat.

I wrote: *Surgery today then. Sending thoughts. Have you explained to her where I am, so she doesn't just think I've buggered off? It's tiring being cheerful but these are lovely people.*

Grace wrote: *Mother is going down for surgery now. The morphine has made her paranoid. She thinks the hospital are plotting to throw her off the top of the building. I told her we are doing a full surveillance all the time, on all staff.*

I wrote: *That's sad.*

Claire wrote: *Where to today, Louise?*

I wrote: *Birmingham. It's surreal. Like I'm in some sort of dream.*

It was fun travelling with a bunch of writers, despite what was happening at home. Perhaps I had done the right thing after all, and this was exactly what I needed. The event in Birmingham Waterstones was packed. I read a different passage in the hope of finding my sparkle. Afterwards, I didn't go out for drinks. I needed to find out how Mother's surgery had gone, so I went back to the hotel.

Claire wrote: *Mother is still in theatre. They're 'closing her up' now and then they will assess where she goes when she wakes. It'll either be recovery for a few hours or to ICU.*

After a while she added: *Good news. She's now back on the trauma ward and good, but very tired.*

I fell straight asleep, exhausted, though only for a few hours.

In the morning Edwin wrote: *Anybody up and about?*

I wrote: *Me. Not sleeping well while away and in different hotels.*

I got dressed again, this time to travel to our final destination, Hungerford. The event that night was our biggest audience, perhaps almost two hundred people. Hoping to liven it up, and bring some of my missing sparkle back, I read a sex scene, much to my publisher's horror. Perhaps I shouldn't have; I didn't sell as many books as I had at the other venues, but you live and learn.

I went straight to my hotel room again afterwards.

I was about to fall asleep when Colin messaged us with a full outline from Mother's surgeon. Her spine had been broken in five places. The surgery had been keyhole so there was very little blood loss. Her sacrum was broken. Bolts and screws were holding her back in place. Her neck was fractured so a brace would be required for a time. They planned to put a frame around her shattered leg and reconstruct the knee, but there was still a high chance of amputation. He stressed that she was a long, *long* way from being out of the woods. I thought again of his grenade analogy.

I thought also of shrapnel. I read a story recently about a war veteran who woke with a strange object in his mouth. It was a half-inch shard of metal that had lodged in his body sixty-five years earlier during combat, and only now worked its way out.

If Mother had stood on a grenade, then we had taken the shrapnel.

I thought the next morning, as I packed to come home, how incredible the body is. It was a week on from the jump; it felt like it had been a lifetime. Our mother was making great physical progress.

Now, I'm waiting to spit out the shrapnel.

Does it sparkle?

If so, when it finally works its way out, we will all light up like fucking fireworks.

14

The Cottage

If you were born in March, then
daffodils are your birthday flower.

It's strange how a house changes.

I don't mean because we paint the walls a fresh colour or buy designer wardrobes or build a huge extension. I mean that we *see* it differently when we look back on the changing phases of our lives within its walls.

When we moved into what I then called The Cottage, it was brand new inside. Old furniture came with us – like the white Formica table and green floral sofa – but the kitchen had modern, brown cupboards and crisp white walls. There was a long back garden, wire mesh fence on one side and beyond, a muddy wasteland and the park. Though not yet spring, it felt like it. Two nearby churches kept our small house in shadow; their bells tolled every quarter hour, even through the night. The sash windows weren't double-glazed but after a while we got used to this noisy marking of our existence.

I slept in what we called the Square Bedroom with Colin – I'm smiling at how we labelled things so simply in the midst of our hectic lives. Claire and Grace were in the Long Bedroom next door. It's curious, I realise, this need to state where we all slept in each house we lived. As adults, my sisters and I often say to each other, 'What room were we in when such and such happened?' And the darker question of: 'Who was downstairs then?' And the darkest of all: 'Who was upstairs?'

I loved sharing with Colin. He was in a cot and I'd pick him up when he woke early, take him in my bed, and tell him made-up stories. I loved the warmth of him; how he smiled at my words. His rapt attention at my tales was magic. Looking back, this must have given my mum a break.

Although the house had no central heating, there was at least a coal fire in the front room and a gas fire in the kitchen, so it was cosy in there. Claire, Grace and I huddled around the gas fire to get dressed in the morning. It was here that Colin took his first steps. My friend called for me to walk to school and she witnessed it too. He was naked – the way toddlers love to be, despite any temperature – and walked across the room with a big grin on his face. We clapped and clapped for him. This memory is bright and joyful; it's indicative of how I felt in that house then.

I loved being able to have my best friend over to play, now we lived in the town again, just a ten-minute walk from school. Our Grandma Armitage knitted coats and dresses for my Sindy doll, and we played with these. My friend had the official Sindy house, car, stables and pool, but I made do with my homemade fashions, and my imagination.

Grace: *When I have on the head of that five-year-old, and I'm walking through Hessle, it all looks different. I don't remember physically moving into that house, but it felt new: I called it The New House. I remember it raining and the kitchen being steamed up with whatever food was being made. The bathroom was nicer than we had had before.*

On Sundays our father picked us up and took us out. He'd wait in his car outside, take us to Scoutwood or to feed the ducks at Melton

– maybe to see Grandma Armitage or Aunt Jane – and then drop us back home. Only occasionally did he come inside, and when he did my parents were amicable with one another. Separately, not so much. My father told us our mum was a clown – comical, to be fair – and she told us, more harshly, that he was selfish, spineless and violent. Unfortunately, I was apparently 'just like him'. The cruellest thing a parent can do is speak badly of the other one to a child. I believed my mum when she said these things about me.

But *why* did she say them?

I've been reading more about narcissist personality disorder (NPD) as I explore the past, though I'm still not entirely sure this applies to my mum. I'm not an expert, so it's all speculation. An article I read suggested that mothers with this disorder are envious of their daughters and so belittle them; that they see themselves as perfect so ignore any undesirable traits. They do this by 'handing them to' the nearest recipient – a daughter. I was repeatedly told I was greedy, spineless, selfish. And I believe(d) it. We are programmed to trust our parents.

Something compels me to read more about NPD.

Something about it… *fits* her.

Edwin: *I don't have many vivid memories of Tower Hill back then, to be honest. I had left Saudi* (where Edwin worked) *and come back to England because I was changing jobs. Me, Allison* (first wife), *and Christine* (second wife) *definitely came. You were all little. I recall the house being cold, which seemed a common theme. Christine felt the cold particularly as back in Canada the houses are very warm. It got to bedtime and your mother said, 'Oh, well, I'll go upstairs and close the bedroom window.' The look on Allison and Christine's faces! Cold as it was, the bloody bedroom window had been open. The three of us slept in one bed because it was the only room available and were plagued by the sound of the church bells all night. There were so many blankets on the bed that once in, it was impossible to turn over or move. Your mother was a little on edge. I don't recall discussing her situation a great deal.*

I enjoyed school, though I always believed I was below average. My father took an interest academically, but anything less than an A was criticised. Understanding him now, as an adult, and in light of realising he probably has ASD, I see that he wanted the perfectionism in me that he insisted on from himself. It can be an obsession for people on the spectrum, especially those with a high IQ. But obviously, as a child, one who was insecure anyway, this criticism hurt me then.

A few months ago, Joe showed me some pictures of 1970s reading books online. I recognised them immediately. The colour of the spine signified their level; gold was Free Readers.

'I loved those,' I cried.

When I realised I'd been reading them from Year Two, Joe insisted I couldn't have been because that would mean I'd read all the levels by the age of six. But I had. I suppose it's understandable with my love of and hunger for words. I was average in all other subjects, but in English I excelled.

Our teacher then was odd. Now there is a much longer word for him. Now he would have been sacked. Let us call him Mr C. He was middle-aged, tall with thin grey hair, and flirtatious. When girls stood next to his desk, he pulled their socks up and kept his hand underneath their skirts. No one wanted to be kept behind, and fortunately I was well-behaved, so I never was.

When Claire and Grace were in his class some years after me, they described how their classmate's father charged into Mr C's classroom and battered him with his umbrella. The headteacher came in and tried to intervene. I tried to imagine how it must feel to have a parent so passionately defend me. He didn't get sacked though. Claire recalls that many years later she saw him with groups of children, on some sort of school outing. Thankfully, times have changed now.

One day I was taken out of Mr C's class early.

The memory was fragmented before; now it's clear. They say that when we remember something, we are only remembering the last time we remembered it. That memories change with us. But this is a first. The colours of it are cut-your-finger sharp.

It was March.

We had only lived in The Cottage for two months.

A woman from the office came into the classroom and whispered into Mr C's ear. I knew he was going to look at me. He did; and I was led away by this woman, who told me my mother had been taken ill and I was to go and collect my sisters from the nearby infant school, something I did every day when I took them home. I always walked in the middle, holding each of their hands, their trust in me absolute. Now was no different, just at an earlier time. They must have asked why we were going home, but I can't recall what I said. And I must have wondered why we *had* to go home because Mum was ill. She had been ill before. We all had. And no one came home early from school.

There were daffodils in the front garden.

And there was a strange woman in our kitchen.

She had reddish hair and wore a grey suit, and she was sitting on the white Formica chair that my mother had sat crying on so many times. She cheerfully told us we were going to our grandma's house for a few days. We must have asked where our mum was, but I don't recall the answer given. If it comes to me, I'll edit this, though then you'll never know I had forgotten it. *(I'm editing to say that I now recall being told our mum was in the hospital, but the woman having no idea how long for.)*

'What about Colin?' I wanted to know.

'Someone's collecting him from nursery,' the red-haired woman said.

'Is he coming with us?' I asked.

'No,' she said simply.

'Where's he going? Why isn't he coming with us?'

She was vague. Not knowing this made me far more anxious than not knowing how long our mum would be away from us. I didn't want to leave without my brother. But we were hurried out of the door and into the back of her yellow Mini. I never got to say goodbye to him. I thought of my Sindy doll upstairs, waiting for me to change her clothes for bed, and of my Tiny Tears doll in her cot. I could have asked if I could go back and grab a toy – if Claire and Grace could – but I didn't like to fuss. And also, I didn't think we would be away long.

I know now that the red-haired woman was a social worker.

I know now that my mother wasn't just ill.

She had attempted suicide.

Give or take two weeks, exactly thirty-nine years before she jumped off the bridge.

My siblings have no memory of it, but absence of memory can be a blessing.

15

RoboTrish

As every flower lover knows, flowers have a language of their own. Every sentiment is expressed in one form or another by these blooms. With a daffodil, it is 'The sun is always shining when I'm with you.'

The first sign that I was home from my book tour was the Humber Bridge, a cement grey welcome waiting for me like a cross parent. Visible from the motorway on the approach to Hull, and arching over the train tracks, it has always meant 'You're home'. But home filled me with dread. I knew Claire was up from Grantham, and that we siblings would be together again tomorrow, which cheered me. But I was exhausted in every way possible, in my bones, physically, emotionally, mentally.

On the train home we had been messaging in the usual family WhatsApp chat. Mother had mostly been drowsy but able to laugh at their comments. She was having IV paracetamol for a high temperature, which can indicate an infection, so this was a concern. But it eventually came down. A few of her friends had visited and, when awake, she seemed to have enjoyed this. I talked to Joe, and he said he felt deeply sad and had had to come home from work early.

The impact of this one, violent act was having such far-reaching effects on all of us. I worried endlessly about how my children must really be feeling. With them away, it was hard to know how much they kept to themselves.

I found comfort in our WhatsApp chat.

Colin wrote: *Joe visited Mother last night. He is kind and clearly fond of her, which is surprising cos she's a cunt.*

I wrote: *I've quite enjoyed your emotional side these last eight days, Colin.*

Colin wrote: *Drink it in. It won't be here forever.*

Edwin wrote: *Have you seen the leg? Or is it covered in Band Aids?*

Claire wrote: *It's got bolts going through it in four places, top to bottom, and is in a temp frame. Keeps bleeding. They should be doing the leg op on Wednesday.*

I wrote: *Has Mother had any sex while on the ward this week? It's a human right.*

Claire wrote: *She hasn't but I sure have.*

Edwin wrote*: Happy International Women's Day!*

Our jokes might shock people. A friend of mine says humour is the wonky mirror for emotions often too difficult to look at directly. Our laughter doesn't mean we don't care – that we're cold or flippant – but the opposite. It's a coping mechanism. It releases the stress when there's no other outlet. When things are impossibly difficult. We have always been this way. We were never allowed to express our concerns as children, so we found a safe vent for our pain: comedy. Therefore, the bigger the disaster, the darker our jokes. Looking back now on those messages as I read them, I've cried at the tragedy – and then laughed uproariously at our silliness.

As Mark Twain said, 'Humour is tragedy plus time.'

Joe was waiting for me at Hessle station, a solitary figure on the platform, shivering in the cold. I'd never been happier to see him. It occurred to me that I was as close to broken as I might ever have been, or at least as far as I could remember being. As he pulled my suitcase home, there was everything and nothing to say.

That night, Ricky Gervais' new show *Afterlife* premiered on Netflix. The series follows Tony, whose life is turned upside down when his wife dies of breast cancer. He considers suicide, but instead decides to live long enough to punish the world for his wife's death by saying and doing whatever he wants, no matter how harsh. Although he thinks of this as a superpower, his plan is undermined when everyone tries to make him a better person.

I watched the first three episodes in bed. It could not have been more pertinent at that moment, not only because Colin had been chuffed when Ricky liked one of his tweets earlier, but because of the subject matter. Tony's dog Brandy saves him from suicide in the sea when she barks and barks as he tries to drown.

I felt sure that the love of my children would stop me.

But how can we ever know, until we are there, in the water or on a bridge, with our feet over the edge poised to jump?

The following morning was a Saturday. Once again, the four of us gathered at Grace's house. At 10am – Tasmania time 7pm – we phoned Edwin and put him on speaker. Most of his concern was for our wellbeing. He may never know how much that touched me, which is a lie because he will as soon as he reads this.

'Your mother is in good hands,' he said. 'She's getting the round-the-clock care she craves, while you're left with the fallout. Take time for yourselves.'

He was still trying to decide whether it was worth flying over to see Mother now or to wait and see how she fared after further operations. He liked the idea of surprising her on her birthday in two months' time. We left it unsaid that there was still every chance she might not make it that far.

When we were done, we took Grace's little ones – Michael and Iris – to karate, had some lunch at KFC, and went to the hospital. As we climbed the stairs, I felt sick. Despite all the descriptive messages, I had no idea what to expect. I had last seen Mother unconscious and fragile. Now she was on the trauma ward on floor four, Ward 40, in a bed by the window. It had quite the view; she later said she was sad to see the trains going by when she was not on one.

'Oh, hello there,' she said to me as I rounded the curtain, chirpy in an unnatural way. It was the morphine. 'Where've you been?'

'London and then the tour,' I said. 'I had my awards thing, remember?'

'Oh yes. Did you win?'

'No.'

'Oh, well, not to worry. You can't win 'em all.'

I was surprised by the difference in just six days. Last time she had been completely out of it. Before that she had been clinically depressed. Now she was mostly conscious, aside from sleeping on and off. She wasn't allowed to eat because she was a swallowing risk – due to all the spinal injuries – so until they could do an assessment, she was being fed via a thin tube that took yellow liquid food through the nose into her stomach. She was also still on oxygen and had fat white gloves on her hands because she kept trying to pull these necessary tubes free. We could hold a sponge and let her suck water from it though, which we did often, her expression agitated, maybe due to the thirst. The scars on her face were healing, but she still looked like she'd just got back from a warzone.

'I hope they don't swap my legs over when they operate,' she said during a lucid moment. 'That won't look right.'

Laughing, we assured her they knew what they were doing.

'The surgeons want to chuck me out of the window,' she insisted.

'They don't,' I said. 'They wouldn't waste time, money and effort fixing you up to do that.'

It was interesting how afraid she was of being so high up when the fourth floor was more or less the height of where she had climbed over a railing and jumped. It was also interesting that the depression seemed to have lifted, but I couldn't help thinking it might be the pain medication that was buoying her.

At times she thought she was on a ship in the North Sea, describing it so vividly that I felt sure the floor was swaying. We took turns going for cups of tea, with her warning us that there were 'weirdos' in the ship's bar. We felt it best to go along with whatever she said, just as you should with dementia patients who are stuck in some past time era.

While she slept, we busied ourselves, chatting with staff about her, and looking at the many cards lining the windowsill. We brought favourite pictures from her house and had a recent one of the four of us printed and framed. Our children had also either drawn pictures or written little notes for her.

The ward was hectic. Some patients stayed only hours before being moved to where was more appropriate. Visitors came and went in various states of distress. Buzzers went off constantly. The staff were clearly overworked but dedicated. During a quieter moment I said, 'Mother, have you seen *Robocop*?'

'*Robocop*? Does he work here?'

'No. It's a film about a cop who becomes a cyborg after being blown apart. Once rebuilt, his movements have cool sound effects.' I did an impression. 'You might have that when they rebuild you. Hopefully, anyway.'

Understandably, Mother looked mystified, but it was after this we changed the title of our WhatsApp family chat to RoboTrish.

As we left after a long day, Grace tenderly held her hand and said, 'I love you.'

'You don't look like you do,' Mother responded.

Claire went home Saturday evening. She had taken a full week off work to spend so much time with Mother; now she had no choice but to leave. Between us, we'd been making sure that someone was with our mother at all times during the day, but it grew impossible as jobs and family and homes and other commitments beckoned. We were neglecting everything else, including ourselves. Caring for and seeing Mother required so much – dealing with a variety of doctors and surgeons and mental health carers, sorting out her house and finances and caravan up north, looking into her future care, and updating the many friends and family members who contacted us. When there's no time to look at how you are doing, you don't realise how far you've pushed yourself until it's too late – until you get ill. We were close to this point.

That night, in the newly named RoboTrish WhatsApp, Grace wrote: *For the first time, I'm getting upset, angry, feeling let down, worthless.*

I wrote: *Take time out. You need it.*

Grace wrote: *Yes. I've given every fibre of my being to her that last week and realise she has never done it for me.*

I wrote: *Everyone here in this chat will understand that.*

Grace wrote: *How many people are in this chat?*

I wrote: *86.*

Grace wrote: *That's fine as long as only 86.*

Edwin wrote: *I thought there were 93 in the group.*

I wrote: *Nah, we got rid of those other seven losers.*

The following day – a Sunday – Mother's cousin and her partner came down from Stockton-on-Tees for the day. She had previously enjoyed visits to them there – and no doubt a drink or fifty – and they had always spoken fondly of her. Grace had decided not to come, but then said she was struggling being away from us, her siblings, so joined me. Colin took a day off. Mother was quite well for the visit, awake often and laughing at jokes, if a little manic. She had been given blood, ready for surgery, which perked her up, and had had some sort of breathing test for her reflexes. She'd also had her hair washed and was finally wearing one of her own nighties.

Knowing her love of all things bovine, Mother's cousin brought her a large, stuffed cow, which she promptly kept on her pillow.

'Can I borrow your shoes?' she asked me, out of the blue.

'My shoes?' I said.

'Yes. They look OK.'

'What do you want them for?' asked Grace.

'To wear.' Mother tutted. 'I don't have mine.'

I thought of the brown ones, left at the bridge, now in her bedside cabinet. Maybe she didn't want to look at them. She still had not mentioned that day yet.

'But I'm a size eight, and you're a five.' I laughed. We were all giggling. 'They'd look ridic. And you don't need shoes here. You ain't bloody going anywhere.'

'But I want to come home with you and Grace,' she said.

'You can't,' said Grace, kindly.

'We can push this bed back to Tower Hill,' she insisted. 'You,' she said to her cousin, 'can distract the nurses, and these two will help me push it back to the park.'

'We can't,' we said sadly.

I felt sorry for her wanting to go home.

I knew this feeling. I knew it too well.

Edwin had recorded a message, which we played for her. He wanted a live phone call too, but we had to plan it so that her being alert coincided with him being on a decent time in Tasmania, and this proved almost impossible. Throughout the afternoon, she kept farting and – perhaps due to all her meds – it was rank, which she found amusing.

A nurse came in to do her vitals, something that happened on the hour.

'I'm going to report this to the police,' Mother said to us.

'They're just doing your blood pressure,' laughed Grace.

'I know. The police need to know what's going on here.'

Clearly, the drugs were making her paranoid. As I have said often, our mother has a rich sense of humour and a wonderful flair for language. Now, she was Tony from Ricky Gervais' *Afterlife* series, saying and doing what she wanted, and causing much amusement for us.

'That nurse is even uglier today than she was yesterday,' she said loudly, with the poor woman still at the end of the bed.

Grace and I apologised to the nurse.

'We don't mind,' said the nurse. 'We love her, don't we?'

'They do,' agreed my mother wholeheartedly.

Before it got dark, Mother's cousin left to go back up north. Mother asked again if Grace and I could sneak her out, somehow fold her up and put her in the car boot. We had to go home alone. It was time for us *all* to go home. To return to work. To get back on with life. I felt desperately sad for this broken, mentally ill, alcoholic woman in the hospital, who just wanted to go home.

Home is a theme I've explored – often unknowingly at the time – in many novels. If not home, then where we belong; where we are supposed to *be*. I've written characters lost at sea, longing for the safety of land. I've written children lost in the care system, longing for a forever home.

My mother wanted to go home.

I had been wanting to go home since I was nine.

16

Thanks Jeels for our meals

Though it may seem weak and easily uprooted by a garden shovel, in the wild, the daffodil can survive hardily.

19th March 1980

Dear Mrs Roberts,

Please find enclosed the family allowance book, which has been countersigned by your daughter, so you are now able to draw child benefit. I have also written to your local Department of Health and Social Security office, informing them of the fact that you are now caring for Louise, Claire and Grace.

Letter from a social worker to our Grandma Roberts

I woke that first morning at Grandma's house – on the day the above letter was sent – and wondered for a moment where I was. It's a graphic memory, as bright as a white firework. I recognised the tiny, box room but couldn't think why I was there. I knew the patterned tan curtains at the window and the limited floor space due to a raised ledge caused by the stairs, and the wooden cross on the wall. But I was alone. Claire and Grace were in the bigger room across the landing. This upset me; I was used to my sisters or brother sleeping near me.

Then I remembered.

Mum was ill.

Colin had been taken home from nursery by a stranger.

We had come to Stockton-on-Tees with a red-haired woman.

I don't recall much else about that first day, other than the moment I woke and realised I was there, and that we had porridge with cream for breakfast, me sitting on the saggy armchair at the kitchen table, Claire and Grace on the wooden seats, and Grandma bustling about before joining us with her brown mug of tea.

These were positions we assumed for each meal, like actors in a regular soap opera, but that day it was novel, confusing, and yet a comfort. It was a Wednesday; I have checked. According to our care records, we started at the Catholic school nearby that very day. I'm shocked by the speed at which we were deposited into this new life. I can't recall my first day at St Peter and Paul's, but I remember thinking that when the red-haired woman told us we were only going to be here a few days, she must have lied.

Why were we starting a new school if we were going home next week?

We had lived in five different places in nine months, but this modest three-bedroom council house opposite a school, with the Virgin Mary's dazzling blue eyes observing us from every wall and shelf – my beloved grandma's home – was somewhere I didn't mind being, whatever the circumstances. That said, I was anxious.

Why was my mum ill? How long would she be in hospital? Where had my brother gone? Who was he with? Were they looking after him? Was someone going to move into The Cottage in our absence?

Looking back with adult eyes, I can't imagine what this sudden circumstance was like for our grandma. She would have received a phone call the previous day. She may or may not have been told that her daughter had gone to a solitary waste ground and consumed all of her medication with a bottle of vodka. She may or may not have been told that her daughter was only alive because a homeless man found her, that she could be in hospital a long time. She may or may not have been told that her daughter had still been awake when this stranger encouraged her to throw up and called the hospital. She may or may not have been told that her daughter had been oblivious, on her way to final darkness.

I've no idea which version is true because Grandma never spoke about it to me, and Mother's two shared versions – one with Grace in later years, and one with me – are very different. Claire also heard an entirely different version, though she can't recall who told her it.

Our care records tell us that Grandma had to admit she couldn't keep the four of us together; it was too much to cope with. She was sixty-one after all, and Colin was a baby in nappies still. She must have been sad about this. She had to give up her job cleaning hospitals, which must have been hard, but with her strong Christian values and good heart, she would likely have just got on with it. She told me once that her colleagues had a collection, to help out financially.

What must Grandma have felt, phone in hand that shocking day, taking it in?

Like we had, getting the call when Mum jumped?

Whatever she felt, she got on with caring for us.

From the moment we arrived, she provided us with a home. A clean house with two large rooms downstairs, the kitchen and the front room, and a coal house leading into a tiny square garden with a log at the end to sit on.

It was a simple existence. One that involved Mary (her favourite) and Jesus, because she was a devout Catholic. One that involved going to church Saturday and Sunday, loving being fussed by the congregation who clearly adored our grandma. One that involved getting into trouble for (God forbid!) turning around in the pews. One that involved home-cooked meals that ended my aversion to food and not being allowed to laugh at the table, having to say grace before we ate – our own prayer that we secretly whispered was *Thanks Jeels for our meals*. One that involved spying on Grandma while she bathed and having her call, 'I can see you there!' One that involved dressing up in her scarves because we had no toys, and making dolls out of paper and playing theatrical games with detailed storylines and characters like Heidi, Patrukal and Shrivel, who basically were always on the run from the evil Madame Charlotte (the *e* pronounced *ay*), and who used Grandma's bed as the horse and carriage on which they escaped.

Claire*: I felt at Grandma's – putting to one side our mum's situation – security and a boring but safe routine that we hadn't ever had. With hindsight, I realise this was good for me, this feeling of always having Grandma with us. Although she didn't play or be childlike, she was always there, stable, totally reliable, not drunk, not depressed. I got from Grandma the nurturing mother that I was missing. I loved us all being together for TV and that she then put us to bed. Mum had never done that. We had to lean over and give her the kiss and then take ourselves to bed. Grandma did things I wanted my own mum to do, so the whole thing was bittersweet.*

My father never visited during our time in Stockton. He was on call as the chief engineer at Hull Royal Infirmary so couldn't leave the area. A practical man, he had apparently offered to have us every weekend if we could go into care during the week. This suggestion was rejected as not ideal. In those days, men worked, and few looked after children full-time, so he would never have been expected to take time off work for us. A note in our care records on 25th June 1980 states that he had, however, visited Colin at his foster home three times, which suggests it had been once a month. Father freely stated that he intended to 'turn Colin against Mother'. Whatever his reasons for not visiting us at Grandma's, they are his, and fortunately it didn't grieve me too much.

Most children, however, find it impossible to detach from their primary carer. There are endless memes and quotes about the unconditional love a mother has for her child. How it is made of deep devotion and sacrifice and pain; how nothing can destroy it. This isn't always the case though. But even so, a child longs desperately for that mum if she is gone.

In bed at night, I often pushed the covers off my body, so I was cold. It numbed the pain of missing her. I didn't cry. My tears froze between my heart and my eyes. I was a loveless icicle. It was safer that way. Such sadness was overwhelming, terrifying.

Edwin was working in Saudi Arabia, at Bakhsh Hospital in Jeddah, during this time. It was an era when international phone calls were not the norm, and though he wrote letters to his mother, our grandma, he says he can't recall either her or Mum sharing the seriousness of this situation with him. He was in the dark about events in England, and only learnt of them now, in the shadow of Mum's more recent suicide attempt.

The bridge tragedy has led to some surprising outcomes.

Despite the sudden change of school, I enjoyed my time at St Peter and Paul's. As a Catholic school, things were a little different, with the school canteen having tables under a large cross and prayers regularly being said. I made friends, mainly two girls called Allison and Susan, who said my accent was strange. I felt special, being different. As always, I particularly enjoyed English and remember the teacher saying I had beautiful handwriting, and me telling her, 'I'm going to be a writer one day.' I still read voraciously and discovered my childhood favourite, *Heidi*, during this time. The story of a little girl separated from her family resonated strongly with me.

On a weekend there was church and a walk to Hintons, the supermarket at that time, or the local shops, where Grandma bought fresh bread and we could pick a treat in the sweet shop.

Sometimes we walked to nearby village, Norton, for a jumble sale. I got so excited about getting a toy once that I couldn't decide which one and rashly picked a flowery, stuffed camel that I cursed because I should have chosen something useful, like a book I could write in. Then we played all afternoon in the tiny back garden, with just our vivid imaginations and whatever bricks, scarves, paper or wool there was to hand.

Grandma told us little about Mum. She must have been regularly updated by social workers, but if it affected her, she kept it well from us. I can't recall particularly asking when we might see Mum again. I felt it might upset my grandma, so kept the many questions in my head. But I got to be the child I'd never been able to be in Stockton. I didn't need to watch Claire and Grace as they slept because Grandma was there. Plus, I had my own room, which though it had at first disorientated me, I ended up liking. I didn't take the twins to school now – Grandma walked us all. In some ways, doing this for my sisters had been a comfort. I liked *giving* that love. Liked being needed by them.

I worried most how Colin was. At night I wondered who would take him out of his cot in the morning and tell him made-up stories like I had. Notes in his care records on 25th April 1980 say he had settled into his new placement, seemed popular with family members, his clothing was sufficient and clean, and the accommodation was cramped but adequate. He also had eczema, which may have been stress related.

I'm glad I hadn't known this then.

Grace: *I still feel the pain now of longing for Mum. Even when she was there, it felt like we didn't have her. The longing was never met, always present, a constant, and I lived in that state. So now we are emotionally retarded in many ways. More so than Mum herself. The worst of it was when we were at St Peter and Paul's school. Maybe because Grandma wasn't with us. I remember the pain. It's the worst pain I've had in my life. No human being has* *broken my heart the way Mum has. She first broke it when I was five. And it will probably never mend.*

According to our care records, Mum was living in The Cottage again by May 1980 and began visiting Colin at his foster home. When I was an adult, she told me she was in hospital most of the time we were away from her. I sought my care records a few years ago – to try and get answers to gaps that come later in this story – and I was surprised to read that she had in fact only been hospitalised for a few weeks. In May, Mum saw Colin once a week, though she wasn't allowed to do it alone. She expressed in one report that she felt guilty about upsetting him, yet little affection, which is sad, and understandable. She wished to resume his care but wasn't allowed and was agitated about it.

On 26th June 1980, when we'd been with Grandma three months, a report describes how Mum 'was adamant she was taking us home'. It states that the consultant and social worker felt she should 'not resume care of her children for the foreseeable future' and that in the event of her trying to get us, an application would be made for Place of Safety Orders. There's a note on the page that her boyfriend agreed with the social worker about leaving us where we were.

Said boyfriend was a man she had met in a nightclub.

One fun afternoon was being taken to see *Dumbo* by Grandma's niece and nephew. I was delighted to have a whole Mars Bar to myself, not a third of one shared with my sisters. I ate it slowly, the edge first, making it last. Claire and Grace were equally delighted to choose their own treat.

Another big day was when we made our First Holy Communion. In simple terms, it's a religious ceremony performed in church by Catholics when a child is seven, celebrating the first time that they accept the bread and wine (known as the Eucharist). This symbolises the body and blood of Christ. It would have been a huge day for Grandma. Photos of that day show us in checked/flowered dresses rather than the traditional white gown, with small veils atop our heads, so clearly it was a hurried affair. I stuck out like a poor bridesmaid at an expensive wedding, not only for the gaudy frock, but because I was tall for nine, and the oldest.

Grace: *I remember watching old black-and-white films like Laurel and Hardy. We made friends with the kids who lived nearby and played with them. We came home once and there were beanbag frogs on the stairs waiting for us. Not sure who bought us them, I think the church people. We loved those. We also got these tiny babies in matchboxes from the Vee Gee shop.*

Grandma had a bottle of holy water on the top of the kitchen cabinet; the vessel was a clear plastic replica of the Virgin Mary. She said it was from a special place called Lourdes, which is a town in France where Mary is said to have appeared to a peasant girl, Bernadette Soubirous, eighteen times. Lourdes hosts around six million visitors every year, a constant stream of pilgrims there to worship. Mary told Bernadette to dig in the ground at a certain spot and sip the water. Cures were reported from drinking there, and countless miracles are supposed to have happened. It is cherished water.

And we often drank it.

I stood on the armchair and reached for it, being the tallest. If Grandma noticed, she never said. However, a holy miracle occurred in the Roberts household that year. As we drank, remarkably the water returned. I knew Grandma was quietly refilling the bottle and perhaps didn't want to tell us off. But I let Claire and Grace think they were drinking magic water.

Grandma prayed daily with rosary beads.

I sometimes caught her, whispering fervently at her bedside, tiny cross glinting in the light. I still know the Hail Mary by heart, and always have a string of those pretty beads in my drawer, just to feel connected to that holiest mother of all to me: Grandma

Roberts. She inspired Nanny Eve in *Maria in the Moon*, and the line, *She'd always hum the same tune, and I'd know that meant I made her happy.* I wonder what she prayed for in her bedroom alone. I wonder if those wishes were answered. I wonder how she feels now, looking down no doubt from her heaven, watching us all.

My prayer was my prose.

As I said in the first chapter, it was following a radio interview question that I realised I'd begun writing – *properly* writing, not just in my head but on scraps of paper – after my mother's first suicide attempt. I did indeed begin scribbling on scraps of paper. They were torn from Grandma's posh notepad in the drawer. I'd steal one or two pages at a time, and then scrawl away in my bedroom. It was a compulsion; I *had* to get the words out. I didn't have a notepad of my own and didn't ask for one because I didn't like to be a nuisance. But when I was done, I'd rip them up into small pieces and hide them in tissue and put them in the kitchen bin. Maybe I was shy about sharing them. Maybe they were private. Maybe they were just too heart-breaking to look at again. I'll never know what I wrote, but perhaps those looped and passionate words were the ones that eventually became every novel I've written.

Claire: *Grandma would walk us to school which was novel because Louise had always done it. I remember pretending to be a majorette – they were a bit like American cheerleaders and often marched past the house. We'd twirl bamboo sticks from the garden next door. We made paper dolls at the table – drawing girls and cutting round them. Grandma taught us how to make wool dolls too. I think we once got those cardboard dolls that you attach clothes to, you know, with little fold-over tabs on them. Father McBrien came to see Grandma once, wearing a black suit, with a trilby on his head. I liked him. Not sure why he came. Perhaps to support Grandma. I think the church community rallied around her when she had us. There was such safety at bedtime, knowing she was downstairs. Sadly, I could never enjoy this as I had a great feeling of anxiety, always, hanging over me. That tinged every memory* *of being there. Thinking, where's Mum? What's she doing? When will we see her again? I don't remember being told anything. I probably just internalised it all. To this day I get nostalgic feelings about Grandma, and that time. It's bittersweet. She probably helped us be decent mothers. What I have done with my children, I learnt from her.*

An enduring image from that whole time in Stockton was the Walsingham calendar in Grandma's kitchen. This is a town in Norfolk famous for its shrines in honour of the Virgin Mary. Saxon noblewoman, Richeldis de Faverches, had a vision of her in which she was instructed to build a replica of the Holy Family's house in Nazareth. The Holy House in Walsingham remains a great place of pilgrimage, one Grandma often visited, bringing us trinkets like silver cups and yet more holy water.

My favourite image was a group of bright yellow daffodils. I believe it was on the Easter month page, so April that year. If I close my eyes and picture those flowers against a blue sky, I can see us all at the table below, trying not to laugh, Grandma's nose dripping (she had a permanent nasal drip) and us hoping it missed our toast, the back door open causing a light breeze, a row of Easter eggs with our names iced on them in the hallway, and the smell of Grandma, unique, indescribable, just *her*.

17

Mum Mum

Toxicity is a major adaptation for the wild daffodil and can save its life. If an organism consumes a daffodil, it will never try eating that plant again, due to the negative association between the consequences and the daffodil.

I had a vivid dream recently. I was on a packed train, trying desperately to tell the other passengers something. They shouted over me, eventually becoming an evil mob that chased me – en masse – along the aisle. I had to fight until I was breathless to push past them and get into the next carriage. They clawed at me, ripping my clothes. Then suddenly I was free and standing in the street outside The Cottage, as we called it back then. I was holding a piece of paper. Everything I'd wanted to say was written there. I knew I was free to share it because I'd conquered the oppressive crowd.

And I walked away from the house with it.

Eleven days after Mother's bridge jump, we siblings returned to our lives. We didn't abandon her. We still tried to make sure at least one of us visited every day, but now we had to fit that around everything else. Grace returned to the medical centre and to her university course. Colin returned to his job in sports data management. Claire returned to her role as medical secretary. And I returned to my theatre usher job, and to the writing.

The first night, my boss asked how my mum was. I started to explain and then broke down. I had to squeeze his hand and excuse myself. It was a hard shift; not the job itself, that was as routine as usual, but carrying the pain around while having to smile and help people. The show was a distraction, but I missed the odd patron using a phone and forgot to pick up enough flyers to give out at the end.

That day I also started my new novel.

It was released almost exactly a year after Mother jumped off the bridge. Life has a way of timing things this way. The words I escaped into during those tumultuous days were born around that anniversary. In the novel, I went to some dark places, exploring self-harm, love, loss, obsession, and the idea of where we go when we die, all set in a theatre. Perhaps I needed to know that – should the worst happen with Mother – there was a place waiting for her. Perhaps when I wrote, *I'm still here, I am dust, I'm those fragments in the air, the gold light dancing there, that breeze from nowhere*, I was reassuring myself – in a way my parents never had – that everything was going to be OK, no matter what.

When I'm sad, I return to this safe place. My anti-depressant. I never get writer's block; this isn't said with smugness or judging those who do, only as fact. I play certain music to get me in the mood. Then I live the words, seeing the characters and scenes as vividly as my own real-life world. In some ways, it *is* my real-life world. One where I choose what happens.

It was time for Mother's major leg surgery.

As usual, we shared our thoughts in the WhatsApp chat.

Claire wrote: *I rang the ward – they're trying to wean Mother off the oxygen machine before leg surgery tomorrow. Her chest needs to be well enough. Anaesthetist will assess her in morning. The shoulder surgery should be next week, if she recovers well from leg surgery.*

Colin wrote: *Jesus, more surgery.*

I wrote: *I have a phobia that I ring the hospital and they say she's dead.*

Claire wrote: *No guarantees she'll be well enough for surgery. I'm starting to see the picture that surgeon Mr Lee painted of her being nowhere near out of the woods. It's going to be a long, long affair.*

Grace included a picture of some flowers.

She wrote: *People should lob themselves off bridges more often. Look at the beautiful bouquet work got me.*

I wrote: *I might tell work my dad's done it too...*

Edwin wrote: *I told people Gabs had been killed by a tiger snake. The man in the paper shop knocked a dollar off my morning paper.*

Grace and I went for a walk that day. A year earlier, we had fallen in love with doing country hikes when we trained for our Wolds Way walk, a seventy-nine-mile trail ending in Filey. We conquered it in four days, wearing wedding dresses, and raising £1500 for type 1 diabetes. Now, we loved walking for the tranquillity, the beautiful scenery, the togetherness, and the silly videos we made that seemed to make people laugh online. We decided that day to walk under the bridge. To go to the spot where Mother had jumped.

For the first time.

Along the river, we observed things we'd never taken notice of before; inscriptions of loved ones' names on benches lining the shore; bunches of bright flowers planted in the slimy mud; wilting, rotten bouquets tied to a post near the Humber Rescue, notes of sadness attached and fluttering in the wind as though to shrug off the words.

Yellow police tape marked the place where Mother would have landed. There was a solitary police cone. Cars raced across the bridge above, echoing around us. I felt sick at how high it was. The concrete square beneath the railing she climbed over was edged with weeds and a wire fence. Grace and I got close to it, studied the area.

I wondered what the scene must have been like that day. Would it have been blood-soaked? Would Mother have woken, in agony, leg shattered, realising it hadn't worked, that she was still alive? Would she have lain there hoping she still might die from her injuries? Was she cold, looking up at where she had left her brown shoes and coat, unable to move? I thought about the poor man who found her. A friend knew him and told me that he'd said he would never get over what he saw.

A parcel had prevented me from being there too.

Despite the questions in my head, Grace and I were silent.

What could we say?

Every time I walk along the river now, alone on my daily hike, and see someone who looks sad or anxious, I wonder if they're going to the bridge. I wonder if I should speak to them. Could I stop them?

I've spoken to people while they die. Many times, when I was a volunteer at the Samaritans for three years. It was something I did to help others, hear the darkest of stories, and perhaps face my own demons. I was trained not to judge if someone rang having taken an overdose or standing at the edge of a train track. We weren't there to prevent them from dying, only to listen in those final moments. I never judged. I never have. Many say suicide is selfish. In the eyes of the Catholic church, it's the most grievous of sins. But how can I judge what I've not experienced? If a human is so desperate that they'll consider ending their life, they need our compassion. Our help. That said, I'm also human. Now, my walks under the bridge, averting my eyes from that horrible place, are often angry, often nausea-inducing, always heavy with pain.

Later that day Colin wrote in our chat: *Just got back from hospital this eve. Mother was the most alert I've seen her, but with that is extremely scared. She was crying for the first fifteen minutes of me being there. The paranoia is present still. The surgeon came by. Surgery will involve a frame on her leg. She'll be mobile. No mention of amputation. Best surgeons working on her by all accounts. Saw X-ray. Not a pretty sight. There're lots of bones to put together. Mother likened it to a jigsaw.*

Grace wrote: *Jigsaw Trish*.

The group name was then changed to Jigsaw Girl.

Edwin wrote: *Happy to have spoken to Mother today. She was lucid and said she's fearful of what's to come – I said we all are. I told her gently that it's not all about her. I said God decided she wouldn't die and it's up to her to interpret that as she sees it. I assured her of my support and told her how marvellous you four have been, that she must be grateful. She said she needed me, which was good to hear. I felt better for the call. My anger is finally abating.*

And then it was the day of leg surgery, Wednesday 13th March.

Edwin wrote: *Today you should all take a day off and go to the pub. You need a break, and you need to look after your brains.*

I wrote: *We can't visit today cos surgery will be long. I'm going to write, which brings me joy, even if there are nine suicides and twenty-eight murders in the novel.*

Mother's surgeon called me at lunchtime to say they were definitely going ahead with it. He described in detail what was going to happen, and what we could expect afterwards. I took notes as he spoke and then photographed them and posted them in the WhatsApp chat for everyone to see. When I looked down at the creased pages in my hand, the looped words looked like a poem.

The Leg
Temporary scaffolding comes off,
to be replaced with more robust cage.
Then connect bones with rods and wires.
Goal is to get leg more leg-shaped
and knee more knee-shaped.
It's completely in bits;
some of the bone is dust.
But we'll put it together like a puzzle.
She can stand with this robust cage on.
Hinges on frame mean she can bend knee.

Likely to get arthritis
and need knee replacement down the line.
Horrendous injury
but bone's a remarkable healer.
Risk of damage to nerves, and infection.
Months of looking after it.
She'll be back on the ward after six.

At six o'clock, Mother was still in theatre. Seven o'clock came and went with no word. It was an anxious wait. We continued to message back and forth, trying to keep our spirits up. Edwin said he was trying to piece it all together, that he thought it sounded like a salvage job. Losing the leg would be devastating, he said, but in the long run it could be the lesser of two evils. I've often thought that had this been twenty years earlier, keeping in touch would have been a nightmare. Technology united us. Joe also sat with me instead of taking his usual fifteen-hour bath.

Finally, at eight-thirty we got the 'all good' call, and nurses assured us that Mother was back on the ward, and apparently alert and well.

There was nothing more we could do.

I went to bed exhausted.

The following day Grace and I were able to visit. It was hard to know what to expect each time we climbed the four flights of stairs to the ward, comparing heart rates on our FitBits and arguing over who was the fittest. Would Mother be alert or unconscious? Would she be desperately sad or manic? Would she recognise us today or not?

'I'm always hoping for *Mum* Mum,' said Grace, 'and we never get her.'

But *Mum* Mum was not someone we'd had for a long time.

If ever.

That day – after major surgery – she was drowsy but fine, delirious but with good colour. At times she was out of it, hardly recognising Grace and me as we sat there, patiently making small talk, tidying her covers, and reading through new cards that had arrived. She couldn't formulate words well and her sentences were jumbled. We knew she was dosed up to the eyeballs with meds though. She hadn't slept much the previous night either, so we just chatted and let her drift off. Grace found it difficult and frequently went to the waiting room alone. I read messages Conor and Katy had sent, over and over, as though their words might cut through her fog.

A doctor told us they planned to get Mother on her feet tomorrow, which we found astounding, just two weeks after jumping from a bridge. The long-term plan was potentially to send her to the rehab ward at another local hospital or, if not, to the mental health ward, and provide physio there.

Colin replaced us that evening. He reported afterwards that Mother talked gibberish, telling him she wanted to go to a duck pond and feed them fried eggs. She also made a variety of crude but funny observations about various members of staff. Joe joined Colin for an hour, and Mother asked him to read her a story from the phone book. He said he would've done if one had been available.

That day, she was the oddest she had been so far. We were hoping she hadn't totally lost her mind forever. Edwin assured us it was post-op delirium. Claire said she would come up on Saturday and 'do her bit'.

At this time, we were also busy trying to sue the mental health team for neglect. We felt the final suicide attempt could have been prevented with appropriate help; that her level of care should have been escalated after the pill overdose and the fact that it *hadn't* been contributed to the bridge jump. Now our mother had horrendous injuries on top of her mental health issues. It was hard squeezing in visits to the solicitor as well as working, caring for our children, and making sure Mother had someone with her in the daylight hours.

We ended up not having a case.

But, on Mother's behalf, we tried.

When I write, a lot of the process is *what if*; what if this happened, what if that happened, what if the other happened. I'm imagining this book as a *what if* too; what if Mother had succeeded? These pages might then have been a long obituary. What would I have written instead? How would that result have shaded what I include from our past? Would my view of it be rosier? Would I edit less favourable stories that paint our mother in harsh light? Would I be kind?

Lie?

I'd like to think not; it wouldn't be fair to the children we were, and what happened then. As I look back again, I need to only be influenced by the truth. I owe it to us all.

Even if it breaks my heart.

18

Waiting for the daffodils

Flowering early in the year provides an opportunity for daffodils to receive much-needed sunlight, before the trees above block the light with their leaf growth.

Today I went looking for those daffodils; the four bunches I saw that early dawn, the day my mother jumped.

On a walk along the river, I hoped that splash of yellow would greet me. But it must have been too early; they weren't ready yet. Perhaps because of the storm that was raging – Storm Dennis. There is news of another storm brewing elsewhere; a coronavirus that has just been given the official name Covid-19. It has been declared a global health emergency by the World Health Organisation.

There are no cases – that I know of – in the UK.

I continued my walk. And I saw a cluster of that other hardy perennial, the snowdrop. Pure white against blades of green, they cheered me up. I took a photograph as I did a year ago of those daffodils. Then I carried on walking.

And I'll keep walking, keep waiting, keep looking, keep hoping. They'll be back, that's a certainty. It's what keeps us going. The seasons continue their cycle regardless, and the sun comes up every morning.

I'll keep you posted.

19

Three girls in a window

The wild daffodil is an autotrophic organism,
meaning that it makes its own food instead of
relying on other organisms for nutrition.

I wrote this paragraph back in chapter three:

I had a scene in my head, just now. Three girls, in a window, waiting for a yellow car. Two small ones, excited and bouncy, one older, more cautious, knowing and hating knowing. Fingers on the pane, net curtains in disarray, a voice from the kitchen telling them not to get the glass dirty.

The three girls are us. The voice is Grandma's. The house is hers. We live there. I have arrived at this moment. The moment when Mum finally came. I've been dreading it. It's one of my most painful memories. They say that the worst pain in the world is the pain you feel just before you pass out from it. I suppose the memories I can't recall are the ones where I passed out; this one is the pain just before.

Claire and Grace can't remember this day. Our grandma is no longer with us to share her recollection of it. Mother now says she remembers little about those days due to repeated ECT treatment, though her memory is often selective. I'm the sole owner of this moment.

I wish I wasn't.

We knew Mum was finally coming to visit us. Grandma asked us what we wanted her to bring, and we all cried 'Our Sindy dolls'. She must have passed this on to our mum. On the day of the visit, the three of us waited in the living room window. I'm not sure how long we had been in Stockton, but I'd say at least three or four months. I don't know what day it was, but likely a weekend if we were not at school. Claire and Grace, naturally, were excited, asking over and over if Mummy would be here soon. I was quiet. I'm not sure if Grandma told me this – or if it was down to my usual, wretched instinct – but I *knew* Mum was just coming for the day. I feared my sisters thought she would be taking us home. But the words were stuck in my throat.

I didn't want to dampen their happiness.

We wore the new clothes we had recently got for a school photo-graph – my dress was covered in flowers with ties at the shoulder, while Claire and Grace wore pale blue T-shirts and floral skirts.

'Don't pull on my nets,' called Grandma from the kitchen. 'Don't leave fingerprints on my clean windows. Don't get your hair messed up.'

She must have been anxious. She had not seen her daughter for months and probably had no idea what to expect. I don't know how frequently Mum had spoken to her during this time.

Then the yellow car I'd anticipated rounded the corner.

It pulled up at the path outside. I knew it was Mum and I told Claire and Grace. They ran to the front door, trying to unlock it, wanting to get out and run up the path. But Grandma said they should wait. I held back, loitered in the living room. I wanted to protect my sisters. *Tell* them. But there was this heavy weight in my chest. I desperately wanted my mum too, but I was afraid to let that feeling in because she would be leaving again.

The door opened and Mum came in with the red-haired lady, the social worker. Claire and Grace leapt on her, clinging to her legs and crying out, 'Mummy,' over and over. I held back. I'm not sure if Grandma told me to – or if I just felt her expectation that I should – but eventually I hugged her, lightly, without passion.

'Hello, Louise,' she said.

She looked tired. Her eyes seemed dead and hardly took us in. She smelled alien and not how I remembered. It was unsettling. I wanted a different mum; one that I could depend on, not be afraid to love. She had our Sindy dolls. Mine was still dressed in the woollen blue coat she'd had on when I left The Cottage. I was almost happier to have this toy than to have Mum because the toy would be staying.

'We missed you, Mummy,' Claire and Grace told her. 'Did you miss us?'

Mum said she had, but her declaration lacked the intensity of theirs.

The duration of the visit is a blur. It could have been two hours; it could have been eight. Mum sat in the floral armchair by the window, her teacup on the brass, rippled coffee table, and didn't talk much. Claire and Grace played with their Sindys at her feet. The red-haired woman seemed to speak more. Grandma bustled back and forth, making endless cups of tea, offering biscuits, making excuses to go and wash up or tend to things. There was a meal – I can't recall what – but I think Claire and Grace insisted on sitting on either side of Mum at the table. She talked about maybe taking us to Scarborough for a holiday and asked what our school was like.

I couldn't eat. I felt sick. Grandma's food that I so loved might as well have been raw sewage.

Then it was time for Mum to leave.

It must have been announced; something like a casual, 'Well, I'll have to get back now.' And Claire and Grace must have realised their mum was not here to stay or taking them with her. They wouldn't let her go. They each clung to her legs, crying out her name: 'Mummy, Mummy, *Mummy*.'

I felt guilt at not having warned them she would leave without us, at not saving them from this pain. I loved my mum, but I hated her for upsetting my sisters. For putting me in a situation where I'd not known whether to say something to them.

'Mummy, Mummy, *Mummy*.'

The red-haired woman tried to placate them. Mum looked anxious, helpless, and did little. Grandma tried to persuade Claire and then Grace to let go of her. I tried to help. I tried to unhook the child Grandma wasn't tending to. They were hysterical. I couldn't bear their sadness.

'Just *go*,' Grandma told Mum, no doubt exhausted and upset herself. Then to the red-haired woman, 'She needs to just go now.'

Somehow, Mum got away. Grandma closed the door. Claire and Grace continued sobbing until they were hot and sweaty. Grandma and I – me the mini adult once again – got them bathed and ready for bed. They calmed eventually; in the way you do following an overly emotional episode. Then they slept, Sindys clutched in small fingers, cheeks flushed still.

I went to bed too. I didn't cry. I had long been trained. I was the icicle I had strived to be. But I was distraught. It choked me like the food I hadn't eaten that day, and I didn't know what to do with it. I wanted my mum. I didn't want her. I was angry. I was sad. Guilty. I sat my Sindy on the hexagonal bedside table.

As I mentioned previously, it was during this period that I discovered the one thing that thawed me. Writing. It still does.

It is now.

20

On Memory

Bulbs allow the daffodil to grow and survive underground, even lying dormant during cold periods, thus avoiding harsh winds, drought, intense heat, and other adverse circumstances.

While Joe and I were on a Caribbean cruise six months after Mother jumped, I saw a CBSN news story about veteran suicide. Naturally, it caught my attention. The report said there was a crisis in the US. Twenty veterans a day take their lives due to loneliness, addiction and broken relationships. One veteran – who had himself attempted suicide – said he arranged surfing reunions with other veterans, so they could all come together on the water. He said something about the Pacific Ocean having no memory, and how it meant that he could give his problems to the sea and not carry them with him anymore. The TV station showed the report over and over, so it formed an endless story on my trip.

The sea haunts me too; it also scares me, which is understandable given my grandad's true sea-survival story, courage I've written about. *The Pacific Ocean has no memory.* I love this. My memories tease me often, like a wave hitting the shore but pulling back before I can dip my feet in. Should I let the ocean keep them? Should I swim out until I'm so deep I risk drowning?

I'll write them.

Put them on this lifeboat that is the page.

21

Fresh out of the asylum

*In the visual arts, daffodils are depicted in three different
contexts – mythological, floral art, or landscapes,
from mediaeval altar pieces to Salvador Dalí.*

The next time Mum visited us at Grandma's house, she was – once
again – not alone. I'm not sure how long the gap was between the
two visits, and I can't recall how Claire and Grace settled afterwards.

Memory hands out her gifts at random.

We must have finished school for the holidays because by now
it was July. I'm sure there had been talk of us going home soon.
Grandma would not likely have told us something like this unless
it was certain, so she must have discussed the move with the social
services team. The only entries in our care records for July are a
brief review of Colin's care – which simply stated that 'health and
everything was good' – and a note that Mum was now seeing him
more frequently.

This time Mum stayed overnight. And she came with her new
boyfriend: Robert.

I sensed that Grandma was not happy. It's understandable. She
had been looking after us for months – alone, with no help – and
our mum brings a new boyfriend the second time she sees us. Could
she not see how unreasonable this was? That perhaps her children
might want her full attention after all this time.

I don't particularly recall the actual arrival, only the fact of them being with us; only the house seeming full, and us feeling we had more freedom to be boisterous without being told off. I didn't dislike him. He had piercing blue eyes, curly hair, and was chunky, sociable and gregarious: completely different to my father. I didn't know what his existence would mean for us, only that it was novel to me, interesting, exciting.

I wonder if he went with Mum when she visited Colin. Probably. He's mentioned in the care records. Mum tells social workers she 'wants to come to Stockton and take us home' but 'her boyfriend' agrees with the team that she should wait.

Grandma always had reverence for the men in our family, allotting them the best seat at the table. In later years, she always said, 'Give him the biggest portion' when Joe or Colin or Edwin were with us for dinner. It was a generational thing, an upbringing in a family where the man was the head. But I can't imagine she gave Robert a more lavish portion of casserole than she did us that day.

Claire: *Robert was a man that Mum met in a nightclub fresh out of the asylum – I feel bad for Grandma now. Mum had been away from her kids for a while and comes to visit with her boyfriend in tow. Grandma loved her daughter, but she must have thought, 'Couldn't you just have come on your own and been there for them 100 percent.' Mum probably knew that by bringing Robert she wouldn't have been grilled by or talked to by Grandma. Bringing him stopped her having to face things. For me, with Robert there, it was like, 'I want Mummy, but I still can't have her, there's a barrier.' That must have upset me so much as a child. She used her illness at times. Act depressed, get sympathy. She manipulated then as she does now.*

Claire's mention of how Mum would *act depressed, get sympathy* I understand, and agree with. Yes, our mum genuinely had postnatal depression. Yes, she had a breakdown and attempted suicide, which must have been terrible. Yes, she no doubt was depressed for some time. But she used this at other times – later times – when her own bad decisions or her heavy drinking or perhaps even a narcissistic personality disorder were the real culprit. When she wanted to do as she pleased and not be accountable. When she wanted to have a break from us. When someone does this – especially a parent – questioning it makes you then seem like a cold, heartless child who has no compassion for depression. When you're angry that you've been let down, or sad that you just want your *Mum* Mum, Other People say, 'Oh, your Mum had it *much* harder.'

But Other People never know the full story.

There was a day out on the nearby moors with Mum and Robert – I'm not sure if it was during this visit or if there was another one before we finally went home. Whatever the case, Mum was more like *Mum* Mum now. Fuller of life. Chattier. Robert seemed to do her good. Of course, I didn't look on it with adult eyes, thinking as I do now how inappropriate it was for her to bring a boyfriend when she should have been bonding with us, making up for the time she had been away, repairing damage, comforting and reassuring us. No, the child-me was delighted that her mum seemed happy. I could eat again. I could hope that we'd go back to The Cottage. That I'd see Colin again. I had adored being with Grandma, but I longed for home – no matter how disruptive – and for my Mum – no matter how imperfect – and for a place where I really belonged.

Grace*: I remember Mum coming with Robert. I went to the box room where they were both sleeping because I wanted Mummy – as the child-me called her – and Grandma caught me and stopped me and smacked me, not hard, just tapped, and sent me back to bed. She was obviously protecting me, frightened of what I would see. The house suddenly felt different when Robert was there. At the time, we were not angry with Mum because we felt that other people – like him, and later other men – were keeping us away from her. But she was an adult. I know this now. She should have challenged these men. After this, every boyfriend validated that she was the important one, and we weren't.*

* * *

I'm not sure where I slept when Mum and Robert were in my bedroom, perhaps back with my sisters, perhaps with Grandma. Only now am I seeing the symbolism of this simple act; of me having to give up the room that had been mine for months to make space for Mum and one of her men. This is where it started. This is when I learnt my place when a man was around; that I was disposable. Easily moved elsewhere. If I shared with Claire and Grace that night, I was likely happy to be with them again.

I doubt it occurred to me that I should feel put out.

I was happy that my mum was happy.

Reading between the lines in our care records, it looks like we finally came home in August 1980. There is a note saying that the plan is to 'get the girls back at their own school and to get Colin back home'. I know we were back at The Cottage before Colin, that there was a month of him still being in care. The records state that his foster family took him on holiday in August, and that Mum was seeing him more frequently, leading up to his return to her. Interestingly, it includes Colin's medical records from then, which are all good, except that he 'does not talk yet'.

This is likely due to the trauma of the sudden separation from both of his parents. Toddlers who are too young to talk about what is happening to them or around them retain lasting sense-memories of these events, which affects their well-being into adulthood. While Claire, Grace and I remained together, and went to live with a family member, Colin lost us all in one day. As a nine-year-old, I knew this.

And it broke my heart.

Before we came home, there was a holiday. Scarborough. And from this brief trip, we returned to The Cottage. I don't remember saying goodbye to Grandma. Perhaps, as the fickle children we can be, I got wrapped up in the excitement of going home. Perhaps I buried the moment as Claire and Grace did the day Mum visited. How alone Grandma must have felt when we left. I have a vision of her sitting at the table, with her tea in the brown ceramic mug she always used, crying, alone, the Virgin Mary watching from the shelf. She did so much for us. I loved her more than any other adult during my childhood. I felt absolutely safe in her presence and she taught me a lot about being kind. But she was not done with having to care for us yet; not done by a long way.

In Scarborough we stayed with William, a family friend. He had a flat in a beautiful Victorian building on a curved, crescent street. Every morning he took us three girls to a corner shop for sweets. He would have known the family situation, so I imagine he made an effort to treat us kindly. There is a photograph of me rowing a boat at Peasholm Park lake, wearing a new puff-sleeved, blue-and-white top that I loved; my smile is natural and even reaches my eyes. It was likely because Mum was the mum I liked best on this holiday – fun, warm, vivacious again. I remember also that William had the Jeff Wayne 'War of the Worlds' album. I loved the spooky music. The cover reminded me of the book on my father's shelf at Hillcrest Avenue. I was only nine, but that house felt like a long time ago. I was only nine, but I felt a million years old.

And then we returned to The Cottage.

The fairytale house in *Hansel and Gretel* was made of bread, cake and sugar to tempt the hungry, abandoned children in from the woods. The witch invited them inside for another meal, pretending to be kind. Instead, she locked them in cages so she could fatten them up and eat them.

That was one of my favourite childhood stories.

It taught me that sometimes home is the least safe place of all.

22

The matriarchal bastion of society

The daffodil is one of the first plants to emerge from the chilly, winter soil, trying to seek necessary sunlight before its peers.

Sixteen days after our mum jumped from the Humber Bridge – on Saturday 16th March – it was Katy's 19th birthday.

It was also the first time Mother talked about her suicide attempt.

Katy had plans with her boyfriend in Lincoln. I missed her desperately. I was still coming to terms with my youngest child having left home, just six months earlier. Conor had been long gone, but now they were both away, I felt lost.

Being a mother fulfilled me deeply, but the hands-on aspect was over. This particular birthday was on my mind. I was nineteen when I got pregnant with Conor, so I felt proud that Katy had gone away to university and was doing all the things I never had. But our life revolved around Mother now, so I didn't have time to dwell on the things I missed or my own life.

Now my siblings and I were starting to wonder about the bigger picture: about the future. We had had time to become accustomed to this tragedy, in the way you do even the worst things, but I began to question if our mother would ever walk again. If not, what would that mean? How would she get about? Where would she live? Her house – The Cottage, as we had called it when we were kids – was not suitable at all with its narrow doorways and steep stairs.

That Saturday, Claire came up to Hull for the day with her husband Julian and youngest daughter Anna. They went shopping in the town centre while Claire and I headed to the hospital. I had tried to go most days since returning from my tour a week ago, feeling I should make the time up that my siblings had given in my absence. The hospital felt like a second home; one that was noisy, overcrowded, and that I'd be happy never to see again as long as I lived.

As we rounded the corner onto her ward, Mother frowned at us and asked, 'Did I get married or buried on Tuesday?'

We knew to go along with anything she said, so without a moment's pause, I said, 'Neither, Mother.'

'Oh,' she said. 'I'm sure I died on Tuesday. But it was supposed to be Saturday.'

'Nope, you're still with us,' said Claire, tidying up her pillows.

'But Louise has arranged the wake for tonight,' she insisted.

'I'll cancel it then,' I said.

'Oh, good. Will you cancel Johnny then because I've invited him?'

Johnny was our long-time family friend and had visited a few times that week. 'Yes, no problem,' I said. 'I'll sort it all out.'

Claire read the new cards that had arrived and tidied up the things on Mother's bedside table. She had lost some of her false teeth in the fall and was delighted that they had been found, cleaned and returned to her. I almost drank from the cup they had been in. Fortunately, she told me in time, and I put the cup down in horror. I dread to think of the consequences had she been unconscious.

'The surgeon who did my leg operation was a total turd,' Mother said suddenly. 'And that nurse is a tart. She goes out partying when she's supposed to be on the night shift.'

We laughed and assured her that everyone just wanted to help. She was in a bossy mood, ordering the staff about, which we thought was a positive because it meant she was getting back to her true self.

Edwin had asked for a photo of the full leg, so we took one and sent it to him. With the sturdy, metal frame and the nuts and bolts and the dried blood, it was like something out of a horror film.

'Can you order us a curry and not tell 'em?' asked Mother.

'They'll smell it,' laughed Claire.

'Oh, bugger you then.'

She had pulled out her catheter at some point and the nurse had decided not to bother putting it back in, so now there was the extra job of lifting her on a toilet.

Two of her friends came that afternoon. We kept the conversation upbeat but everyday.

'Was Johnny there when I got buried?' she asked again.

'We never buried you in the end,' insisted Claire.

We fell silent, the hum of machines and buzzers our eternal backdrop.

Then, for the first time so far, Mother mentioned that day; the bridge jump. She spoke factually, with little emotion. 'I strolled up to the bridge,' she said. 'I walked farther out to where the road is, but I was scared. It's so high, and I didn't want to hurt anyone else. So, I came back in more. Then I climbed over the barrier and went dum-dum-dum down. Then my leg was the wrong way.' She paused, adding, 'I was very selfish.'

'You weren't,' we said gently.

I didn't know what else to say. Her words were so simple and yet so graphic. I knew it was something for her to have said them. That she was thinking about it now. When we later messaged the family, Colin admitted that this was quite horrific, and Grace said she was heartbroken for how Mother must have felt in that moment.

I wanted to ask some of the questions I'd thought of when we stood around her bed that first day at the Emergency Department.

Why the bridge? Why that Catherine Cookson book? What was in your final note?

But Mother changed the subject; then said no more about it.

We told a nurse what she'd said, and she thought it was good that she was starting to remember. But with memory, you must face the trauma as much as the event; the emotions as much as the physical. Was she ready for that? I hadn't been ready to look at some things in forty years. Was sixteen days' time enough?

While Mother's friends were still there, Claire and I went to the hospital café to give them space and have a breather ourselves. Julian and Anna met us there. Claire told them Mother was the funniest she had been so far.

'She's chatty but she's not showing any emotion,' she said, sipping her latte. 'I think her mind is fragmented – she's disassociated from that day. She talked about the bridge, but it didn't distress her. And it *should*.'

It was not lost on me that we too had disassociated from a painful past.

After the hospital, we went to Mother's house and picked up the post and got rid of food that had gone off. Joe went to visit her that night. She told him she was frightened and wanted to go home. This saddened me because whatever she had done to us, I could never bear the thought of anyone feeling that way.

On the Sunday I took a break. Stayed at home. Chatted to the kids. Wrote. Sat in silence. Then wrote some more. My new novel began to take hold of me. It helped me be strong.

There were plenty of WhatsApp messages to keep me up to date that day.

Grace wrote: *Mother is the best I've seen her so far. She said a magician came to see her this morning.*

Claire wrote: *Lucky her – I never got a magician when I had my hysterectomy.*

Grace wrote: *She told the doctor that when they meet in social circumstances, she is going to sneeze all over his meal. Now that she is clearly more 'normal' I might take Michael and Iris to see her.*

Colin wrote: *They are checking her swallowing soon. If it goes well, she will be able to eat normally again, which is good because she won't shut the fuck up about eating steak. Today's visit has left me hopeful.*

Grace wrote: *She doesn't seem to be in any pain, but she does keep trying to get out of the bed. The surgeon came this morning and is satisfied with the leg. He said Ward 29 is excellent for rehabilitation and she should go there. Mother said she's happy that this seems to have brought us all closer together again.*

I wrote: *How close will you get to me if I do it?*

Grace wrote: *Anally, at least.*

Edwin wrote: *I'm only hearing about the physical intervention, which is marvellous, but not much about psychiatric input. What of that, anyone?*

Grace wrote: *She is visited daily by the mental health team. They think she currently has post-traumatic amnesia and will assess further as she improves.*

Colin wrote: *The clinical psychologist said her mental health is a high priority. Mother's priority, however, was trying to fix me up with one of the nurses.*

On Monday morning Edwin told us he'd be arriving at Heathrow on the 12th May. We were delighted, and ready to see him. The plan was to surprise Mother on her birthday the next day, so we had to keep it secret. Many times, we almost mentioned it and were grateful that she was more interested in the 'Scottish bastards' who were apparently coming for all her belongings.

Grace and I visited that Monday. Mother was more agitated than she had been; she was paranoid about people stealing her things and kept asking us to lock the door. Each day was different and therefore a challenge. Our patience was tested to the limit at times. I know that she had the toughest ordeal, and that's why I gave everything I had, but we never knew which mother we would get.

'I'm the matriarchal bastion of society,' she said, during that afternoon.

Grace and I fell about laughing.

And changed the WhatsApp group name to Matriarchal Bastion of Society.

We also spoke to a psychiatrist, telling her we thought Mother was in denial about what had happened. She agreed, saying she thought Mother was still at risk mentally, though she couldn't fully assess her until all the surgery had been done, and the after-effects had settled. Shoulder surgery was set for Thursday; another risk; another hurdle.

On the drugs round, a nurse offered Mother pain relief. She glared at the tiny, white cup containing two pills and said, 'I will not be fooled by a paracetamol wearing the disguise of a moth.'

The food tube was finally removed, and Grace fed Mother a yoghurt, which she devoured noisily. The ward was a busy place; nurses came on the hour to do checks, visitors breezed in and out, patients were rushed away on beds, buzzers went off, and a variety of specialists called by. A woman from the Citizen's Advice Bureau brought some leaflets for Mother. She had bright pink hair, matching a striped shirt.

'Oh, you are a colourful lady,' said Mother. 'What do you want, love, a packet of apples and two bananas?'

'I'll have a bag of oranges,' she laughed.

'And what do *you* do?' Mother asked her.

'I generally go around annoying people and giving them my leaflets.'

'How marvellous! Now, are you short of an umbrella cos I've got five going for a pound?'

While funny, Mother's comedic words bordered on hysteria. Her eyes were wild and her mannerisms jerky. The unsettled environment – people coming and going constantly – didn't help.

Though I needed this brief lightness, I knew darkness might still engulf us all when it fell silent. When we let it in.

Later that evening Mother called Grace, distressed, wanting us to go and get her. The following night she sent me video of the floor and a message saying she was at the docks and wanted to be picked up. It was an exhausting cycle of laughter followed by tears. The hope Colin had expressed was being dashed.

I wrote: *She's not even the woman she was on Saturday for Claire and me. She's more disorientated now.*

Claire wrote: *I feel we're losing her.*

I wrote: *Yes, I felt that today, but don't know how to get her back.*

Edwin wrote: *You lost her a long time ago?*

Grace wrote: *It's so complex. Forty years of ups and downs, getting her back, losing her again, getting her back, losing her – our whole lives.*

Edwin wrote: *You can't get her 'back'. This is extremely complex. You need to look after yourselves. All that sensory overload on that open ward is too much for her.*

Claire wrote: *We are going to limit how many visitors are there at once.*

On Wednesday, the day before shoulder surgery and almost three weeks after the jump, Mother was bright and alert. Now she could eat, she was devouring yogurt after yogurt. She went on and on about wanting wholemeal bread, so much that in the end Colin brought a loaf in and we kept it on the nearby windowsill for her.

This was also the day medical staff first had her sit up in bed. It was horrible. I stayed for the process. Colin couldn't do it. Mother was extremely distressed; understandably, she was irate and shouted at the nurses for hurting her. I held her hand and tried to comfort her. The nurses insisted she stay up for ten minutes and then let her lie down again. I settled her as best I could, and Colin returned. They would now be sitting her up every day.

After, Mother kept trying to get up and go home, becoming agitated when she couldn't. For the first time she started saying her leg was hurting; that she also had pain in her ribs. We were assured that this was part of the healing, and nothing to worry about.

And then it was Thursday and time for yet more surgery.

23

A White Christmas in October

*From seeds, daffodils take a long time to grow into
a full plant. It can take between five and seven years
for a daffodil to bloom from a dispersed seed.*

We arrived back at The Cottage in time for Claire, Grace and I
to return to our old school. I was worried my friends had forgotten
me, but they seemed excited to have me back, saying my accent was
'weird'. Clare – a schoolfriend of Claire and Grace's – describes how
she remembers them being in the dinner queue; then they were gone;
and the next minute they were back, but with 'posh' voices.

I began my third year in junior school. In the first lesson we
had to write an essay on who we were; very *The Breakfast Club*. I
wrote that I was nearly ten, had blue eyes and brown hair, and that
I'd been away and was finally home again.

A visit that I don't recall by a social worker is described in our
care records; Mum was 'going out to buy a bed for Colin' so clearly
he was still in foster care. These notes state that we three girls were
'wary of the social worker'. This is understandable, especially if she
was the red-haired lady who had 'taken us away' just six months
earlier. I don't recall being asked anything by them. It was all about
our mum, which we knew anyway, and just accepted as normal life.

I remember going to see Colin at his foster home. The details are hazy – other than there being a narrow, leaf-covered back garden – but I know my joy at seeing him again was immense. He had grown, but he was still chubby with pink cheeks, and was wearing brand new chunky brown shoes. Reports at this time state that Colin would 'play up' on being returned to his foster home after seeing Mum. He was no doubt confused. I have no idea how upset he was when we left that day without him, but I do know that I was sad and longed for him to be ours again. His foster parents had a daughter, also Louise, who insisted he was *her* brother now and I was never getting him back.

But Colin did come back.

On 20th September 1980, according to our records. There is a photo of us all around this time; Mum, Claire, Grace, Colin and me. In the centre, Colin claps his hands and smiles broadly for the person taking the picture. We girls gaze only at him, mirroring his claps, looking as happy as he does. I always thought our joy in this picture was because we were finally home. Because we were with Mum again. But I know now that it was because our little brother was back.

Another person who lived with us then was Robert.

Mum's boyfriend.

I'm not sure if he was there when we arrived or if he moved in sometime after, but he was soon part of everyday life at The Cottage. As I said when we first met him, I liked him. He was what you might call a handsome man, with a look of Oliver Reed, burly, magnetic. He was generous too and we probably lapped the attention up. He bought Colin a luxurious brown teddy bear, and we three girls a tin packed lunch box each; one was Star Wars, the other was Buck Rogers, and I had one emblazoned with Disco.

Grace: *I had the Buck Rogers tin. I remember there being a flask inside it, held in place by a metal spring. I remember also taking them to school and having Farmer Browns crisps. They were shaped like a farmer, and I can still taste them now.*

* * *

Robert also bought us our first pet.

I came home from Brownies one evening and there was a gorgeous black-and-white kitten in the living room. I fell in love immediately, even though she scratched me the first time I picked her up. Her name was Duchess. We didn't have her for long though. I was allergic to her fur. She also exacerbated Grace's asthma. In the end, we had to give her away, and I felt it was my fault, even though I'd never asked for her and I couldn't help my physical reaction to her.

It's worth saying at this point that our ailments were rarely tended to.

I had chronic hayfever from the age of nine; it meant summer was a misery. I was never taken to the doctor where I could have been prescribed some sort of antihistamine. I sought out my medical records a few years ago, looking for answers to the missing parts of our childhood, and mine were almost blank; a few random sheets of paper. The first time my hayfever was dealt with was when I made an appointment myself, aged fifteen, and I finally got some pills that relieved my symptoms.

Claire suffered endlessly with severe tonsillitis; she did eventually have them taken out aged thirteen. And poor Grace had asthma. Quite seriously, she is lucky to be alive. We sisters called it her 'breathing thing' because we didn't have a name for it. We just knew that she often struggled to breathe, especially at night. I can still hear that awful rasping if I close my eyes and recall when we shared a room.

It was years before she got an inhaler.

Our ailments were merely an irritant. Mum had her hands full. She had four children, on her own. There is no doubt it must have been immensely hard. But I realise now that we deserved better care. Was my mother depressed during this time? She seemed like our happy mum to me; the lively, fun one.

The narcissistic mother apparently needs to be the centre of the world, and her children being ill gets in the way of this. She will therefore often neglect their medical care; bones don't heal, scars don't get stitched in time, dental visits are infrequent. This leaves children believing they're not worth taking care of, and they end up with ongoing health problems.

This lack of care has shaped how I value myself as an adult; or, rather, how I *don't*. Though I walk five miles a day, eat plenty of vegetables, don't smoke, drink occasionally, and take vitamin supplements, I rarely see a doctor. I have my smear tests, but that's all. I often joke with Joe that I'd have to be 'bleeding out of my eyes' to go. And even then, I wait and see if it clears up. I can't ask for help. When I'm ill, I hate it and want no fuss. Yet, I'll happily care for others who are suffering.

We saw our father every Sunday during this time, though I can't remember much of it. There's a photo of us with him, somewhere like a farm – the colours autumnal – which suggests we went places.

While Robert lived with us, there were also days out at the coast with him, to a field where his daughter rode horses. His son came with us once. I remember being excited that we were allowed to sit in the back of the car, in the large area where the dogs went; we watched the road falling away from us as we travelled. He misbehaved on the way there and Robert stopped the car and left him in a field. My anxiety as we drove away was sky high. Were we going back for him? We did, eventually. The boy was sitting there, chewing a piece of straw, as though he was accustomed to being abandoned.

I was once on the receiving end of Robert's discipline too.

Grace: *We were all in the kitchen. Louise was in the corner near the sink. Everyone else – including me – was sitting, eating, on the wooden table and bench we had then. Robert stood up and suddenly he smacked Louise across the face. I ran to her. Though terrified, I was more overwhelmingly sad for* *her. I was crying and hugging her. I was devastated that someone had hit her – it felt worse than if someone had hit Mum. Mum did nothing. Just nothing.*

I can't recall what I'd done that day; whether I'd been cheeky (which would've been out of character back then) or maybe not eaten some food I was supposed to eat. I know now that there was no excuse. It didn't matter what I had 'done'. I was nine. Robert was a well-built man. And he hit me hard enough to knock me almost off my feet. I didn't cry; I'd had enough training to know there was no point. A small part of me hoped that my mother would come to my rescue. It was soon crushed. It was a pivotal moment. Like when I fell into that muddy stream. A chance for my mum to show she loved me more than Robert.

An anger began in me that day; a rage of knowing that I'd never let anyone treat those I loved in this way. Curiously, I've never dated a violent man. It's like I have a sense of them and avoid at all costs. But not for *me*. For those around me.

If a man hurt my children, I'd destroy him.

In October I was admitted to the hospital. According to our care records, I had severe abdominal pains, and a social worker took me to see a doctor. They must have been acute for me to tell someone about them; perhaps I was simply unable to hide it. I went to a children's ward for observation. Nothing else is revealed in my care documents. My medical records simply state that I was assessed for three days and released with no further treatment needed. I felt too old to be on a children's ward despite being nine; I felt I was wasting everyone's time. I loved the array of books in the tiny library. My only visitor was Robert. He brought me a donut and a yellow I LOVE ELVIS pin.

Is there something I don't remember?

How can you even know if you *don't* remember?

Sometimes you *know*.

But on this occasion, I can't recall the physical pain I apparently had. With hindsight, I imagine it was a belated reaction to the trauma of being separated from our mum that year. Maybe my mind needed care, not my body. Maybe my heart was broken, the pain presenting in my stomach, which is a common thing, and affects me now as an adult.

It was around this time that I began a diary. Plum red, it was one of those small Five-Year Diaries with a tiny padlock. I lost the key. What I'd give to have it now or recall what was in there. I can't imagine it was particularly honest or dramatic if there was no way of locking it up; but then I can't imagine anyone being remotely interested in it either. I don't have any of my childhood writings. If I did, I imagine there might be pointers there about the things I can't recall, about things buried, hidden carefully in those neat words, like hints in a game of Cluedo.

Soon, Robert had gone.

I don't know why, only that Mum must have ended it.

But he came back.

Grace: *I remember being in the front room, all of us. Mum was standing at the wall where the telephone was, and she rang the police. She was quite calm about it too. Before that, Robert had come into the house, via the side door, with a cheap wooden crate full of food, as though everything was normal. I think he wasn't living with us by then because I was surprised to see him. Mum told him to leave. He ignored her and carried on, being chatty, unpacking this food, and she said the police were coming. Eventually the police came, more than one. They got Robert from behind, pulled him back, and he banged into the door frame. It was quite the kerfuffle. They got him into the passage. There was a lot of shouting. I don't remember how I felt but I guess I should have been scared. Another police officer turned up with a Grandways trolley and they somehow got him into that — I think they handcuffed him to it — and carted him off up to Peeler House. He sang 'White Christmas' as he went, though it was only October. We all just carried on doing whatever we had been doing, because that's what we had been taught to do.*

Somehow, during this ruckus, Robert took the luxurious brown teddy bear off Colin, making him cry. I wanted to get it back, but was afraid, and hated myself for my cowardice. I remember choking back tears while in class the next day, and then later at home when Abba's 'The Winner Takes It All' played on the radio. It wasn't that I wanted Robert back; he ruined our homecoming. He darkened our precious Cottage. He was the wolf threatening to blow it down.

It never felt the same after that. I stopped calling it The Cottage. We just called it Tower Hill then, after the street it was on.

I didn't wear my I LOVE ELVIS pin again.

I think I threw it away.

24

This is your life

Due to toxic sap in their stems, daffodils should not be kept in a vase with other plants as it can harm them.

When we got our care records a few years ago, it was not unlike when Eamonn Andrews surprised random celebrities and people of note with his big red tome on *This Is Your Life*. Except the pages in our large black, plastic-sheathed book describe a life I never even knew we had.

According to these records, at the end of October – when we had been home for just two months – things went downhill again. I don't know whether Mum's depression returned or if it was the fact that she had gone quickly into a relationship with a man that turned nasty, but social worker notes give facts I might otherwise never have known.

A 31st October report says: *Discussed plans for children's future. If possible, plan to be Mrs A* (our mother) *and Colin at Mother and Baby Unit, and three girls at Hesslewood Children's Home for a brief period. No beds available at Hesslewood, and no money to pay for them. Beds at Manor Way – three have now been reserved.*

Only three days later, on 3rd November, this is updated with the following: *Maternal grandmother is not going back home for at least a month so there's no need for the girls to be received into care, at least in the immediate future. Manor Way been informed. Visited Mrs A and she said BLOCKED OUT NAME* (could only be Robert) *had been around, crying and wanting to come back.*

I have no recollection of this period.

It's like the time my mum went away after the twins were born. Nothing.

It's curious how I remember many things from those days, and yet other chunks are completely absent. My memory is much like our care records; some words are typed in bold and easy to read, some are handwritten and faded so harder to see, and some are completely blacked out. I would have celebrated my tenth birthday in her absence; this could be why I have zero memory of it.

Grandma Roberts stayed with us a lot during our childhood, sometimes because Mum went away on holiday, sometimes because she needed a 'break'. It would appear from our records that she lived at Tower Hill with us for the whole of November, and into December, while Mum and Colin were in a mother-and-baby unit.

I have a single memory of my packed lunch being different to usual; of opening my Disco tin in the school canteen and there being an extra cake inside. A teacher noted that I had 'quite the hearty lunch there'. This piece of cake made me feel so loved. I wonder now if this was when Grandma was our mother again during the winter of 1980, and if she had given me this extra treat.

How must I have felt at my mum disappearing again?

At Colin being away?

How must Claire and Grace, aged only almost six, have felt?

Were we all so accustomed to these upheavals that we simply accepted them? Is this why I don't remember, because they are customary, routine, everyday? Children are resilient. They adapt like chameleons. But everything clings to us. Shapes us. I imagine we were happy to have Grandma with us again, but not for the reasons we did; the key word there is *imagine*. I've imagined many stories over the years, but it's strange to do it with my own. I should know it, but I don't, not all of it, not yet; maybe never.

For now, this is your life, Louise, written in notes by others.

On 15th December 1980 there is a detailed report on a Case Conference meeting, the conclusion of which was that we four children were placed on the Observation Register. It lists who is present: a variety of doctors, social workers, teachers and health visitors. Also, it states that the police were invited but did not attend. I'm not sure why, but this is an alarm bell to me. The discussion is about the degree of risk it was felt we were subjected to, raised by staff at the mother-and-baby unit, after the five-week period of Mum and Colin residing there.

Various things are discussed, including how we girls are doing at school. Little is said of me and there is 'no knowledge' of how I'm functioning there. Claire and Grace were apparently now 'more stable and progressing well' after a bad start. Colin attends nursery three mornings a week with 'no problem'. It is, however, a doctor's concerns about Colin's 'unfulfilled emotional needs' and the fact that he is 'more aggressive than usual' that dominates the debate.

A sister from the mother-and-baby unit describes how Colin is not talking yet and is not toilet trained, though these things alone do not cause undue concern. More worrying is that Mum slaps him frequently, is always shouting at him, always 'wanting to get rid of him', and finding endless excuses not to see him.

The conference concludes with a debate on what should happen. The nursing officer feels there are times when we're 'at risk'. The social worker argues that the risk is negligible as Mrs A always rings up when she is 'going down'. The doctor feels that 'the emotional problems will be more prevalent than the physical ones' in the long-term for us. The others present don't think this warrants inclusion on the At Risk register. The final bullet points are that we should be placed on the Observation Register and that frequent visits from the social services team should continue.

The biggest reveal for me in this report was one line; that my mum had 'required help and support' after my birth. I had never known this until reading it right now. What prompted it? Mother told me once that she left me in the pram at the shops. Did she edit her tale to best suit herself, sharing what paints her in the best light, ignoring what doesn't?

I don't want to do that with my story. I want to be honest. Admit my many flaws and where I've failed. I have sympathy for my mother's early struggles; the depression may have manifested in her lack of care for us; the blackness of such an illness may have caused her aggression, self-hatred, and therefore dislike of her own offspring.

I'm no perfect parent. I've snapped at my kids. I've made bad decisions. Who hasn't? But is depression an excuse for neglect? Our mum wasn't depressed the *whole* time, much as she now paints it that way at times.

I've not yet reached my mother's chronic forty years of alcohol abuse – an abuse that has dampened my sympathies and almost destroyed what compassion I have – so it may seem I'm unkind about her at times. But in these drinking years yet to come, she was well enough to go out, to have boyfriends and see friends and go on holidays. Of course, she deserved this joy. But you can't say you were too depressed to love your children if that love is in your heart for other people in your life.

I try to understand. I struggle with anger.

With being able to forgive her.

Visits from social workers after this meeting were indeed frequent. They occurred at least weekly for a good four months. The details of these calls are detailed, though much is blacked out, which means names mentioned and situations described are confidential. Mum is said to be 'generally well' though 'floundering somewhat' at times. Grace is described as 'very clingy' and to be 'having trouble with her bowels', which the social worker suggests to Mum is likely a reaction to the upheavals of the last few months. The twins still bed-wet, which must have meant a lot of work for Mum. Colin has begun going to the nursery five mornings a week to give her a break and is apparently upset when he watches us three girls going off to school without him.

I have zero memory of these social workers visiting, despite the reports saying that we were present. Either they never spoke to me – which would be odd as really, they should have done – or I have buried it.

There's an official note on 9th April 1981 which states that approval has been given for the children to be 'admitted to Hesslewood as and when necessary'. Mum was 'going down' again.

In my second novel, *The Mountain in my Shoe*, I explored ten-year-old Conor's search for a real home. He has lived in foster home after foster home and is now missing. Those who love him are trying to find him. In the novel, I used a Lifebook to give Conor's background. This is a real-life document, used to record the childhood of an LAC (Looked After Child) so that when they leave the care system at eighteen, they know their history. I first came across them when I volunteered for SOVA, a service that pairs an adult with a LAC, to be their friend. I knew immediately what an incredible narrative device a Lifebook would make in a novel.

Now I think about it, though I named this fictional boy after my own, and though I gave his character certain traits belonging to my son, really, he was Colin. I often wonder if life imitates art, as the saying goes; if the notion that an event in the real world is inspired by a creative work is true. Or if it's the other way around?

Many times, my fiction comes true. Is it that I knew it all along? Or that it *already* happened?

Whatever the truth, this is your life, Louise. This is your art.

This is your Lifebook.

25

Still waiting for the daffodils

Wordsworth lost his mother when he was seven, and his father at thirteen. As if that were not enough, three of his children preceded him in death. This gives his 'I wandered lonely as a cloud' poem even greater meaning.

I saw some daffodils on a recent walk.

But they weren't the ones I wanted to see; not the ones I captured forever in a photo. These were a sunny cluster in someone's front garden. I was hopeful, thinking mine would have arrived too, in that riverside spot. Not yet. Almost. Small green stems pushed through the overgrown grass near the water.

I read the news on my phone as I walked. Covid-19 continues to dominate headlines. Cases have been confirmed in the US and numerous other countries but not here yet. A cruise ship docked in Japan has been quarantined and confirmed two deaths aboard.

I find it surreal.

Joe and I have been on a cruise recently. Imagine a holiday ending like that?

I walked home again. Would my daffodils bloom later this time? Would Covid-19 continue to bloom or hopefully die out now?

I'll keep you posted.

26

Eternal jokers

Humans can suffer from the daffodil's toxic properties. If sap from the wild daffodil touches our skin, a rash known as 'daffodil itch' – and resembling eczema – will form.

Thursday came – by now it was 21st March – and Mother's shoulder operation was delayed. We were happy, knowing the risks of surgery and the aftereffect of the drugs on her state; *she* was happy because she could eat. She has always loved food, piling her plate with steak or casserole. I couldn't visit on this day because I was working, but Grace took the kids. And something else.

We all caught up, as usual, in the WhatsApp chat.

Grace wrote: *Mum loved seeing Michael and Iris today. I took her a McMuffin, which she savaged. She said she's glad she survived and that she doesn't care if her leg is damaged, as long as her mind heals.*

Colin wrote: *She sounds almost sane now?*

Grace wrote: *She's much more lucid. And when she was paranoid, she could identify it. Probably because post-surgery drugs are out of system now. Shame there have to be more operations.*

Edwin wrote: *Has she asked how you all are? I have been affected.*

Claire wrote: *Not asked me.*

Grace wrote: *She said to me that she feels bad at her selfishness.*

*   *   *

The following day I spent a long time alone with Mother. It was the hardest yet. With recovery – and fewer drugs in her system – came frustration and irritation. Understandable, but tough to deal with. One moment she was snapping at me, another she was weepy, and another making jokes. I tried to go with whatever mood presented; tried to be patient when she wasn't.

It can't have been easy, still being in the hospital after almost a month. Two friends from Dove House Hospice (where she volunteered) came for an hour, which was pleasant. The other local hospital physio came by too and told us Mother was second on the list for a bed, so hopefully she would move there next week, where intensive work could begin on getting her walking again. Despite the delays and difficulties, I felt things were progressing.

Mother thanked me that day for being good with her, admitting she had 'put me through the wringer'.

She also ate enough food to kill a large horse.

I reported my day in the WhatsApp group.

I wrote: *Just leaving hospital. Been here five hours. Really shattered.*

Claire wrote: *Go and do something restful and pleasant now, Louise.*

Edwin wrote: *I spoke at length to a nurse. Shoulder surgery may be done electively much later. They are planning for her to stand with a frame on Monday. The nurse said you had a meeting with the community mental health team.*

Colin wrote: *I've no recollection of it.*

Claire wrote: *There has been no such meeting.*

Edwin wrote: *How bizarre.*

Colin wrote: *Maybe we're all suffering with delirium and Mother is sane?*

I wrote: *That could be a novel.*

Grace wrote: *It really could – guess who's sane.*

I wrote: *Yeah – it'll be my memoir.*

Grace wrote: *With a twist at the end where we're the insane ones and it was to protect us from the baddies.*

I wrote: *You couldn't make it up…*

That Sunday I didn't go to the hospital. I needed a day off again. I often felt guilt at not going but tried to ignore it; my family reassured me that I had every right to take care of myself too. I caught up with my kids; they needed me as much as − perhaps *more* than − my mother did. I also wrote.

Writing continued to be my saviour. No matter what's going on in my life, I return to fiction. I've been called a machine for how much I've written in a seemingly short time, but there's no mechanics to it, only compulsion. When we lost our house in the East Yorkshire floods of 2007, my first novel was the shoulder I cried on. Frenziedly, I typed words on a rickety metal desk on wheels while our home was being rebuilt around us. Finding the story was like when the builders peeled off rotten wallpaper. Would the brick below be intact or had the paper been holding it together?

Could it be rebuilt or was it ruined?

It feels that way now. Am I going to be OK when this is done? I'm finding my way to the truth. To the memories. But how will I feel afterwards?

Colin shared some thoughts after his visit that Sunday.

He wrote: *Mother was improved again today. Not ratty at all. She asked after you Eddie and said nice things about you.*

Edwin wrote: *Glad to hear it. What is the progress on the mental health treatment?*

I wrote: *I haven't heard any more on that since I was there with Grace on Monday, and she saw the psychiatrist. Mother, not Grace. There isn't one alive that could deal with Grace. I know Mother is on all her usual medication.*

* * *

The next day, Monday, there were more messages.

Colin wrote: *Just had a voicemail from Mother. Sounds chirpy. Been visited by the physio, the surgeon and the psychiatrist this morning ... and she's been upright on her feet!*

Edwin wrote: *I've just had this message off her ... ALL LIGHTS ON GREEN. HAVE BEEN STANDING ON MY OWN TWO FEET UNAIDED. WE ARE GOING TO MAKE OUR DREAMS COME TRUE!*

Colin wrote: *Have they put Ecstasy in her IV?*

I wrote: *She must've been on Grandma's holy water. Hail Mary!*

Claire wrote: *I've just spoken with her and told her not to try and walk about alone!*

On the Tuesday, Claire came up to Hull. We spent the afternoon with Mother, who was lively, if a little frenzied. Claire then stayed at mine. I love having my sisters sleep over; it takes me back to the times we shared a bedroom when we were little. The following morning, Claire headed off to see Mother alone because I had a guest arriving: my dear friend Madeleine.

We met through our books. I read *Unbroken*, her raw and powerful memoir exploring the healing process after having been brutally gang-raped by two men when she was just thirteen years old. When we first met at Leeds train station for an event we were doing on trauma and healing, I felt I'd known her for many lifetimes. Like we had been supposed to meet.

Now she was coming to Hull to appear on Fiona Mills' BBC Radio Humberside *Unheard and Uncensored* show with me, talking about the #metoo movement. It was an unforgettable night. Afterwards, producer Phil White said, 'That's what you call award-winning radio.' The studio had fallen into absolute silence as Madeleine shared the story of her brutal attack and the journey to recovery and forgiveness. She has, since then, given up her job in psychotherapy to speak all over the world, encouraging others to share their stories and heal too.

Claire, Madeleine and I went for a walk under the bridge.

Madeleine: *You showed me the spot where your mother had jumped. The yellow tape from the police was still there. I looked up and thought, 'That is high. That is a big jump.' This wasn't accidental but very determined. It was eerie. Then we went to the hospital. It was surreal seeing your mother because here she was – not that long ago having jumped from a bridge – and she was excited to meet a new person. It wasn't quite the picture I'd had in mind for someone just having tried to end their life. She was very interested in me, asking lots of questions. She was flirty with the nurses, making jokes, and seemingly making quite light of what had recently happened.*

Madeleine left for Leeds the next day, where we were both attending a book event on the Saturday. Claire spoke to the psychiatrist about Mother's seeming lack of emotion, the denial and not facing reality, and her unrealistic belief that the depression had now lifted altogether. The psychiatrist deemed Mother as still a high suicide risk and said she wanted a psychiatric admission for full assessment after the physio.

Mother finally had shoulder surgery at the end of the week. She was done by 6.30pm and described as 'perky'. On the way back to the ward afterwards – knowing she had missed teatime – she asked the recovery team to make her a sandwich.

That night Edwin wrote: *You all need to pull back in a big way now that Mother is recovering. She needs to do it herself now. You all need to preserve your energy and sanity. She will become (more) demanding otherwise.*

Grace wrote: *I'm having night terrors. I'm a child again and Mother is how she was when we were small. It's horrific.*

Edwin wrote: *Shit, that's sad. How can you deal with it? Sounds like you should see someone.*

Grace wrote: *I will, but there's a waiting list. These are the mental health services that failed Mother remember.*

Colin wrote: *I'm eating.*

Grace wrote: *Is that a separate contribution to the conversation or did you need it off your chest?*

Colin wrote: *Just venting.*

As Edwin had suggested, I pulled back in a big way and met Madeleine at the book event in Leeds. While there, author friend John said to me, 'For some reason, your mum survived when many others wouldn't, and you wonder if there was a reason for that.' After a thought, I responded with, 'Maybe to give us chance to heal and to make peace with her?' I drank wine and smiled but I felt lost. Just like my mother had all week, I joked and made light, but my chest felt as heavy as lead. Did my mother feel like that when she flirted with everyone who came across her path?

The next day was Mothering Sunday. Colin, Grace and I visited her, bearing practical gifts like puzzle magazines and books for her to read. She seemed her 'normal' self but a tad irritable; anyone who knows her would laugh at the words *a tad*. Colin described her as being 'in a showing off mood'. How well I knew that trick for hiding my sadness; I'd done it all day yesterday. How often Grace and I joke about how no one would want to be around when the laughter stops. But you can't cut a Joker-esque smile into your face every minute of every day.

I smile because it's genuine, and my disposition is that way.

I smile because I'm burying hurt, and that's learnt behaviour.

I smile because I don't want anyone to feel sad, and that's from years of anxiety about my mother being depressed.

Smiling is the complexity of my relationship with her. Though she's hurt me more than any other person, she's made me laugh too. She can observe the minutiae of life in such a perceptive way that she has you sick with laughter. She can sum up a situation – weave a witty tale – with a few carefully selected words that Victoria Wood might have stolen. We once spent three hours on a train laughing at a newspaper article where a variety of people had ended up in the wrong beds at a hotel, and I'm sure everyone wanted to throw us out of the carriage.

This is where the deepest hurt lies. When someone makes you smile that much, it reminds you that you love them. Makes you forgive. Makes you go back to them after the hurt. But the hurt is bigger. The hurt is too much.

Laughter is as much a release as crying is. I've got forty-nine years of crying to do, and who the hell has that kind of time? I've shed some tears here. But I've laughed too. Both leave me feeling exhausted.

Both leave me wishing our mother...

I don't even know the end of that sentence.

27

One daffodil

Fair daffodils, we weep to see you haste away so soon. – **This line by Robert Herrick is on the gravestone of my dear friend Joanne's sister Helen.**

I saw a daffodil on my walk this week.

Just one. Buffeted by the wind, barely blooming, but there. As if to reassure me. A new cycle begins; seasons change; life goes on. It made that shocking day feel as close as ever. I wanted to see the four bunches from last year to know that everything would be OK.

But those ones are never coming back.

I read the news on my way home; the headlines said that more than two thousand people have died from Covid-19 in China, and numerous people elsewhere, including a few in Italy. No one here. Yet. I have to hope it stays that way.

For that moment, I was happy with my one bit of daffodil sunshine.

28

The queen of not remembering

The line 'they flash upon that inward eye' from Wordsworth's poem reveals that he not only still has the physical memory of those daffodils, but also the memory of how they made him feel.

On 18th May 1981, Claire, Grace and I finally went into Hesslewood Hall Children's Home. According to documents, we were there just three days that time, and then Grandma Roberts came to care for us at home. But we know there were other occasions; we remember being taken to and from school in a blue van with other children. Our memories of the place are too vivid and numerous for us to have stayed once. I was now ten, Claire and Grace were six, and Colin two.

This letter was sent to a variety of relevant people from the head social worker.

To whom it may concern,

In the event of Mrs A contacting you in a state of distress and being admitted with Colin to the Mother and Baby Unit, it may be useful to have the following information. Claire, Grace and Louise can be received into care under Section 2 of the 1980 Children Act, and be accommodated at Hesslewood, if they have vacancies. Humberside County Council Social Services will sponsor the children.

Leading up to this admission, social workers observed that Mum was looking after us. The report on one visit was that Colin seemed 'fine and contented' and wandered happily in and out of the garden; there was also fresh baking on the kitchen work surface. Just a week later, however, Mum queried the possibility of others caring for us, like a nanny or a boarding school. Grandma Roberts had been told not to come every time Mum demanded, as this was not helping.

On the morning we went into Hesslewood, Mum admitted she 'couldn't be bothered with the children'. Apathy is a sign of depression. But did she just want a break? Was it yet another symptom of a personality disorder? Is she a narcissist who *also* happens to have chronic depression, who later used alcohol as a crutch? There are lots of depressed mothers who manage to put their children first, so to blame this illness for why my mum neglected us isn't fair.

The social worker, quite understandably, warned Mum of the effect on our emotional well-being if we continued to be moved about. The fact that she had to be told this is sad; could she not see it for herself? Still, that afternoon, the record states that we three girls were placed at Hesslewood until Grandma could come mid-week.

I've no memory of being taken there. Reading the facts in our documents is at times like reading a novel; I never know what might happen at the turn of a page. A report quotes me as being the 'most concerned' and asking if the social worker would visit us the next day. I imagine I was anxious about how long we were going for. No doubt – after our indefinite time at Grandma's the previous year and the hysteria I'd witnessed when the twins finally saw Mum – I was terrified of being 'forgotten' again, and of being unable to console my sisters.

I do remember the place itself.

Another high-ceilinged building like The Cliff and the school we lived in. Another bedroom to get used to. At least the three of us got to share. Our room was shadowy (it could, of course, be my little girl eyes seeing it that way) and had three narrow beds in a row along a wall. I had nightmares that the room was swallowing me up, that the walls grew taller and taller, like trees do in old horror movies. This dream reoccurred many times after. Even now, when I'm ill, I dream of sleeping in rooms that don't want me there.

Claire: *I remember the three of us sneaking out of the bedroom to go to the toilet at night. Louise was taking us. We got told off by a woman and sent back to bed. I vaguely remember that woman – I don't think she was particularly nice. There were soggy cornflakes for breakfast. I had to have a bath with someone other than Louise or Grace, so that wasn't very good. The beds were skinny. Basic room, big windows, big wardrobe. We were allowed to pick a toy. I picked a black sausage dog with a zip. I took it into school on a show-and-tell day, so I must've liked it. There was a real mixture of kids – sadly, they likely had lots of issues, difficult family backgrounds, etc. As usual, I don't remember particular feelings.*

After the three of us sneaked out to the toilet, our bedroom door was locked at night. This made me anxious. What if there was a fire? We were on an upstairs floor. I often looked out of the window, wondering how high it was. I felt such a weight of responsibility for my sisters; no ten-year-old should have to deal with that much concern.

According to our care records, as she had promised, the social worker visited us the next day. She reported that we were 'enjoying' being at Hesslewood. Claire and Grace apparently said they wanted to stay, but I wanted to go home. This only makes me think that we can't have been probed very much; children – especially vulnerable ones – will say what they think an adult wants to hear. Perhaps the social workers saw what they wanted to and then wrote our story as duty.

Like Claire, I find it hard to access feelings from these long-gone events. Apparently, children of narcissistic mothers often have a disconnect between their thoughts and feelings. They are so used to their emotions being dismissed that they don't know what they feel about a situation and have to make special effort to tune into it. Reconnecting the severed mind-body chord takes work. Whether or not my mother has a personality disorder or not, there is some comfort in reading psychology articles and thinking, yes, that's me.

If I look at how things make me feel today, I can imagine my trauma then.

When my home was destroyed by the 2007 floods and I had to find us somewhere else to live, I was ruthless. I viewed a dilapidated property with fifty other flood victims. I didn't even look around; I went straight to the landlady and asked, 'What will secure this house *right* now?' She said, 'A hundred pounds.' I wrote a cheque, and she wrote a receipt on the only thing handy – a napkin. Conor was sixteen, Katy seven, and the idea of not giving them a home filled me with abject fear.

This is how I know that the upheavals of my childhood have deeply impacted me. God knows how I coped back then when I had no control over what happened. I kept my bedroom very tidy; at Tower Hill the orderliness of my room was in direct relation to the disorderliness of our daily life. This has stayed with me. My OCD is consuming. I find safety in order. If my home is tidy, nothing can hurt me.

Grace: *I remember bread-and-butter sandwiches and getting dropped off at school in the blue van, so we were there during the school week too. Luckily our friends didn't make fun of us, which we were worried about. I hated butter so I couldn't eat my lunch. I can't remember being locked in the bedroom, but we may have been. Baths were humiliating as they were shared with other boys and girls. There was a huge field behind the building, and we played in there. There was a woman who for years after I saw with a dog, witchy looking; she worked there, and she wasn't very nice. The dining area was like a classroom.*

I remember hating our packed lunch too. It was basic. No love; no care. It exacerbated my food issues again. I couldn't eat it. My throat felt tight all the time. The evening meal was some kind of stew, and tepid. I was cold at night, even though it was May. Perhaps, like I had at Grandma's, I kicked the covers off to try and freeze my feelings.

Everything must defrost at some point though.

Grace: *The place had a 'big house' smell; institution, polished wood. When I go in places like that as an adult, I'm taken back to it. I don't recall missing Mum. It just felt like an adventure. And, after all, we had our 'real' mum with us: Louise. And there was routine. We craved that.*

That time, we went home after a few days, when Grandma arrived. The social worker signed us as 'discharged from care', picked up our clothes, and got the twins from school. I apparently went home from school myself, as usual. Mum remained in the mother-and-baby unit with Colin for a few more days, though she complained that the other residents were 'a bit rough' and that Colin hadn't settled this time.

At the end of May 1981, Grandma was back again.

Colin now went to nursery fulltime. The owner of the place kindly offered to not only pick him up first thing in the morning, but to also bring him home at night. She had expressed concern previously about Mum's 'handling of' Colin. She said she had never seen any sign of physical injury but that she kept an eye on him, and on us three girls too.

Mum admitted that she 'had no feelings for anything'. The social worker asked the doctor to assess her medication and wrote in a report that it was clear she was not going to get better at home. She asked if Colin could go with us to Hesslewood if needed and was told yes.

There is a large chunk of information blocked out of our care records here. It seems, from what I can piece together, that on May 29th Mum went missing. I have a vague memory of knowing she had gone. Of feeling nothing. A social worker wrote that if she hadn't heard anything by 3pm she would call the police. Then it's all blacked out again. Did Mum go into the mental hospital again at this time? Was there another suicide attempt? A breakdown? Was this when we returned to Hesslewood?

It's not clear.

The report then jumps a few months. The in-between is a mystery. Were those pages destroyed or just lost? We got warned when we applied for them that some might be missing after all this time. Is fate being kind and protecting us?

And I can't remember.

Like Catherine in *Maria in the Moon*, I'm the queen of not remembering. Through me, she said: *There was something else: something I couldn't remember. Something as black as feverish, temperature-fuelled nightmares. Something that couldn't be fixed or replaced. Something that stopped all the singing in our house for a long time.*

It was around this time that Mother met Peter.

I never liked Peter.

The biggest wolf is here, and it's time to open the door.

29

The miracle of the returning pigment

*The wild daffodil's interactions are diverse
and crucial to its survival.*

April arrived with developments: a new ward, some home truths, a humorous conversation about Mum's ex, Kenneth, and reality.

For the first fortnight of the month, Mother remained on the busy trauma ward at Hull Royal, her bed now on an opposite wall, her ward-mates changing daily. Weaning off strong pain medication meant leg ache. Doctors insisted this was part of the healing process, and not necessarily an infection, though this of course was a constant worry. There was a high risk of bone infection with such an extreme injury.

As always, we discussed the issues in WhatsApp.

I wrote: *If the leg doesn't fix properly will they remove it, do you think?*

Claire wrote: *I knew a doctor who shattered his ankle skiing – after a rebuild and five years of problems, he asked for amputation below the knee. His life was much better.*

Edwin wrote: *I'd take amputation any day over a non-functional leg.*

Grace wrote: *Me too! My ambition when I was six was to be in a wheelchair!*

Mother was also frustrated with her left arm because it didn't work properly; she couldn't raise it or grip with that hand. Unfortunately, it was another result of the jump and might never be right. Constant urinary infections meant doses of antibiotics. Physio commenced, which simply meant Mother being walked up and down the ward occasionally. Privately, a nurse told us her irritation was born of realising what she now had to face. We knew it already; the bubble had burst, leaving the bleak reality of the results of her suicide attempt. Fewer visitors – they had all returned to their lives – meant less drama, less fuss, and having to therefore face this new future.

Edwin wrote: *Thinking of you all because I sense a shift in emotions now with the reality of all these chest infections and UTIs and kidney issues and pain. Looking forward to seeing you all in May. Be kind to yourselves. Have a meal. Get drunk.*

Grace and I often visited Mother together. It was easier in twos; strength in numbers and all that. We often helped her on and off the commode, which was no easy task. It clearly caused her a lot of pain, but she was determined to do it. One day, we assisted a nurse: I got behind Mother, Grace supported her torso, and the nurse had her shoulders.

'Thanks, love,' said Mother, out of breath but safely in place on the commode. 'What's your name again?'

'Grace,' she joked. 'Your daughter of forty-four years. Now move that Robocop leg and get on with it…'

It was sad to see her so physically frail yet making great effort to get about. Whatever her mental state, Mother has always had the constitution of an ox. Now she was thin, gaunt in the face, trembling at every exertion. Her leg inside its metal frame was bent at an odd angle. Yet her hair was getting blacker by the day. We laughed at this curious return to her youthful colour.

'Have you been dying the bugger?' I asked. 'You've fewer greys than me!'

'No, I swear.' We knew she hadn't; she could barely wash it, let alone dye it.

'It's bizarre,' said Grace. 'They should experiment on you – find out why.'

The miracle of the returning pigment.

That afternoon, when the frenzy of the ward seemed to pause for a moment to give me the opportunity, I finally asked if Mother still had that last note, the one written before the jump.

'It's gone,' she said.

'What did it say?' I asked.

'Just sorry… and goodbye.'

What more could I say?

'Why did you take that book?' asked Grace. 'The Catherine Cookson one.'

'No reason,' Mother said.

There is always a reason, but she clearly didn't want to share it, and that's her right.

I wanted to ask, 'Why the bridge?' but I didn't. I never did. Never have.

That was it. Those were our answers.

On 11th April, Mother finally moved to the physio ward at another nearby hospital. It was a much nicer place, less chaotic, with stricter visiting times so fewer disturbances, and not as many emergency buzzers going off. The turnover of patients was also slower so she could bond with her ward-mates. It was on a ground floor and had a view of a pretty garden with a bench and paths snaking around the building.

As a non-driver, it was much harder for me to visit though; it was farther away, and buses only went once an hour. Also, the visiting times were in the evening and on a weekend, when I work at the theatre.

Claire wrote: *Mother loves the rehab ward – she said it's like The Ritz.*
Grace wrote: *I'm happy for her. I'm feeling very low though.*
Edwin wrote: *Are you seeing anyone?*
I wrote: *The sad thing is that unless you pay, there's no mental health support on the NHS. I asked for it in 2012… still waiting.*
Claire wrote: *I'm seeing a physio today about my excruciating neck/ shoulder pain, which I'm certain is due to feeling tense for weeks.*
Grace wrote: *I'm on high-dose antidepressants.*
I wrote: *I'm writing furiously.*
Edwin wrote: *It cost me $170 to see the shrink. I'm billing your mother for that, and for the airfare when I come.*

Mid-April, I went to Edinburgh for a weekend break with Joe, and our friends Vonny and Neil, celebrating our upcoming 20th wedding anniversary and Neil's 50th birthday. It was heaven to escape for a few days, where it wasn't work or a book event; we ate out and drank wine and chilled and watched Saturday night TV at the huge flat, like everyday people who don't have a mother with one and a half legs.

Back home, the psychiatrist reported her thoughts to us. She said Mother was not facing reality, and therefore still at risk. Her plan was that following six weeks of physio, she should be admitted to a psychiatric ward. Mother's 'happiness' now was either a deliberate act or a denial state. The psychiatrist was concerned that she had shown no guilt or remorse or embarrassment, which wasn't 'normal' after such a serious suicide attempt. She also noted that Mother enjoyed the attention of staff and visitors; she was concerned she'd crash after being discharged. Mother, however, was resistant to the idea of a mental hospital; she said she would think about it. In reality, she might have no choice. The psychiatrist said she would invoke Section 2 if necessary, so they could keep her in for twenty-eight days. She could then be fully assessed.

We wondered what it would reveal.

'Mother's often used the depression card to get what she wants,' said Grace afterwards. 'Yes, on occasion she's really suffered with it, but there were times it got her the attention she craves. Now it means she has to do what *they* want.'

'Exactly,' said Claire. 'She doesn't want to go on a psychiatric ward because she isn't depressed now.'

We've spent a lifetime trying to work our mother out. Claire has read many books on narcissistic personality disorder and thinks it most accurately describes her. An explanation like this helps me cope. But we are not psychologists. At times, the depression has been real, this is fact. At other times, she has used it to justify bad choices or inappropriate behaviour. Now? We had no idea.

One day during her hospital stay, Mother said she felt like a queen when surrounded by us. That we were completely at her beck and call. She adored the attention. Another time, I expressed concern about Colin, about how things might be affecting him, and she was flippant, saying, 'Oh, he'll be fine.' She might have been feeling off that day, but it struck me that there was little care for how *he* felt.

I've been trained to fill her attention-tank since I was small.

It has always been about her, above all else.

Easter arrived, and Katy came home from university for the week; I wanted to squeeze her and never let her go. She visited Mother for the first time. Her training – even though she was only in the first year of her Mental Health Nursing degree – meant she was patient and asked all sorts of questions I might not have thought of. While we had Katy, we visited Conor and met his new girlfriend, Ieva, for the first time. It gave me great joy to see him happy; she was exactly the girl I'd have chosen for him. I hugged him and told him so.

Back at the hospital, Mother reckoned she would be on the physio ward for a full year. We tried to gently tell her this was unlikely. An X-ray revealed that the leg was healing well. She could now bear her full weight, though the leg frame could be on for another six months; she might be discharged in it. Despite the positive news, she sounded down again. She said it had been a hard weekend, quiet, with less staff and fewer visitors; that we had been busy with our families over Easter. We knew we'd have to warn her that there wouldn't be round-the-clock care forever. Colin had already tried.

By the end of April, Mother was depressed again, and scared.

It seemed real. It was hard to witness; it felt like she might never be OK again. She was no longer the wide-eyed, frenzied joker. She opened up to Grace and me, admitted it was finally hitting her. She'd had time to reflect on everything. We reassured her, acknowledged that she was bound to have low moods with all that had happened in the last ten weeks.

'It's fine to stop being jolly and go with it,' I said.

'Open up to the psychiatrist,' said Grace. 'That's what she's there for.'

'I will.' She sounded weary, and we didn't know if she would.

We wheeled her out in the grounds regularly. There were expansive views of green fields, and spring was bursting into life around us. Most of the daffodils were dying now but other colourful flowers brightened the barren soil, hopeful promises. Other patients passed us with cheery hellos. Mother was no longer full of such cheeriness. It took me back – as it does every time – to being small and helpless and unable to make her happy. We siblings all find different aspects of our mother challenging. Her sadness is my biggest trigger. I'm afraid of being dragged down with it; afraid I'll never surface; drown.

Edwin wrote: *This is her new reality. This is the consequence of her actions. She is getting plenty of care. You aren't. You can't be at her beck and call when she's discharged. She needs to adjust to that. You need to get back to your own families.*

He was right.

We realised that Mother needed to know this and prepare for it. We talked at length about it; about how we should be firm but kind, reassure her that we were *there* but make clear that it could not be daily now.

I watched a series called *The Trials of Gabriel Fernandez*, in which the mother of an eight-year-old boy was sentenced to life in prison, and her boyfriend to death, for torturing and murdering the child. It was a hard watch. What made me sob was the beautiful Mother's Day card Gabriel made for his mum weeks before his death. Children will find a way to forgive even the cruellest, most abusive mother. They will look for some small thing to love about her, no matter what.

I cling to memories of the funny *Mum* Mum who fills me with laughter. I cling to memories of the emotional *Mum* Mum who enjoys a weepy film as much as I do. Even at forty-nine, I have days where I long for her unconditional and absolute love.

As always – despite our advice to Mother to 'stop being jolly and go with it' – we returned to our refuge: the humour. We joked in WhatsApp about a boyfriend she'd had years ago.

Claire wrote: *Is Kenneth still alive?*

Grace wrote: *I hope so. I saw him on Prestongate last week.*

I wrote: *He was alive five minutes ago when he left my bedroom.*

Claire wrote: *I miss him.*

I wrote: *I wonder if he's aware now that he truly exists?*

Claire wrote: *I think he'll sense it.*

Grace wrote: *Just think, he thinks he's normal…*

Don't we all.

No.

Though Kenneth was a man we liked, some of our mother's past boyfriends were as dangerous as the fairytale wolf in the woods…

30

Peter

Wordsworth compares daffodils with the 'continuous stars that shine and twinkle on the milky way'. This reveals that he is more comfortable thinking about the afterlife than real life. There's a sense of disappointment in earthly (early?) life.

Peter was vomited into our lives from the womb of a badly dressed 1970s sitcom, frizzy-haired, wearing ridiculous white flares and thin-rimmed glasses, and so drunk he had to be helped into our house by someone from the pub.

This was some time in the spring of 1981. It was definitely after Prince Charles and Lady Diana got engaged – which was 24th February – because Peter arrived with the most bizarre gifts for children he had not only never met before, but who were all under ten: four commemorative dinner trays with a picture of Charles and Diana on them. In mannerism, he was one of Mum's more gentle boyfriends; wiry, bad-skinned, beady-eyed, softly spoken, slow in movement.

He was never violent. Didn't swear. Didn't slap me across the face.

But still, from the moment he staggered into our kitchen, I didn't like him.

Grace: *I remember him in white flares, walking in Hessle Square with him, and he was pissed. I remember him being with us when the Humber Bridge* *opened in July. Also, we went on the Lincoln Castle (a boat anchored at the foreshore that sold drinks aboard) with him, and we got a Coke and crisps.*

Peter was lodging around the corner from us, having moved to the area from Jersey. Mum had begun going to the pub and having a social life. They met there. I don't know how soon he moved in with us, but it was definitely by the summer because on 15th September Mum expressed in our care records that the house was getting small with us 'all being there'. She told a social worker she was 'looking forward to moving to the Chestnut Avenue house'. I remember talk of this large house on a leafy street in the town. Peter and Mum also talked about adopting another child.

Neither of these things happened.

Peter paid me attention, something I'd never really had.

But I still didn't like him.

Once we were walking past the church – just the two of us – and he said I should stay a child for as long as possible; play with my Sindy and enjoy it. I remember thinking that I'd never felt much like a child. I had, however, always dreamt of growing my hair long. Mum kept it short; I felt scalped, boy-like. I must have mentioned this because Peter said he would talk to her. In a picture a few months later, my hair is growing out.

But I don't look happy.

And I still didn't like him.

According to our care records, in October Colin was wetting himself again, and then laughing about it. Mum reported that she tried smacking him, but it didn't work. The social worker suggested she simply ignore it; that he would grow out of it. I wonder now why no one looked further into why a child who had been dry for some months was regressing.

At this time our records also state that Claire came home in tears one Sunday when our father had hit her across the face. 'We *were* a bit noisy,' she admitted. I remember this. It was on the stairs in his flat. Mum, however, told the social worker she still wanted us to go to his flat the following Sunday because she had plans with NAME CROSSED OUT (clearly Peter). The social worker told Mum she should talk to her ex-husband about this behaviour but wasn't convinced she would.

There is little detailed mention of Peter in our care documents, apart from on Bonfire Night when we went to a firework display and Colin was apparently frightened. Peter took him away from the main scene while we girls stayed. Did Mum paint the picture she wanted social workers to see? She is reported as looking well at this time, dressed fashionably, and with a perm 'which looks nice'. She tells one social worker she is 'happy with Peter' and that he gets on 'very well with the children'.

Clearly no one asked us, not that we would have said anything negative. We would probably just have given an answer we thought they wanted.

I find it odd that social workers didn't seem concerned about a man moving in so fast with a recently depressed woman, when the previous boyfriend had been violent, and she had four children on the Observation Register. I suppose someone *might* have spoken to us; my unreliable memory means I can't recall. In adult years, when we've asked her, Mother has been vague about Peter and this era, claiming memory loss after ECT treatment, and that she was 'ill'.

I often wonder if she knows more. She lied a few years ago when Grace asked her for Peter's surname so we could do research, find out who he is, his history. Why? What would she have to hide?

I think Mum started drinking around this time. She had often enjoyed a drink before now, but this was when it began in the life-changing, excessive way that would ruin our lives. I remember Peter and her, sitting in the front room, smoking. I hated the way he looked at me. Not with unkindness; something far worse.

Grace: *I remember Peter sitting with his legs crossed like a lady, smoking a cigarette and putting the ash in this tall 70s ashtray, his glasses, his wild hair, pointy collars, just a thin, shady thing.*

Mid November, reports state that we hadn't seen our father much due to us being 'busy on a Sunday'. He was unable to visit on Saturdays because of band rehearsals. The social worker asked if Mum had taken it up with him about hitting Claire and she 'looked shame-faced' and said no. The social worker emphasised that we 'looked to her for protection and care'. She suggested that Mum invite our father to see us one weekday teatime. We four could eat with him, while she eats with Peter in the kitchen. This would leave weekends free for her, Peter, and us four to get together as a new family.

I believe Peter was encouraging this 'new family'.

Late November, Mum complained that 'the girls were playing up'. Apparently, we were 'forever fighting and arguing'. This is unusual for us. It has never been said anywhere else in our records. What prompted this change in our behaviour? Why did no one check it out further? Ask us? The twins were apparently clingy. Grace was anxious when Mum went out, asking over and over if she was coming back. It's understandable; I remember trying to console her.

Peter made every effort to separate us from our mum. He sent us out to play, saying, 'She's having a bad day today, you need to leave her alone.' Then he locked the door so we couldn't get back in. Colin was in the back garden, crying for us.

Mum has since claimed that at this time Peter manipulated her because she was 'so ill'. Our records suggest otherwise; that she was well and liked this new man. When I told her in recent years that his behaviour had definitely been predatory grooming of us kids, she said he 'groomed her too'. There was no compassion for our experience. No acknowledgement. She felt she was the true victim, not us.

Grace: *I remember being at the side door to the house and we couldn't get in. He came down the stairs – I could see his shadow – and he opened the door a crack and said, 'Your Mum's poorly, go back out to play.' And that was a mantra for months. He always sent us out.*

During the day, we were dismissed. In the evening, it was different. When we were inside the house, it was a dark, unsafe place, far more than the outside world. People worry about strangers, the dangers of the unknown, but it's often those closest who hurt us the most.

The wolf was inside the house. He smoked posh cigarettes. He walked about naked, often in a state of arousal. He left sex books scattered carelessly around. I can still see those graphic images, feel my confusion and fear of them. He and Mum had loud sex when we were close by, particularly in his caravan in Withernsea where we often stayed, all of us in the living room with barely a partition between us.

What would social workers have done about this if they had known? *Did* they know? Where are all the missing pages in our care records, between June and early September, at a time when weekly visits were occurring? Was so much blacked out that there was no point in including them?

Or did the wolf huff and puff and blow them away?

31

Eighteen seconds

'And then my heart with pleasure fills, and dances with the daffodils.' This Wordsworth line gives the sense that he's caught a glimpse of heaven. It leaves the reader yearning to find a place of utopian peace.

My mother once said to me, 'I wish you could feel the way depression does for eighteen seconds. Just eighteen seconds, so you'd know how awful it is.'

I thought about it. Realised we could all learn a lot from being in another person's head for eighteen seconds. I imagined it for many things. Eighteen seconds inside Katy's head when she got diagnosed with type 1 diabetes at just seven. Eighteen seconds inside Grandma Roberts' head as she sat alone with her evening cup of tea, us three girls upstairs in bed. Eighteen seconds inside one-year-old Colin's head when he woke up in a foster home without any of his family.

Eighteen seconds inside the head of a girl waiting for her bedroom door to open.

32

Blacked Out

'You have to be bashed about a bit to see the point of daffodils, sunsets, and uneventful nice days.' – **Alain de Botton**

During the time that Peter lived with us, the bedroom situation in the house changed. I had always shared with either Colin while Claire and Grace were in the next room, or with the twins while Colin slept alone. Now, I was alone in the Long Bedroom, Claire and Grace were next door in the Square Bedroom, while Colin – I can only presume – was with Mum in the back bedroom. It's hard to be sure. But I do feel sure that Peter instigated these changes as he integrated himself into our family. As he divided and conquered.

Memories from then are fragmented. I hear songs from that time and a sickly dread consumes me. I recall clothes I had, like the cheap, quilted, pale blue dressing gown that I remember fastening right to the top, and I can't look at the image for too long.

Grace: *I remember Peter vividly, in the back bedroom, standing with an erection. I don't know where Mum was. Or where anyone was. But I was there.*

I remember the sound of my bedroom door opening at night.

It wasn't Mum; she rarely came up to us, not for bedtime stories or if we were ill. The door scraped because there was a raised step into the Long Bedroom. Slowly, slowly, slowly, it moved. I hated the sound of it for months after. An ominous tugging, like a gift that doesn't want to be opened. Even now, I hate anyone coming unannounced into my bedroom, and I can't sleep unless the duvet is wrapped tightly (*safely*) around me, no matter how warm the night.

I knew it was Peter.

I pretended to be asleep. This I know too. I'd lie as still as a statue, my eyes tightly shut, breathing as slowly as I could, hoping he wouldn't stay long. I wished I was invisible. I remember the woodchip wallpaper when I briefly opened my eyes; trying to see patterns in those dots; concentrating on it; *willing* him to go. If I push hard to see – to *remember* – I can hear his breath too, feel the weight of him sitting on the bed, a hand on my back, over the top of the cover.

But nothing more.

There's a nauseous feeling as I write this. I just went to the sink, thinking I'd throw up, but I didn't. I stood there, my heart pounding. It's like a closed patio door that you don't see until you crash into it when you try and go into the garden. I can recall his presence, and then *bang*, nothing else.

Door shut.

'You have to be good or your mum could get ill again.'

I know Peter said that.

Not only to me but to my sisters.

Not only at night, but during the day.

'You don't want your mum to go into the hospital again, do you? You don't want to be the reason she's poorly?'

I can hear him saying this too. I believed him. Without question. It had happened before, and it could happen again. I can feel now the anxiety I had then that she would disappear again. That this time she might never come back. And I know I would have done *anything* to stop that happening.

But no matter how I try, I can't access the memories.

I can't see beyond him sitting there. I can't see what... *happened*. And yet I *know* there is more.

I thought writing might free it, the way my fictional stories fully emerge when I sit down at the computer and let them in. It feels torturous not to remember. But is it better this way? Maybe ten-year-old me isn't ready to share; maybe she never will be; maybe I have to accept it. She kicked off the bed covers to freeze her feelings when her mum left. Maybe this time – with Peter – they are permanently frozen.

But just to see these words in black-and-white – my own acknowledgment, on the page, for the first time – I know *something* happened. Something I didn't like. Something I didn't want. Something so insidious that I buried it so deep I can't find it. I can *feel* it though; my stomach churns with it; my throat constricts with it; my heart chugs with it; a rage I have buried all this time shows itself in other, easier-to-deal-with experiences.

The body remembers what the mind can't.

The *soul* remembers.

Grace: *Mum seemed to spend a lot of time – weekends and summer holidays – upstairs in bed. I used to think, 'I just want Mummy.' If I think of Peter now, I get a seedy, dark, foul, festering, disgusting feeling about anything to do with that era. I remember it hurt 'down there' when I wiped after going for a wee. These are my six-year-old words. They were dark days.*

People might read this and ask, 'Why didn't you tell anyone?'

Who would I have told?

A mum I was terrified of losing again, who dismissed every thought or ailment I ever had? An absent father more interested in his band rehearsal? A beloved grandma who might never look at me the same way if I shared my shame? I was a good girl. I had been taught from a young age to be quiet; to never complain; that I didn't matter; to smile with my teeth showing. And Peter was a clever and predatory adult telling me the most terrifying thing I could hear.

That my mother might again disappear.

Go into the asylum.

Shame silenced me too. Something 'felt wrong'. I was told not to speak of it, so I felt guilty. Disgusting. Like *I* was wrong. I believe I *wanted* to speak. I had a dream at this time that I remember vividly. In it, I came downstairs during the night. Shaking, I descended the steep steps. It was dark. As I gripped the banister, my hand found something. I went into the front room. Peter and Mum were laughing and drinking and smoking. I looked down and realised I was holding a severed arm. I woke in a cold sweat. Just as at Hillcrest Avenue I got in trouble for going downstairs, I knew that rule still applied.

So, I buried it.

Like Catherine, a child in one of my novels, did her abuse.

She said: *I think Uncle Henry was never here. I think we all made him up. It's easy to forget a story. You just close the pages, and all the words suffocate. The pictures take longer to dissolve though.*

It was around this time that I began comfort eating. Treats were not readily available in the house. All credit to Mum, we ate a healthy diet of home-cooked meals and very few sweets. Children will find a way to self-comfort though. I started stealing chocolate from a corner shop near our house. It was on my route home from school, so perfect. I'd sneak in, try and look inconspicuous, and take what I wanted. Looking back, the shop owner must have known. Perhaps she simply felt sorry for me.

It was my eleventh birthday that November. I didn't want a party at our house, but I know there was one. I don't recall much of it, other than someone giving me felt-tip pens that smelled of their colour (oranges for orange, strawberry for red) and being nervous that Peter would be around.

There came a time when he left.

It's not written in our care records, at least not visibly, not without being blacked out. When I asked her recently, Mother claims not to know why he went. I think it was Christmas time;

I remember a particular Santa bauble on the tree and wanting to cry for no reason. I don't know if something specific happened that Peter would suddenly be gone as fast as he had arrived, in a blur of awful hair and clothes.

Has my mother really forgotten those days?

Did she know Peter came into my room at night?

Would it be possible to hide that from the parent of a child in the same house?

Perhaps yes. Perhaps he waited until she was asleep. Perhaps that's why they drank every night. Or – even worse – perhaps she has simply rewritten history to save herself. Someone with a narcissist personality disorder might do that. It's called gaslighting. Deny an incident even happened if it doesn't suit their narrative. But if she knew and looked the other way, that means there were two wolves in the house.

And how would I come to terms with that?

Is it better to believe she didn't know?

Peter came into my bedroom for a last goodbye. For many years, I thought this memory was of my father, so confused I am about this time. I realise now that I was placing a safer face on the person in order to look at the moment. Peter was crying. Saying sorry. Hugging me, suffocatingly tight. I remember lying still, stiff as a board. Waiting. Just waiting for him to get out and go.

Grace: *He came in our bedroom when he left. I was in the top bunk. He said, 'I've got to go. Goodbye.'*

The words 'got to go' are interesting. Like, he didn't want to. He had been told to. He had to. But by whom? I wish there were answers. I wish there were non-blacked-out pages.

Then he was gone.

Then I shared the Square Bedroom with Claire and Grace again.

And we all got on with our lives.

33

Bedtime Barbie

(A poem I wrote in recent years, inspired by the Peter time.)
Cherry paper catches stars
from the Christmas tree by the
scratchy wicker basket.
Pink wrapping rips fast,
except where Sellotape tugs tight,
resisting, putting up a fight.

Bedtime Barbie sleeps
through jiggling and jerking and pulling
and slippers coming loose in the box
to smack her in the face.
She needs a kiss goodnight
but goodnight is a forgotten wish,
remember.

She smells of blanketed babies.
Lace nightie tight at the neck,
skin beneath not yet wrong.
Wavy hair is brushed and plaited and patted
and persuaded by a boyfriend to be kept long.

18 Seconds

Discard cherry paper
in tangles of sheet and pillow and ribbon.

No, save the wrapping - it'll get used again,
for something small.

But the stars are ruined.

34

Thirty minutes, three drinks

Picasso said that no one has to explain a daffodil. Good design is understandable to virtually everybody. You never have to ask why. – **Hugh Newell Jacobsen**

On 5th March 1982, a social worker wrote this note in our care records: *Problems appear to have settled down to the point where social workers can withdraw, unless approached by the client.*

It was two months after Peter left. Maybe this was why they felt our 'problems' had settled down. But despite his departure, we were still deemed to be at risk, and the four of us remained on the Observation Register until 28th February 1984, oddly thirty-five years to the day before Mother jumped from the bridge. Little observation was actually done for the final two years of us being on this register though, at least as far as I recall, and of course I'm the queen of not remembering.

Just before this withdrawal note, Mum was described by a social worker as 'seeming to be rather high' and 'looking a bit wild'. She explained that her appearance was because she was growing out her recently permed hair and insisted that she felt well.

This description takes me to a scene in *The Prince of Tides*. The film is based on the book by Pat Conroy and tells the story of Tom's struggle to overcome psychological damage inflicted by his dysfunctional childhood in South Carolina, mainly via a narcissistic mother. After her three children are brutally assaulted in their home, she simply insists they clean up the mess, put their clothes back on, and continue as though nothing happened. The camera zooms in on the daughter, sitting at the table, dress on backwards. Apart from the mother's manic speech and mannerisms, this is the only clue that something is untoward.

For a time, we had our clothes on backwards too.

The care records observed that Claire and Grace were bed-wetting badly and had been taking some medicine on a six-week trial, which was helping. This shows how distraught the twins were. Grace is described as 'the most unsettled'. She regularly declared that she 'hated Mummy', swinging between clinginess and rejection. Colin was sleeping with Mum at 'his insistence'; it was a habit I know Peter started. Mum apparently tried telling him he would have to go in his own bed when he went to the 'big' school. The social worker suggested she did this much sooner than that.

And that's it for our care records.

There's a letter two years later saying we no longer need risk observation. I find it baffling that the service withdrew after Mum told them she would ring if she needed them. They simply took her word and left us in her care. She had received all the attention she wanted, and she was done. She felt 'well'. I must close the big, red *This Is Your Life* book. Now, it's just me and what I can remember.

I think the reason Mum dismissed the social workers is because she had something else to replace them. She had a new support; a loyal companion that would see her through the next thirty-eight years, that she would choose over not only us but, in the end, her men and her friends.

Alcohol.

With Peter gone, our bedrooms returned to normal; I shared with Claire and Grace again. This was one of the joys of my childhood, until I was a teenager and wanted rid of them. We talked until we fell asleep, giggling about the silliest things. The only sad moments were hearing Grace when she struggled to breathe with asthma, and Claire being prone to vivid dreams when she had a fever.

One night, when she had tonsillitis, I comforted her.

'Please tell those children to go away,' she said, looking behind me.

I was terrified to turn, my imagination creating ghostly, horror kids waiting behind me with black eyes. I looked; nothing. She was hallucinating.

'There aren't any children,' I insisted, my heart beating fast.

This aside, I was glad to be with my sisters again. If we spoke in the dark about anything Peter had done, I can't recall. But I doubt we did. Shame is powerful, more so than anger. Predatory adults are clever at silencing and guilting children, especially those who are vulnerable. Instead, we laughed at him; we mocked his ridiculous fashions and mannerisms. This deflection of real feelings has remained in adult life. We deal with the dark by using light.

During most of 1982 I was in my final year of junior school, with one of my favourite teachers. I had my first crush on Mr W; it was likely a father figure thing because he was kind to me. I was ill one day, and he pulled my hood protectively around my face and told me to go home. I hated that coat; it was a too-big second-hand thing with a furry hood that made me feel ugly. There is a picture around this time of me wearing it and I look desperately sad in it. But when Mr W touched it, I felt loved. His kindness made me feel pretty. I wore my newly longer hair loose that summer and made extra effort in his English lessons.

'Your drawings aren't very good,' he said.

I asked why not, and he said they were cartoonish.

'I'm a writer though,' I said, excited for him to read my stories.

He gave me a B and I was ecstatic. At this time, I started filling exercise books with 'novels'. I wrote my own sequel to childhood favourite, *Heidi*. Themes in my novels always had people finding home; often 'poor' children being taken in by kind, wealthy adults, and living happily ever after. Nothing else existed when I wrote.

My best friend had an album that was a collection of sci-fi music – including the *2001: A Space Odyssey* theme song – and I recorded it and wrote space-inspired stories to fit the music. I read them aloud into a tape recorder. My first foray into reading for an audience of one; me.

There was a girl in my class who was cruel to me about my parents being divorced, and my mum being 'a lunatic'. She hounded me relentlessly about it. I knew her mum had died when she was a baby but couldn't bring myself to hurl this at her. One day, I was queueing on the stairs to our classroom in front of this girl. She continued to taunt me. On and on and on she went. A rage built and built in me, which I know now was because I was recovering from trauma. I spun around and punched her hard enough to knock her down the stairs. I'd never hit anyone in my life.

Only it wasn't her.

She had moved and I knocked a female teacher over. I was mortified. My rage died and I felt sad, sorry I'd hurt someone. Guilty. Afraid of the trouble I'd be in.

Mr W spoke gravely to me. 'This isn't like you,' he said.

I couldn't respond in case I cried; I was too old to cry.

'I'm disappointed in you,' he said. 'I thought you were a nice girl, Louise.'

I remember knowing that I wasn't a nice girl. Feeling that I was a dirty, unpleasant girl. I can't remember what my punishment was. I don't know if my mum found out. I only know that I was consumed with a hot mixture of guilt and rage and unhappiness; it churned inside me and I didn't know how to deal with it.

I met Mr W recently when I did a school workshop, much the same, just older. He flirted but said he didn't remember me. I understood; I was a forgettable child. But part of me was angry. Part of me thought, how could he not see how sad I was then, how much I had needed an adult to see what had happened to me? How dare he flirt with the adult-me if he couldn't remember the small-me? I was cold with him then; the kind of ice that must have made him question if he existed. It's not a nice side of me, but it's triggered by unresolved childhood trauma; when you're not allowed to let out your feelings, you freeze them, and the people who hurt you.

He was another adult who disappointed me.

At home, Mum was drinking. When it first started happening, it was exciting. After a few drinks, she was warm and vivacious and fun. At a workshop some years ago, I did a free-writing session, which is where you write solidly for five minutes, without pause. I wrote a piece called 'Thirty Minutes, Three Drinks'. It was about how for that length of time – and that number of drinks – my mum was lovely. Her mood lifted. She told funny tales about people we knew, in her articulate, engaging, witty way, and I'd be happy for a moment in this glow. Children, as I've said, cling to the best of their mother. She'd also more or less let us do what we wanted. Tea was hastily prepared chips and a sausage roll; naturally – as kids – we loved this more than stew or fish. Bedtimes were less strict. Freedom occurred in some ways. Not so much in others.

Now I was the babysitter.

Mum went to a local pub. To be fair, it was only a two-minute walk from our house, and I was eleven, not a baby. But I dreaded the responsibility. There was an old-school telephone on the wall in the front room and Mum stuck the number of the pub next to it. In the end, I knew it by heart. I can still recall some of the digits.

'Just ring if there's an emergency,' she told me, looking beautiful and ready to go out. 'The landlord will come and find me.'

I worried about what constituted an emergency. With my child-hood experiences that far, it was hard to know which events were the everyday and which were worth reporting. I dreaded that Mum would be cross if I disturbed her. While I was glad that I could stay up late and watch what I liked on TV – mostly horror films that were highly inappropriate for my age – I got scared being alone.

I found it hard to comfort the twins when they asked if Mum would be coming back. Especially Grace. She came downstairs over and over, upset, asking where Mum was. The anxiety I'd had that day at Grandma's house when Mum left to return to The Cottage, and we couldn't console the twins, resurfaced.

'Please ring the pub and check,' sobbed Grace.

Grace: *I remember whenever Mum was out, in my mind the world had ended. I thought: She is not coming back. And I was beyond terrified. Because until I could see her again, no one could convince me that she was coming back. As in, it wouldn't matter how Louise tried to say, 'It's OK, I'll ring the pub,' I just knew she was never coming home. The only way I could believe it was when I physically saw her. She had this cough she would do to clear her throat. That was what I waited to hear, coming up the side passage. To this day, I remember the relief of hearing that cough. And the smell of her. There's no pain like that pain.*

Sometimes Claire followed her, quieter in her grief, a little shadow.

Claire: *As usual, I don't have many memories. It's really weird. But I do remember clearly sitting in the front room, on my own, waiting for her, being cold, and wishing she'd come home. She must have been at the pub. She finally came and I was so relieved. She wasn't hammered, by her standards, but she'd had a few drinks. I remember that beery, lager-y smell. To this day I don't like that smell.*

I'd ring the pub. The landlord always answered cheerily. I explained that the twins wanted to know when Mum was coming home. There was the clunk of the receiver going down; the sound of laughter and music in the background. After a while, he'd return, not Mum, and explain kindly that she wouldn't be long. Occasionally she came to tell me herself that I should get the twins back to bed, and she wouldn't be long.

Not Long are vague words for seven-year-olds.

Being just three, Colin must have been asleep in Mum's bed, so mercifully he was unaware that she had gone. Can I be sure though? Might he have woken in the night, alone, anxious? I don't like to think of it.

The best way to describe this time was that Mum wasn't *there*.

She lived with us and she had tea with us after school and there were some pleasant times like in any family. We had holidays in Whitby and a visit to Ireland and days out at Scarborough. There were evenings when we watched Dynasty and Coronation Street and laughed at Bet Lynch and Deirdre Barlow. But this felt like foreplay to the *real* evening. I think because she knew alcohol was waiting for her – as escape and comfort – she could be pleasant in the early evening. She could 'cope' with us.

When we went to bed, and she was at home, she never came up and read stories. I was too old for that at this stage, but the other three might have enjoyed this. We had to kiss her cheek while she remained in her chair in the front room and take ourselves up.

It must have been hard being the sole parent of four children. But if you love them, you try your best, even if it isn't perfect and you make mistakes at times. Mistakes can be forgiven. Outright neglect, not so much. I asked Mother recently why she never said she loved us then, and she said she 'didn't have time'. But you can say it while you iron. While you wash the dishes. During tea. It takes a moment to say it, and its power lasts a lifetime.

We *gave* the love.

She *took* the love.

We saw our father again, now that Peter wasn't dictating family life. The four of us went to Sunday school in the morning, and then church, and then our father picked us up, waiting outside the house and rarely coming in. He said that Mum was a clown.

Even after everything she had put us through, I hated anyone saying unkind things about her. A friend called her a murderer once because she had a dead butterfly in a frame on the wall. I told this friend that even if my mum *was* a murderer, she didn't look like the back end of a bus like *her* mum. It's curious how loyal a child is, no matter what.

I started to hate Sundays.

I dreaded coming home from being with our father.

Mum often wasn't there.

The problem with alcohol is how it changes you. If the first thirty minutes and three drinks made Mum fun, it was what came later that we learnt to dread. It was when the loud music started in the early hours; when we wondered if she would stay out all night; when we wondered who would come home with her if she returned; when we wondered who might be there in the morning; what state she would be in. It got worse when she made friends with a woman who moved into our street. Geraldine. That's where she was when our father dropped us home. She left a half-started Sunday tea in her wake. I had to finish making it, and take care of my siblings.

35

A darker place

Deprivation is to me as daffodils were to Wordsworth. – **Phillip Larkin.**

As I write up the murkiest moments of my childhood, the world now is a darker place than when I began my story. I buy my cheap bunches of daffodils for the back room, but their colour feels diminished.

Now, Covid-19 has changed everything.

It has come to the UK.

People have died here: *died*. It feels so… unreal. As though now that I'm writing fact, the world out there has become fiction. We've been advised to self-isolate for fourteen days if we have symptoms of a new, dry cough or a high temperature. Schools are still open, but we've been 'strongly urged' to avoid pubs and restaurants. My theatre has closed, leaving me indefinitely out of work, and a little bit lost. Joe is working from home. People are panic buying, mainly toilet rolls and pasta, which is bizarre.

We're in unchartered territory.

And I return to three months after the bridge jump; to a place that felt then like the end of the world.

36

Morning Dad

*A schoolboy is on a mission to prevent suicide in the
wake of Caroline Flack's death; by handing out bunches
of daffodils to strangers* – **the Birmingham Mail**

In May, while still on the physio ward, almost three months after
the bridge jump, Mother was depressed again.

She cried a lot of the day and it was hard to witness. The illness
had never really lifted; she had it for months before the suicide
attempt, and it had lingered in the background for the past ten
weeks, masked by the opiates taken for her leg pain, and the drugs
taken for surgery. Now, in the absence of this camouflage, it took
over again. The psychiatrist upped Mother's mirtazapine dose to the
max and increased her venlafaxine too. She also considered adding
lithium to the mix. A psychologist started visiting her twice a week.
Not only was the initial depression resurfacing, but now Mother had
her physical injuries to deal with and was approaching seventy-one.

We did what we could; we wheeled her around the pleasant
grounds, offered practical advice and comforting words, and took
Grace's little ones to visit her. She had many visitors; people came
from her local pub, from her singing group, friends near and far.

Grace was doing exams and still managed to get 93 percent.
Claire continued to have tests for her health issues. I was a guest

on panels at two book festivals. One of my favourite parts of being published is meeting readers. My new book had been out for a month and reached Number 1 on Kobo as I sat on a train. Just for that day and the next, I was the most-purchased eBook. I could see a ten-year-old me scribbling away in a notepad; I wanted to give her a hug and say, 'Keep writing, keep dreaming, it's going to happen.'

We planned for Edwin's imminent arrival the day before Mother's birthday.

Edwin wrote: *Have you booked a restaurant for the first night I'm there?*

Claire wrote: *Yes, a Michelin star place, since it's your treat.*

Colin wrote: *Steak is only £105.*

Claire wrote: *Champagne is £95. And I only drink two bottles when I'm there.*

Edwin wrote: *Do they do cheese on toast?*

Grace wrote: *That place near the bridge?*

I wrote: *Yes. Close by if I fancy a jump.*

Claire wrote: *A family jump?*

I wrote: *That would be a beautiful moment.*

Grace wrote: *Who'll take the selfie?*

I wrote: *Me. I've perfected the falling fast angle…*

On 9th May we got the shock news that Mother was deemed medically fit for discharge; the orthopaedic surgeon just wanted her to remain on oral antibiotics. Her leg looked red and swollen still. When we asked hospital staff about her general future, all we got was, 'It's too early to tell.'

As a result, the psychiatrist said she'd raise the Section 2. She was concerned about Mother's continuing plummet into depression, and the risk of suicide again. There were no beds in any mental hospital in the UK – that's how desperate the service was. Mother would be sectioned to her current physio bed until one was available, hopefully somewhere local, though this wasn't guaranteed.

Colin wrote: *Fit for discharge? She can't walk alone and has fucking scaffolding attached to her leg!*

Grace wrote: *If they section her will it be in a strait jacket?*

I wrote: *Can we request it?*

Claire wrote: *It's official – she is sectioned – she gets told at 3.30pm. All your dreams of having her live with you are OVER. You can appeal this though…*

Colin wrote: *I already have. I want to live with Mother forever.*

Claire wrote: *Police are on their way to arrest you.*

I wrote: *I'll get her out.*

Finally, Edwin arrived in the UK. We had someone to take the weight of it all off us for a while. No matter how old you get, you look to those relatives above you for support, guidance and protection. It's usually your parents. Edwin became our surrogate parent for a fortnight; our Uncle Dad.

Edwin: *It was a strange trip to plan and execute. I've never been on a journey for such a purpose before. It was not fear I felt but nervousness about what I was going to find. Particularly how I was going to find you guys. I hadn't seen you all since Grandma Roberts' funeral and obviously that was a spectacularly enjoyable time, as you all recall; she wouldn't mind me saying that, as it was a celebration of her life.*

I must admit I was heartily relieved when Claire met me at Heathrow and looked well. It was nice to see Julian too. They brought me up to scratch. It gave me a chance to relax in their home and collect my thoughts before seeing all of you in one big hit. In hindsight, a good thing.

It was fantastic seeing you all; I fully understood what you must have been feeling mentally but your physical appearances buoyed me. That first meal we had together was great. When I looked at you all, I thought, 'Oh shit, what have these guys just come through in the last few weeks.' My sole reason for making the journey was to see you four and offer support. Lots went through my mind. How much had I missed? Fortunately, those gaps were filled, and I got to know you all better during those two weeks. To love you more as family. And that really cheered me up.

I loved having Edwin stay at our house for the week. He had a simple routine, much like mine; we arose promptly, had a cup of tea or coffee and a social media catch-up, he said, 'Morning, Dad,' in his jolly way when Joe came down, and then we walked along the river and had breakfast somewhere afterwards.

One morning, I showed Edwin the spot where Mother jumped. From the top, looking down at the far away ground. It seems higher from there than when you look up. There's an urgency caused by traffic whizzing past. There's a peace below, an emptiness, trees, contrast to the hustle and bustle on the bridge. Edwin was speechless that she had survived. It's one thing seeing a photo of it and quite another seeing the reality.

On our way back we passed a beautiful, new show-home on a luxury estate and found that the door was open for viewers. Perhaps to jolly ourselves out of that horrible reality check, we went inside and enjoyed a play around in the state-of-the-art kitchen and a 'Can you imagine if we lived here?' moment in the living room. Edwin pretended to urinate in the not yet plumbed toilet.

I still pass that house now. Someone has bought it and lives there.

I think of Edwin every time, and wish it was him.

Edwin*: As I set off to see Mother, my thoughts were downbeat. I wasn't sure how I'd react. When I went into the room, basically, your mother looked at me and said, 'Eh, what are you doing here?' as though I was a cleaner or a doctor going in to take her temperature. She said to the woman in the opposite bed, 'This is my brother, he's come from Australia.' She didn't seem excited. Didn't offer a hug. It felt anticlimactic. I thought, 'There's insanity but with a frame on the leg.' She was gaunt and her eyes were cold. Little emotion. As time went on, I approached the issue of the suicide and of her reconciling with you guys. I felt at one point she wanted to proceed with this but to my knowledge it's never been done.*

While Edwin was here, he spoke with many of the professionals, not only to gain a greater understanding of Mother's health but to offer his thoughts; as a physiotherapist too, he had his own opinions. He was told that there would be a discharge meeting the week after he went home and he tried to prepare us for what would happen, assuring us that we had every right to speak up if we disagreed with anything.

Edwin: *Apart from the circumstances, I had a wonderful time staying with the four of you. I'd never spent quality time with you all. I thought that in spite of all that your mother has done over the years, and what transpired on the bridge, you were holding up and supporting one another. I saw what trauma was behind your physical appearance. I don't think that was an effort to show me how strong you were, it's just how you all are. I thought about Joe and Brent and Julian, and what they must be going through. Colin just looked like an absolute trooper. He detached himself emotionally and I think that helped. I felt Grace was suffering badly.*

My latest book launch happened while Edwin was with us. On a sunny evening, with the doors wide open, we drank wine and I chatted with an intimate audience, and my uncle who lives thousands of miles away was there too. To date, it's my favourite launch. Colin and Grace took Edwin to see Ricky Gervais in Manchester one evening too. We did pleasant things so that his trip wasn't just about seeing Mother, which was difficult and challenging, and something he did most days, alone.

I also got him a ticket to see a show at my theatre, which he thoroughly enjoyed. When he had gone home, and the show ran for another four weeks, I watched it with some sadness, looking at the seat where he had been. Curiously, it was empty every time, as though no one else should sit there after he had.

Edwin: *Despite the years apart, we still had a very close family bond. I had always loved you all, but this just reinforced it. It was a very strong emotion. I* *really was sad to leave you four. I was keeping up a brave face because I shed some tears on the way home. All this time later, you're doing well.*

Grace wrote: *I'm going to really miss you when you go, Edwin. I wish you were staying longer.*

Edwin wrote: *Don't make me cry.*

And when he had gone…

I wrote: *I missed you this morning in your spot in my back room.*

Colin wrote: *It's such a shame you are on the other side of the world.*

Claire wrote: *I won't forget the good times we've had.*

Finally, Edwin sent us a picture of the brown fedora hat he always wears during his travels; it was resting on his pillow. He was home. Sometimes the world is too big; the people you want close are too far, and the ones who hurt you most are too close. But that's life. And it goes on.

37

An actual proper human

If I were living in a utopian world, then it wouldn't be political commentary; it would be about daffodils. – **Emily Haines**

At the beginning of June, it was Mother's big discharge meeting; most professionals were present, including the physio team, the mental health team, the crisis team, a charge nurse, and Mother's main psychiatrist. The social services team weren't invited; in a phone call to Colin afterwards, they admitted it was frustrating. Essentially, it would be their responsibility to oversee and support Mother's movements once she left the hospital, so this was a big oversight.

I went along with Mother to support her. She begged me not to let anything happen that she didn't want, and I assured her I wouldn't.

Working evenings at the theatre meant I was the only family member who could attend; Claire, Grace and Colin had taken every available day off when we were seeing Mother around the clock in her early recovery. I was dreading it. Mother was deeply depressed, and I was her sole voice in a room of medical professionals who dealt with this kind of thing every day, and likely had a plan already in place.

In a stuffy hospital office full of the kind of mismatched chairs you use during Sunday lunch when extra relatives come, we gathered,

Mother in her wheelchair, me at her side on an uncomfortable high seat. I took notes to share later in our WhatsApp chat.

The charge nurse welcomed us all in his soft voice. 'This is a goal-setting meeting,' he said, legs crossed in the delicate, affected way Peter used to assume. 'We'll discuss plans for Mrs L's discharge. Let's begin by introducing ourselves...'

And we went around the room, like it was an AA meeting.

Hello, my name is Louise, and I wish I was at home eating my own weight in Dairy Milk rather than here...

The lead physio began by summing up how Mother was doing, describing how she had come on well physically, saying that she could walk for approximately sixty metres outside, could get on and off the bed, stand briefly without a frame, and get herself to the toilet and back. She hadn't attempted stairs yet, but she managed her frame well and had independence. Her low mood obviously affected her efforts with these tasks.

The charge nurse repeated what the physio had said, as though perhaps it sounded better coming from him. 'Mrs L is progressing so well now that she's almost too good for the physio ward.' He paused as though he expected laughter to follow. 'She can do self-care and is able to take a shower.'

Mother tried to speak, but he continued over her depressed voice.

'My mother wants to talk,' I said.

Mother said quietly, 'I've only had three showers in seven weeks.' And she began crying.

'Are you *sure?*' he asked her.

She's depressed, not demented, I wanted to say.

If I hadn't been there to intervene, he might have ticked the *Can Shower Herself* box. If they all agreed – wrote it in their notes – they would be able to discharge her. I understood how desperately they needed the bed, but so did she.

'She's sure,' I said, trying to comfort her.

'Well… *well…*' He trailed off. 'OK, we don't know quite how she is in showers, but we can do more of that.' He continued with, 'We'll also test her soon on kitchen tasks, so she is prepared for that.' He paused. 'I for one believe she can leave here, go home, and live there with support.'

'From who?' The words sprang out of my mouth. It was absurd. 'Have you seen the place you're suggesting she go and live in?'

No one spoke, so I knew not.

'It's a two-hundred-year-old cottage with steep stairs, steps up to both main doors, narrow doorways inside, and the only shower is upstairs. You said you haven't tested her on stairs yet.' Mother was crying while I spoke. It was unbearable. 'How will she get a frame through those doors? Down the side passage?'

They directly asked Mother, 'Would *you* like the option of going home?'

'I would prefer to be there,' she said softly. 'But I don't see how.'

'Do we rule it in or out?' the charge nurse asked her.

'Keep it as an option,' she said.

He looked at me like I was a troublemaker.

Her mental health seemed to be low on the list. I kept trying to bring it up. 'I'm concerned that if you send her home, she'll attempt suicide again,' I said.

One of the medical team, with a pained look, said, 'This really isn't the place to talk about that.'

'Where is?' I asked.

When she's at the bottom of the bridge again? I wanted to scream.

They were just doing their jobs. But I had to do mine; make sure my mother got the help she needed. In my frustration at feeling inadequate and not knowing medical jargon, I said, 'Look, I might not be an actual proper human but my sister who's a nurse is one, and if she could be here, she would be. I may not know what you all know, but I know my mother.'

The room fell quiet. Then the crisis team discussed what medication Mother was on. They said they didn't want to increase it yet as they thought she'd improved.

Mother looked more distraught at this. 'I'm not fine,' she sobbed.

'She's not fine,' I said, exhausted.

One of the women said kindly, 'We can treat Mrs L's mental health needs wherever she is. We've already done some anxiety management with her. We'll continue to visit three or four times a week, up to twice daily. Even if she went home, there's always the possibility of a mental hospital admission if it doesn't work out.'

I didn't have the energy to argue that Mother had been telling us for weeks that none of the mental health team went to see her. I believed her, but what if it wasn't true and I made a fool of myself? I knew they wanted the best for Mother, that they were bound by the criteria that had to be met, by the immense pressure on the NHS.

The meeting concluded with the suggestion of an in-between place – a reablement home where Mother could live independently but with twenty-four-hour support. Then she could get accustomed to socialising and doing everyday activities. In the meantime, they would assess her current home, as I'd requested. The matter of the leg frame coming off was to be discussed at a later date.

By this time, I had to get the bus from the hospital to the town centre and go straight to work. I was mentally, emotionally and physically exhausted. Mother thanked me for having her corner. I would never have done anything else in such a situation. What actual proper human would?

I reported what had happened in our WhatsApp group and everyone suggested I take a break from visiting for a while.

Mid-June, Mother's depression plummeted again. The physio ward was still pushing for her discharge. The psychiatrist looked into a possible mental health ward again. Mother insisted she didn't want to go, but Claire stressed that it was the safest place. Mother admitted to Grace that she hadn't told the mental health team how afraid she was in case they 'carted her off in a straitjacket'.

No matter what she had ever done, my heart broke. I hated seeing her frail and broken, blank face, dead eyes, no emotions, no motivation. She used the word *guilt* a lot, though she wouldn't explore it any further. We said that when she felt stronger, she should address it; acknowledge it; look at it; deal with it. She needed constant reassurance which we gave her, but it was exhausting. We had been saying the same thing for months; *you will get better, you will get better, you will get better.* Other days, particularly during a conversation with Edwin, she scored herself as a five out of ten when he asked how low she was and said she just 'felt flat'.

We believed she would attempt suicide again.

This was what I'd tried to say in the meeting, and they had shut me down. At times, Mother was overwhelmed, which is understandable. It was the not knowing where she might end up. We insisted that we were doing our best and would make sure she got exactly what she needed.

The psychiatrist doubled her dose of anti-depressants.

And in the end, Mother agreed to the psychiatric ward.

I felt cruel, but sometimes I wanted to scream in her face, 'You should have stopped drinking and you wouldn't be in this state! We told you over and over and fucking over to *stop*, that it was destroying your body and mind.' But I didn't. I turned my rage and passion into words. I turned my emotions into a fictional story, as I have always done. I was close to finishing my next novel. I worked on it every day. That night, as part of the other world I created, I wrote: *What if I let go? What if I fall? If I let go, what will there be?*

Our WhatsApp messages at this time were quite serious as we discussed the aspects of where Mother would go and what would happen. There were still some funny moments though.

Edwin shared a photo of himself in bed.

I wrote: *No camouflage pyjamas like you wore when you were here?*

Edwin wrote: *Just camouflage slippers.*

I wrote: *Ah, yes – I can't see your feet.*

At the end of the month, Mother moved to a mental health ward. We were told we would be invited to the next important meeting.

I dreaded it but knew it was necessary.

The same day, my publisher got in touch to tell me that my book had been picked as *Best* magazine's Book of the Year in the Big Book Awards 2019. We were both invited to a ceremony for the prize-giving in London later in the year. After losing out on that previous award, after crying over the many rejections for ten years, after the year we had all had, this news was glorious.

And yet I would have handed back that award in a flash if I could have changed that day in February when the daffodils slowed me down for a moment; if I could have prevented the pain that was life now for my family.

38

The past and present colliding

She has a daffodil beauty, but in repose her face is strangely tragic – **Edith Sitwell about Marilyn Monroe**

The now is a strange place as I face the then.

The UK is in full lockdown due to Covid-19. We are to only see those we live with, which limits my daily world to Joe. We can take one form of outdoor exercise – my riverside walk, thank God – and we can go to the shop for essentials like food or medicine. Schools are closed, football matches cancelled. Hollywood has shut down and foreign travel doesn't look likely to happen any time soon. All the book festivals I usually do are postponed.

I can't see my children; I can't see my beloved siblings.

But this is small stuff when hundreds of people have died of the illness.

I wonder how we'd have coped with last year's tragedy in a pandemic. We wouldn't have been allowed to visit our mother. She likely would have received far less attention from health professionals. And my siblings and I wouldn't have been able to support one another in person; this is the thing I can't even imagine.

The past and the present are colliding within these pages.

For the first time since I started this book, I'm more afraid to look ahead.

So I go back; to 1982.

39

How to not be gormless

The flower that blooms in adversity is the rarest and most beautiful of them all. **– The Emperor, Mulan.**

I'm entitled to a life.

This line was the chorus in the constant, repeated, badly sung song we heard from 1982 onwards. We heard it when we nagged Mum to stay home on a Sunday; when we pleaded with her to please not go to her friend Geraldine's and to eat Sunday tea with us instead. We heard it if I rang Mum at Geraldine's house, at the twins' request, asking when she would be coming back. We heard it if we asked for the basic things that children require from their mum; her time, her reassurance, her attention.

I'm entitled to a life.

I used to wonder why she didn't see *us* as her life.

I felt guilty for stopping her having this life she was entitled to.

I'm not saying mums shouldn't enjoy a social life. Of course not. Every hardworking mother deserves a break; nights out; an occasional weekend away; a holiday with a friend. When I got pregnant aged nineteen and became a single parent, I got baby-sitters and went out. But Mum wasn't having a break. This was general life. She put her desires above our needs.

Geraldine reprimanded me if I called her house when Mum was drinking there. I had my siblings with me, and they just wanted their mum. She was yet another adult who sided with Mum, and not only separated us from her, but tried to make us feel bad for the fact that we wanted her. When I rang there, Geraldine said, 'Let your mum be. She's entitled to a life. You're older, you should know better.'

When reading about narcissist personality disorder, and speculating once again on whether my mother suffers with it, I discovered a word for the people who become attached to someone with NPD; the flying monkey. These flying monkey friends do the bidding of the narcissist. They support them, and gaslight and twist the truth on their behalf, often unaware that they have been tricked into such a thing. There were other friends who thought we were terrible children when we tried to get our mum's attention. Friends who were fed a one-sided story about how demanding we were, the bitter irony being that we only wanted what most children do.

I didn't want my mum that much by then anyway.

At the end of 1982, I started senior school and turned twelve. I liked it when she stayed out all night because it was calmer, quieter. I'd lock myself away in the bedroom and listen to my new obsession – Duran Duran – and write novels. But the little ones still wanted her, and it tore me apart.

CPTSD (complex post traumatic stress disorder) is a psychological condition that develops in response to prolonged, repeated experience of trauma, where the individual has no chance of escape. This includes chronic sexual, psychological, physical and narcissistic child abuse or neglect. The sufferer experiences PTSD along with additional symptoms, such as difficulty controlling the emotions and feeling very hostile or distrustful towards the world. Reports show that sustained verbal and emotional abuse causes it too. Dysfunctional parents react contemptuously to a child's natural call for connection and attachment. This contempt is traumatising for a child; it creates fear, self-disgust and shame. Their effort to bond and get acceptance is hindered, and he or she is left to suffer the frightened despair of abandonment.

This perfectly describes how Claire and Grace behaved. Colin – being much younger, still only four – did not outwardly show such distress. But this only saddens me more; where had he put all his pain? Perhaps in other behaviours. Some adults who were in our life then have since described Colin as a 'handful' though I don't recall him this way. And if he was, is it any surprise? I only remember the pink-cheeked boy who held my hand and listened to my stories.

Claire: *I remember collecting Mum from Geraldine's. Me and Colin. God knows how young Colin was. Maybe four if I was eight. She fell. She literally took us down with her, onto the neighbour's fence, into his garden, all three of us. It was dark. I remember lying on the floor with her and the fence. Our neighbour must have come out with the noise. How drunk must you be to fall and take a fence with you? We tried to walk her down the garden and into the house. As always with my memories, the feelings aren't there, which is disassociation as a protective mechanism. Looking back now, I wonder what does an eight-year-old do with that? Did I just go in the house and get on with my life? How did I feel? What did I think? I spent most of my childhood burying stuff.*

Sometimes we went to Geraldine's with Mum; the younger ones more than me. I was happier being away from her when she was drunk because she could be cruel. Once the *thirty minutes, three drinks* warmth passed she pointed out our many flaws while telling us what a wonderful mother she was, and how grateful we should be. Grace's flaw was that she was grumpy; Mum called her Madam and Mary-Ellen, in a derogatory way rather than with affection. My flaws were that I was lazy, gormless and selfish.

I just typed this and stopped to look at it. Tried to imagine even *thinking* it of my daughter when she was twelve, let alone saying it. As I've said previously, children believe what their parents tell them. With my father I wasn't quite good enough because I didn't get all As. With my mother I was lazy, gormless and selfish.

As an adult, I constantly try to disprove these things to myself. I'm a perfectionist in my writing; I edit and revise and over-analyse so that I don't look stupid on the page. I find it hard to switch off in case I'm being lazy; I always feel I should be doing something. If I'm unkind (a form of selfish), I feel guilty. If I find out I've hurt anyone, it upsets me deeply. (Unless you hurt me first, of course; then I'll hurt you back, twice as hard.) To be fair, I don't understand how to not be gormless. Maybe someone can advise me on that? Tweet me with tips.

Grace: *Sometimes we went to Geraldine's with Mum and played there. I probably found that easier because we were at least with her. I wanted her but hated who she was when she drank. She'd drunkenly tell me how grumpy I was. It was awful – I wanted to say that it was because she was drunk, but I didn't know the word for it then. Geraldine had these skinhead cats, so I wheezed and wheezed, and obviously had no inhaler at this point. Mum used to say, 'No wonder I drink.' And, 'Can't you just give me some peace? Can't you leave me for a minute?' She would say to us all, 'Oh stop nagging me,' if we asked why she'd been gone so long.*

Geraldine's house was fancy; it had three levels and a balcony overlooking the park. She once flashed the poor people having a stroll there. She had some strange pets – a goat, a tarantula, a long-haired dog, and multiple cats. She cooked some very odd meals too. One such dish looked very much like the cat food in the nearby bowl. Another time she served us this curious meaty stew just after the goat had gone missing. She and Mum drank the whole time they were together.

I can't remember who bought it, but around this time we got a tortoise. I loved him. We called him Terence and he lived in the coalbunker out back. When he opened his mouth for lettuce, he had a little pink tongue. He moved fast; he zipped along the sparse grass in our garden. I loved taking care of him.

That love for him inspired the first full-length novel I wrote in a large notepad. It was about a girl who found a bear cub in the field behind her house. He had escaped from a nearby circus. She hid him in her bedroom, which resulted in a comedy moment of her trying to disguise the noise he made while she was with her family downstairs. In the end, he was taken back to the circus and she was heartbroken.

In winter, tortoises hibernate. Geraldine offered to take care of Terence during this time, in the cupboard under her stairs. To this day, I'm not sure why Mum agreed to it. Maybe she thought we couldn't be trusted to leave him alone to sleep. I was sure he'd have been fine in the coalbunker. But off he went – to Geraldine's. I don't recall who told us but come the spring he was dead. Apparently, Geraldine took him out of his box on Christmas Day, and gave him some brandy and wrapped him in tinsel. The shock no doubt caused his death.

I cried alone on my bed.

I couldn't express my pain to anyone. Mum was drunk downstairs, and I knew she'd tell me not to grumble because I didn't know *The True Meaning Of Depression* – another oft-sung song that was number two in the chart after *I'm Entitled To A Life*.

Geraldine took us four and her daughter to see *ET* that winter; she dropped us off at the cinema and picked us up afterwards. It was the big film, not only of that year but possibly the decade. It had a huge impact on me. I was in a dark place after the death of my pet. I lost my heart to this alien, alone, just wanting to go home. Geraldine's daughter smoked in the theatre – it was allowed back then – and I thought she was a rebel.

On the way home in the car, I was staring out of the window and thinking about the film, and Geraldine said to me, 'I think you're the most morose child I've ever met. Why don't you laugh like other children?'

I didn't say anything, but I thought, 'You killed my tortoise. You drink with my mum and keep her away from my brother and sisters.' I was angry that she misjudged me. She didn't know me at all. One thing I knew how to do was laugh. It was ironic; she had no idea that the twins and I laughed at her all the time, at her large hair and ludicrous, inappropriate fashions.

I was envious of friends who had normal home lives; who didn't have to help their mums down the garden path when they were pissed; who didn't have to cook Sunday tea and then be told they were lazy; who didn't get woken hours after falling asleep to Thin Lizzy or Paul Young full blast downstairs; who didn't hear the voices of pub people arriving late at night; who didn't wake in a morning wondering when their mum would surface and what state the house would be in.

I particularly loved one friend's mum. When I slept there, I'd go and sit in the kitchen while she made breakfast for everyone. She was kind and asked how I was, and I wanted to live there. Weirdly, this friend thought *my* mum was cool. She was young and fashionable, vibrant, and she made people laugh. Cool doesn't keep you safe though. Fashionable isn't dependable. Vibrancy can't replace security.

Sometimes our house was full of people.

We just wanted it to be quiet.

Grace: *All sorts of people came. A local councillor. Other people from the pub and some of our neighbours too. This man who was a known paranoid schizophrenic threw up in the sink when there was some kind of party. I remember feeling our tiny kitchen was full of people. And when that man was sick, I was terrified.*

Mum had a new boyfriend by the end of 1982: Kenneth. I liked him. He was a decent man, someone she stayed with for the next seven years. He must have gone to Geraldine's house with her. He taught me the word *apprehensive*. He was at the house one night when I wrote an essay about how I'd felt starting high school. It's strange the things you remember when there's so much else you've forgotten.

I remember a word but not childhood abuse.

Here's another word.

Grandma.

She had no idea about Mum's behaviour.

We never told her; we were well versed in keeping secrets. Even if she *had* known, I'm not sure what she could have done. We went to stay with her at Easter, in the summer holidays, and while Mum went on holiday with Kenneth. I loved going there. It was the safest place in the world. Nothing could hurt me there because nothing ever had.

We resumed our simple routine from the time we lived there – nice meals, regular bedtimes, the Virgin Mary watching all we did, *Thanks Jeels for our meals*, no parties, no drunken people, no disruption. One summer – aged thirteen – I went there alone on a National Express coach. Some of the houses on the estate were being renovated so it was a ghost town. It was all over the papers that a man was breaking into the empty homes. But I knew Grandma's house was safe; I knew absolutely that nobody would come in.

They didn't.

Not then, anyway.

I was thirty-four when I got a call to say that Grandma was in hospital. She'd been found unconscious at home, amidst chaos, amidst knocked over furniture and emptied cupboards. It appeared that intruders broke in and scared her. The story made the national papers. We were fingerprinted to be eliminated from the investigation. Locals offered a reward to catch these criminals who had 'scared an eighty-six-year-old widow woman to death'. The last time I saw Grandma, I arrived at the hospital to see her familiar face on every newspaper front page in the lobby shop.

In the end, they decided she'd had a stroke and – in her con-fusion – had caused all the carnage herself. We may never know the full truth.

When I believed that someone had broken into Grandma's home, it destroyed my faith in everything for a while. It meant nowhere was sacred. There was no such thing as a safe place.

Back in 1982, Claire, Grace and I created our own, in the shared Square Bedroom. With laughter. While Mum was at Geraldine's, after we had eaten the Sunday roast I'd attempted to finish (I hate cooking to this day) and after I put Colin to bed, we talked in our beds until we fell asleep. We laughed at David Banner in TV show *The Incredible Hulk* because of his dated and often ripped clothes and his badly painted alter ego. We laughed at Mum's drink friends. We laughed because it made us feel better.

If Geraldine hadn't tragically hanged herself years ago, I'd invite her over to watch some of the funny videos I've made with Grace, and ask her, 'Who's laughing now, bitch?'

I wouldn't really.

The angry child in me just said that.

But it felt good to give voice to the child who wasn't allowed to be angry; to give voice to the distressed child who wasn't allowed to address the distress; to give voice to the sad child who wasn't allowed to be sad.

To not create a fictional character using these experiences.

To finally look at the real girl.

40

The world now

The daffodil is tall: it can reach six to twenty
inches in height, depending on the variety.

The world now is this: we patiently queue two metres apart to
be let into supermarkets on our necessary (as in infrequent) food
shopping trip, we then queue this same distance inside when
waiting for the till after having tried to keep that far away from
other shoppers going around the aisles, we pay by card not cash
so we don't touch the cashier, and we then go home where we
must isolate apart from one daily walk, again avoiding all other
people. The key words are social distancing and isolation and
lockdown.

We're back on our WhatsApp group, chatting daily as we did last
year, sharing tales across the ocean, and jokes and memes to get
us through this new difficult time.

Colin wrote: *I can hear my neighbour − I think she's hosting a dance
class.*

Edwin wrote: *That's a good initiative.*

Claire wrote: *Join in!*

I wrote: *Why don't you follow along in the garden?*

Colin wrote: *I was peering through the window with my leotard on but the police removed me.*

I wrote: *I might host an Eating All The Easter Eggs Early class.*

In many ways – with the solitude that writing requires – I've been preparing for this for years. It's hard to look outward; my only view is from the window. And so, I look inward. I've all the time in the world to think. I've all the time in the world to write. I've all the time in the world for this.

41

A load of screaming humans being flung in the air

Gay as a daffodil. – **Freddie Mercury**

In July, five months after the bridge jump, Mother was in the mental hospital. Despite talk at the previous meeting about her going home or to an in-between re-enablement place, this had not yet occurred. She at least had her own room for the first time, one with a pleasant view of grass and trees, but without mirrors or sharp corners or scissors or any other things that might be used in a suicide attempt. She wasn't even allowed a phone charger, so we gave her device a quick zap when we were there.

There was a delightful garden, rich with a variety of insanity-reducing flowers and foliage, where we often sat. This ward was the hardest to get into – and to escape from – and meant waiting for buzzers and signing books.

There's a certain smell to these places, no matter if the building is old or new; it's a mixture of bleach and old radiators and cheap soap. We've been to a few. When Mother was incarcerated in 1994, I had to take three-year-old Conor with me on the bus to visit her. One time while there, I turned my back for a second and a zombie-like old man grabbed Conor's bottle of water and handed him a cigarette in exchange.

When we sat in the garden with Mother now, a woman, another patient, would come and stand behind us, staring vacantly at some distant land in her head. Mother told us that one morning this woman was lying naked in front of her bedroom door when she tried to leave in the wheelchair. Another night she screamed for hours. It must have been a distressing place to live.

Not much seemed to be happening with regards therapy, either physical or mental. Psychologists kept missing appointments. Physios didn't turn up. Mother insisted she was doing all that was offered, except it 'wasn't much'.

'I just hang around in the garden and play puzzles,' she said. 'The physio only comes once a week. The nurses sit around gossiping while the lunatics wander.'

There is such a huge strain on the NHS, and I admire the staff immensely, especially the care they gave Mother after her jump. But here it was different. Perhaps this is due to how poorly funded the mental health services are, I don't know. Possibly there were boxes to tick and they had to cover themselves, which must be stressful. Claire tried ringing constantly and never got an answer.

Edwin wrote: *I tried ringing Mother. Why doesn't she ever answer?*

I wrote: *Maybe she's in the garden?*

Edwin wrote: *They are called mobile phones for a reason.*

Colin wrote: *Maybe she's having a massive wank.*

I wrote: *I hope so. She deserves it.*

Claire wrote: *I finally managed to speak to a human today. We discussed Mother's anxiety. She's engaging to work on this. They're giving her strategies to cope. She attends group sessions. She's depressed but motivated. Good signs are that she gets up in the morning. She's sleeping and eating fine. The psychologist who didn't turn up the other day was apparently ill.*

Edwin wrote: *Why do I have déjà vu? Mother said not much happens. That she's on her own and has no motivation. She never mentioned group therapies. If the above is true, why isn't she mentioning it? I'll ring her today. She sounded happy about some pins coming out of the leg, but it still being infected five months on is worrying.*

Mother returned to Hull Royal Infirmary for an afternoon and had the top part of the leg cage removed, which gave her a little more freedom. Within days though, she confessed to being in a lot of pain behind the knee. We encouraged her to report this. The nurse explained that because she was now using muscles she hadn't used for months, it would ache intensely. This sounded fair.

Mother's mental capacity at this time, strangely, began to improve. Perhaps the higher dose of antidepressants had finally kicked in. She expressed the desire to go home, despite it not being ideal. She was, however, frightened to walk; it hurt too much. I had to carry her to the toilet during one visit. She was sad because all the skills recently acquired – like using a stick or frame – were gone. The staff pushed her to try and walk, insisting she should be able to. If she hadn't been in pain, I felt she would have been even better mentally.

I was sad for her setback.

One afternoon, Grace and I arrived to the sight of a fairground on the green next to Mother's bedroom window. It was like something out of a surreal comedy. Who the hell would build gaudy, noisy, fast rides next to a mental hospital? Someone with a bloody good sense of humour. I suppose it might have cheered the depressed for an afternoon. Mother's view that day was a load of screaming humans being flung in the air.

Mid-July, I went to stay with Katy for a few days in her student accommodation. She gave me her bedroom – immaculately cleaned because she knows me – while she stayed with her boyfriend. Being a young mum, I never went to university, so it was an experience to wake up to three trolleys in the living room, multiple empty vodka bottles in the kitchen, and only the hope of a pot noodle for breakfast. Katy and I went to see a film, *Midsommar*, but we walked out after an hour. I'm a huge horror film fan, but one graphic scene was too much; a man leaps from a cliff and ends up with a smashed leg, horrified to be alive.

I left Katy with the same sadness heavy in my heart that I always do but was cheered by the next destination; Conor and girlfriend Ieva. They only had a small one-bedroomed flat then, so I stayed in a nearby Mansfield hotel. It was the escape I needed. A long walk with them both in the nearby woods, a home-cooked meal – being Latvian, Ieva made some tasty stuff – and catching up on the other things in life aside from suicide and hospital meetings and destroyed legs. I observed the way Conor looked at Ieva, how he let her take her rightful queenly place in his life; I felt contented at his happiness, glad the adversity we had started out in – without a home of our own – had come right now.

When I got home, another meeting was called for mid-July. Grace could come this time, and I was glad. We were led to believe it was a discharge discussion, that all options were open. However, the main physio asked Colin to go with them beforehand to Mother's house so they could work out where a bed might fit downstairs. We were aghast at the idea of this as she was barely mobile. At this stage, the physio was telling her *not* to weight-bear and yet they expected her to go home. Her knee was shocking: a big red balloon. They promised a scan after the meeting.

Edwin wrote: *Good luck with the meeting today. Have your wits about you.*

I wrote: *I will have both my tits and my wits.*

Edwin wrote: *But no fits.*

I wrote: *My bits?*

Edwin wrote: *Bits yes, fits no, tits for sure.*

* * *

Before the meeting, Grace and I arrived early and sat in Mother's room. The nurse told us she would come and get us when the meeting started. I needed the toilet.

'Light,' Mother cried when I sat back down in the armchair.

'Pardon?' I didn't know if she had just noticed one somewhere.

'*Light*,' she repeated, brusque.

I realised I'd left it on in the toilet.

'Don't speak to Louise like that,' said Grace, firmly. 'There's no need to talk to her like a dog.'

Mother switched to self-pity. 'Oh, don't say that. I'm in pain. Don't tell me off.'

'It's no excuse,' said Grace. 'We've taken time off to come to this meeting and we'll leave now if you talk to us like that.'

This impatience meant Mother was returning to normal – good in some ways, not in others.

Ten minutes after the meeting was due to begin, we were still waiting so we went down the corridor and knocked on the door. They were all in there; they had started without us. *This doesn't involve you*, they said without words. I dreaded that a decision had already been made.

We joined them in a stuffy room, my chair so low that I had to look up at them all as though in worship, Grace at my side, Mother in a wheelchair like Ironside. There were staff from the physio team, social services team, mental health team, and Mother's psychiatrist. It was warm and I wished they would open the window, offer us a chilled cocktail.

The psychiatrist said, 'We were just making a risk assessment for Mrs L's care, based on historical information. We can, of course, never rule out suicide again. There will be a support package in the community, both from the social services and the community mental health team. The risk assessment will be ongoing.'

'Why isn't there an orthopaedic clinician in the room?' asked Grace. It was so helpful at times that she was a nurse who knew such procedures.

'They've been saying your mum is medically ready for discharge for a long time,' said the psychiatrist. 'We've fought for her to stay. That's the challenge we have with that service.'

We realised they were going to send her home.

'What about respite care *before* going home?' asked Grace.

Abruptly, the physio asked, 'For what purpose?'

The room went quiet, perhaps in united surprise at her brusqueness.

'Well,' continued the physio. 'Right now, mentally, Mrs L is fairly stable. Physically, it's just the infection, and she's on antibiotics for that. She's fully independent. She will go home with a care package.'

'She needs more care than can be provided by a few calls a day,' insisted Grace.

'She walks everywhere,' said the physio.

'I had to carry her to the toilet on Sunday,' I said. 'She's in agony.'

'It *will* hurt,' explained the physio. 'She's had it in a cage for months. The muscles haven't been used.'

'What if we're missing something though?' asked Grace, perfectly reasonable.

'That would have been looked at prior to the top of the cage coming off.'

'Why is she booked in for another scan then?' asked Grace.

'It's quite normal to keep having scans.'

'I thought it was to check for infection,' I said, confused.

'Has the wound been swabbed recently?' asked Grace.

'Yes,' said one of the nurses. 'She also started new antibiotics yesterday.'

'It's leaking now,' said Grace.

'That's been ongoing,' said the nurse.

'But that's not acceptable, is it?' said Grace. 'There's a serious risk of infection.'

'It was clean yesterday,' said the physio.

'I sense a lot of defensiveness,' said Grace, calmly. 'I'm not comfortable with it. I feel as though we're being attacked every time we ask anything. We're here to work *with* you.'

'It was like this in the other meeting,' I said.

The physio looked like she'd happily have strangled us both with one of the hundred phone charge wires that had been removed from patients. I saw her try and bury this desire in the name of professionalism.

'I'm not medical like Grace is,' I said. 'But this leg is the worst I've seen it.'

A nurse kindly explained that it was due to Mother moving differently now that half of the cage was off. It made sense. Then the psychiatrist explained that if Mother went into respite care and *then* home it meant two changes, and too many could be traumatic.

'We're trying to limit this,' she said, kindly. 'I think it would be too busy for Mrs L's mental health in a care home than in her own home. Is it better to just take the plunge and go home? I think it is.'

What could we say? It sounded fair. We had to agree.

Mother looked fine with it.

The physio spoke again, her tone gentler. 'It will be another eight to twelve weeks with the remaining cage on the leg. She might have to go in the hospital again for a brief period when it's removed.'

A discussion of Mother's medication followed, what she was on and what she would continue to take. As part of the care package at home, a district nurse would come and give Mother her medication. It would be locked away until the next time so she couldn't overdose. The team would monitor the situation to see how she coped and decide if the care should be increased or decreased. Someone would do her shopping too.

'I live close to the shops,' said Mother, helpfully. 'I've a lovely local butcher and you know I could—'

I laughed here. 'Mother,' I said, 'I think they'll go to Aldi for your bloody meat.'

The end of July was suggested for her discharge home. I strongly felt this had been decided before we joined them.

'It may sound soon,' said the psychiatrist, 'but we need a date in order to start the care package.'

We would have to sort out a key safe so the carers could get in.

'The district nurses will look after the leaking leg and dress it,' said the physio. 'An ice pack can help stop the swelling.'

'I've got a bag of peas at home,' I said.

We mentioned that the only shower was upstairs, but Mother said she could wash at the kitchen sink. 'We can hose you down in the garden,' I said. Mother laughed, and I added, 'She thinks we're joking.'

And that was it. Meeting done. Decision made.

Colin wrote: *Not totally sold that an early discharge is the right thing but, as suggested, it might be worth her taking the plunge.*

Edwin wrote: *Well done, Louise and Grace. On the surface, the plan sounds good. Once the leg rights, I wonder will she focus anxieties elsewhere? I hope not. The plan sounds reasonable, it has just come about very suddenly.*

Claire wrote: *Couldn't agree more. Louise and Grace should be proud of how they conducted themselves in what sounded like a difficult meeting.*

The results of the leg scan came back clear.

And Mother went home.

The NHS is in the news a lot. Doctors and nurses are dying from Covid-19 while working on the frontline; real, actual humans who sacrificed their lives for others. We've been going onto doorstops across the land to clap for these care workers. The sound carries up over the rooftops. I clap for the ones who cared for Mother too; even the ones who argued with us and occasionally seemed to get it wrong.

We're all flawed; we're all actual humans.

A caterpillar stays inside its chrysalis for up to twenty-one days: hidden away, it metamorphosises into a beautiful butterfly. I thought about this on my morning walk today. Maybe when we emerge from our Covid-19 cocoons, we'll be different too. Maybe we'll appreciate the things we've not had, seeing friends in person, going to the pub, doing events, going on holiday, shopping for clothes, working in a theatre.

Or maybe we'll still be a load of screaming humans being flung in the air.

Grace has changed the name of our WhatsApp group to *Us 5*. It was about time. The title has always been to do with Mother. It should really have been about us. When we said goodnight to Edwin one evening as he was rising for his day, he wrote one simple message.

Edwin wrote: *I'll keep watch*.

42

Nice Mum/Other Mum – The Narcissist Mother

Sketch the trees and the daffodils, catch the breeze and the winter chills. – **Don McLean**

My mother is warm and funny so it's understandable that she's popular. She makes people laugh with her humour and witty tales. This is the complexity of her. Despite the neglect, she can be Nice Mum. Other people just see this aspect of her personality and tell us what *awful* children we are to our *wonderful* mother. This causes the difficulty; she has hurt me acutely with her dark actions but then melted my heart with her occasional sunshine.

As children, we got up every morning hoping for Nice Mum. Sometimes we got her, and we clung to that. Then night fell and – like a werewolf in the light of the moon – Other Mum arrived. Other Mum was often there in a morning too, grumpy from a hangover. She was there when we got in her way, when we asked for anything, when we needed care, were ill.

Another description could be Narcissistic Mum.

I think that's what she is.

I'm no expert, this is only my opinion, but nothing else makes sense. Some of the main signs are these: insulting your children to feed your superiority, lying, laying on the guilt, not listening to or caring about your children's feelings, gaslighting them, never being wrong, hating criticism, and keeping your children dependent on you.

If she did have NPD, would that mean her behaviour is excused? Because it's a condition, one can argue that she can't help it.

No. Because she's still a human.

It's difficult to be officially diagnosed with narcissistic personality disorder. These people rarely want to think anything might be wrong with them, so won't seek treatment. If they do, it's more likely for symptoms of depression or alcohol abuse or other mental health problems, which very much fits my mother. Complications of the disorder can be depression, suicidal thoughts or behaviour, and relationship difficulties.

Here's what I think, rightly or wrongly: Mother has the disorder and due to this, she found it harder than most to deal with her postnatal/clinical depression, needing constant attention to cope. She then turned to drink as a crutch when these wants weren't met. The personality disorder is the foundation of her house. The depression is the broken wall inside. The alcohol is the cheap plaster she used to repair it.

My siblings and I are the people who had to live there.

Because of her vivaciousness, Mum had many friends during our childhood, some of whom we really liked, particularly the ones she'd known for years, before the drinking began. But we also liked the odd drinking buddy. They might have been her flying monkeys, but to us they were drinking buddies. Not all of them were Geraldine, who after a few years Mother must have fallen out with because she didn't visit her as much.

There were Alice and Sarah, both of whom I liked. They were intelligent and kind, particularly Sarah who I had great affection for. Drinking didn't turn them nasty. I used to wonder why our mum became the monster she did, while others were simply silly or loud after wine. Even with the neglect and loud music and insecurity, I could have perhaps coped with that. I know now that it was her real personality. It simply came out when the inhibitions were obliterated by booze.

Grace: *I remember Mum getting drunk with Sarah, but it wasn't unpleasant because Sarah was nice. She always had her drinking partners. She would then fall out with some of these people. With all the drink-fuelled parties and Mum's behaviour and personality, she probably argued with Geraldine, ending the friendship. She could be fickle. The main thing she had in common with the majority of them was alcohol.*

Occasionally, family members or friends saw Other Mum. Now – long after – some people have realised what we went through in those years. Some have apologised to us for not seeing. Others still think we kids should be grateful we had such a 'wonderful mother'. I could be angry that no one came to our aid, but that wouldn't be fair. We were the masters of silence, of doing as we were told and staying quiet, of putting up and shutting up, so how could anyone have known?

Mum's cousin came to stay once with his new girlfriend. It was a beautiful day, so she had a barbeque, and we all sat on our garden's burnt grass and uneven patio, with the sound of children playing in the park nearby.

Grace: *We were sitting on the garden benches; I was facing the house. Mum was being her usual drunk self, so me being feisty, I challenged her. Probably called her a witch or something. She said she was going to have me adopted. I remember thinking, 'She probably will. I'm the black sheep. And we've been sent away before. So, it's probably gonna happen.' I thought she'd tell social services how vile I was and that I bit myself. I believed they would think I was troubled and violent and take me away.*

The look of horror on our guests' faces when Mum said she'd have Grace adopted was intense. Perhaps they just thought this was a one-off; that she had got drunk and was having a hard time being a single parent. She burnt the sausages, but we ate them anyway, coated in ketchup. Grace went inside and I went to check she was OK. She would only have been nine because I was thirteen. I hated my mum at that moment. My anger simmered like the barbeque coals, but there was nowhere for it to go. I found the courage to address it with her.

She became Nice Mum, taking me into her confidence, a warm place I desperately craved. 'She tests me the most that one,' she said of Grace, not unkind.

I nodded, trying to be sympathetic but not disloyal, torn between defending my sister and having Nice Mum shine her light on me. It messed with my head.

'But if there was a fire,' continued Nice Mum, 'and I could only save one of you, she's the one I'd save.'

Another thing that narcissistic mothers do is have a favourite or 'golden' child. This can change, depending on the moment, depending on who she's trying to win over or control.

I believed every word my mum said.

I believed she *would* save Grace in a fire.

I was happy for Grace, knowing she was safe. But now I had a new anxiety – what would happen if the house burnt down? Who would get everyone out? I knew it was down to me because Mum would be too busy carrying Grace out. I knew the sash windows in our bedroom were easy to open, and that the drop wasn't too high – being a two-hundred-year-old cottage – so I figured I could do it. From then on, and into adulthood, I made sure I had an escape route out of a house. I wrote a short story on this theme and in it I repeated the line *If a fire started tonight, I'd know exactly what to do* over and over and over.

Colin was growing older now, no longer the chubby, pink-cheeked toddler. He was present for all the childhood events I've described, a small boy in the background, but he remembers very little.
Colin: *I don't have many memories. The ones I have are vague pictures. I*

remember being in Dad's flat and watching the film Grizzly, *which was very scary. Then I remember when he lived with his mother, and we went there. In his drawer, he had a large hunting knife in a sheath. He often took us to Scoutwood. With regards to Mum being annihilated, because it was such a regular occurrence there aren't any memories that really stand out. I remember Alice coming for tea and telling us the world was going to end – I was terrified. She and Mum were pissed. I remember mince and mash for tea, and it was gristly and cold, with carrots that were rock hard. Once I sat there for three hours because I wouldn't eat them. Me being a stubborn bugger, I thought 'Fuck her, I'm not eating them.' That's about all I remember.*

Mum's drinking became routine; the norm; everyday life. It didn't take long to forget that there was ever a time before it. Children adapt quickly to new situations. But they carry what has gone before, like suitcases with previous passports hidden in a pocket.

I might have buried what happened when Peter lived in the house, but it left hidden wounds. A scar always forms over an injury. Even with an untreated infection beneath, it heals enough for you to get on with life. Unless you scratch it, it remains intact. But some things make it itch. The teenage years were a major irritant.

As I went into these years, I struggled with self-loathing and my self-worth. There wasn't a word for self-harm back then but I'd often bang my arms against the wooden bed headboard until I bruised, needing to see that injury, feeling better for it. I destroyed things I loved; things that were mine, that I had previously taken care of and had pride in.

Once, I cut up some curtains that I'd saved hard for and bought. They were striped, pale grey and daffodil yellow. I was fourteen and had used the money from my Saturday job in a care home. I loved how they matched the bedroom walls that I'd also painted myself.

'What the hell did you do to your curtains?' demanded Mum, understandably cross.

I had no answer. 'I didn't like them anymore,' I said sheepishly.

She never thought to probe any deeper, to see if I was OK, like *I* would if it had been my daughter. Was I crying out for attention? I'm not sure. It's more like I felt I didn't deserve to have them.

'You just won't have curtains now,' said Mum.

I didn't, until I saved up again.

But I could see the stars all night.

I started writing angry poems at this time; typical teen angsty things. Some were light-hearted, using my humour to mock things. Most of them explored self-image, self-hatred, and how I sometimes wished I didn't exist. The latter sounds like a suicidal thought, but I think it was more that I wanted to be invisible. Occasionally they were profound for the fact that they seemed to glimpse a future I could not yet have known. I had a large black book that I stuck them all in. I can still picture it, even though I no longer have it. A few of those poems have travelled with me through my life though.

Moon...
How can you move the tide
but not the woman on the bridge
to a safer place?

After The Fall
What did you think lay ahead
for friends who could never be
strong enough to save your life?
Imagine how they feel.
I would have told you;
it's easy to be free.
And when I fell, down, down, down,
I would have screamed.

THIN
If I was thin,
I wouldn't be,
so in the way,
permanently.

I became obsessed with my weight. Anorexia is nothing to do with being thin. It's about control. One study found that thirty percent of abused children end up with an eating disorder. When someone is told over and over again that they are not loved, or that they are a problem, they believe it and take it on as their identity. Survivors of abuse often ignore their emotions, rather than learning how to deal with them appropriately. This can lead to acting out, impulsive behaviour, completely shutting down, drug use, promiscuity, and bingeing on or reducing food intake as a way to numb painful emotions.

I starved myself.

There was acute satisfaction in doing so.

The weight loss was a plus.

I added up my daily calories. I was allowed six hundred a day. If I went over, I had failed. I weighed food; measured the tiny portions. I ate it slowly. One day, I was so hungry I ate six pieces of toast, one after the other, ramming them in my mouth. Then I was hysterical, wanted to make myself sick, but I couldn't do it.

Mum walked in on me in a state. 'What the hell's wrong?' she demanded.

I admitted what I'd eaten.

'It doesn't matter,' she snapped. 'It's just toast. What's wrong with you? I should take you to a doctor.'

She never did but the mortification of maybe being taken to see one – which would have been odd since she never took us for anything else – made me see sense for a while. I tried to eat more normally, but extreme dieting has reared its head many times over my life. In those moments, I'm that little girl sitting at the table, hiding her food in a striped apron pocket, choking, choking, choking, unable to swallow anything.

Claire: *As we got older, we became very self-sufficient. Very capable. Because we had been abandoned. So, we just got on with our lives. We couldn't turn to Mum. We couldn't rely on her. We couldn't explore thoughts, feelings or worries with her.*

Nice Mum once told me she wanted the words *She Loved To Love* inscribed on her headstone. Aside from humorously thinking, 'Pray tell, when will that funeral be?' I thought, 'Loved to love *who*? Men? Alcohol? Herself?' And it occurred to me what a gift she had wasted that was right in her hands; that if she had loved us as she should, she would have four children who adored her with every single beat of their hearts. Because we have a huge capacity for that, and it's all we've ever wanted to do.

43

Quite the writer,
aren't we, Louise?

*Never be afraid to be a poppy in a
field of daffodils.* – **Michaela DePrince**

The teenage years are a minefield, no matter what your homelife is like; it's that fragile time when you shed your childish skin and emerge as an adult. I often felt I'd never been a child, and in that regard, nothing fazed me. But with all these new hormones, in many ways I was more vulnerable than when I was nine.

Though I still loved them, I wasn't as close to Claire and Grace. This is natural – what fourteen-year-old wants their kid sisters hanging around them? I sulked now when I had to babysit instead of being able to go out. Once *they* hit fourteen, we were close again, causing mischief and laughing together, but for now I preferred my own friends.

I didn't feel I fit in though, because I was kind of gormless and not streetwise. Despite Mum liking fashion and being pretty, she rarely encouraged or took an interest in me, or showed me how to apply make-up, or let me have a stylish haircut, insisting I kept it short, and she always bought me the cheapest, ugliest shoes. I sympathise with her having to be economical, being a single mum to four, but what she lacked in money she could have made up for with attention. Narcissistic mothers criticise their daughter's looks; they will shame them for their body, hair, clothes and face.

At fifteen, I took control. I had money from my Saturday job and bought clothes and cosmetics. A friend gave me a makeover – heavy foundation and lipstick, the works – to go to a party. I felt like a film star. When Mum saw me, she said it looked awful and told me to wash it off. I pleaded with her not to make me, knowing my face would be red and blotchy from scrubbing. But she insisted.

It was during my teenage years that I fell in love with Marilyn Monroe.

I saw a black-and-white poster of this gorgeous, open-mouthed, heavy-lidded woman in HMV. I had no idea who she was, but I was mesmerised. I hung it on the wall above my bed. That night I dreamt that she and I were swimming together. 'I'm going to let go now,' she said. 'I'm going to sink.' I begged her not to. I woke briefly in the dark, sure there were tears on her face on the poster.

I told my friend this the next day.

'You weird freak,' she said, staring at me. 'That's Marilyn Monroe and last night was exactly twenty-three years since she died.'

After that, I read everything I could about her. Learnt that she too had a mum who spent time in asylums. She too had an absent father. She too was abused and moved from home to home as a kid. My obsession has been lifelong. At fifteen, I longed to look like her but had no confidence in my appearance.

The only place I was confident was when I wrote. I knew how to conjure up stories. Reading Jackie Collins in the dark, and Stephen King and Virginia Andrews and Paul Zindel, I dreamt of being published too. I began my own magazine after I got sacked as sub-editor of the school mag for arguing with the editor. Then I sent a story to our local radio station; the DJ read a segment each night. It was a comedy about my chemistry teacher and his magic test tubes. It made me popular, and garnered my teacher's sarcastic comment of, 'Quite the writer, aren't we, Louise?'

I basked in this positive reaction.

I felt seen; accepted; clever.

It was maybe this radio experience that led to an interest in the spoken word. I applied to a hospital radio scheme to learn how to DJ. There was an interview, which I was terrified about, and had no idea what to wear. I borrowed trousers and a blouse; I mention my clothes only for the later relevance. The man who interviewed me – balding, middle-aged – was a DJ at the hospital.

'You did well,' he said. 'You have a nice voice. It's between just you and one other girl.' He studied me from across the desk in a high-ceilinged, dusty room, with a small studio nearby where the shows were broadcast.

I was chuffed. A bit speechless. If I got accepted, he said he would train me twice a week there, show me how to work the equipment, what radio DJing entailed.

'Maybe I'll take you both on,' he said. 'You and this other girl. See who does better. You can come back next week.' He paused. 'Wear a skirt though. I prefer skirts.'

I didn't even question that this was odd. Victims of abuse often have trouble knowing when something is unacceptable. I was fifteen but, in some ways, barely ten. I wanted to do well. Make something of myself. Impress my parents.

I went back the next week, wearing my favourite white skirt.

'Much better,' he said.

Now, looking back at this man of probably forty-five-plus, I feel sick. I want to march into that room, grab him by the neck and ask him what the fuck he thinks he's doing, talking to a child like that. But then, I supressed any instinct that it wasn't quite right. The gut feeling was there, I just hadn't the confidence to trust it yet.

Training involved me being in the little studio and him behind my chair, showing me what to do, his breath warm on my ear, and his body that bit too close. I didn't like it. I was repulsed. It must seem ridiculous that I didn't leave then. But no one had ever told me that my body was mine and I didn't have to do anything I didn't want. My childhood had taught me people *could* do whatever they want. I thought that was all he would do; lean a bit too close. I thought, *Maybe this is bearable, and I'll leave when I've learnt these skills.* I thought, *He's an adult, and who would I tell anyway? What would I say? He hasn't really done anything wrong, has he?*

Each time I went there, he took things a bit further. When he wasn't in the studio with me, he blew kisses through the tiny window. I feel sick now even remembering it. I'd avoid looking up. Other times he was in there with me and patted my knee, just above the skirt he always insisted I wear. I continued what I was doing and tried to ignore him.

But he was persistent.

'Part of your training involves going away for a weekend,' he said. 'Just you and me. To a conference. That's what we'll tell your parents anyway.'

Men like that can probably spot a vulnerable kid. He didn't pick me for my skills but for my lack of them. I don't think I'd recognise him now if I saw him. I can't remember his name. Maybe that's a good thing. I didn't want to go anywhere with him. I didn't want to be near him. But I wanted to do well. I didn't want to fail and be criticised by my father who I'd proudly told I was doing this.

When I got home after each session, I felt ill and went to my bedroom. Mum asked why I was moody, but I couldn't speak. The words were stuck in my throat, deep down, right in my gut where all the previous trauma was buried.

On our final training session, he grabbed me while we were in the tiny studio and made me sit on his knee. I said I wanted to get up and tried to pull free. He laughed at my efforts and squeezed my wrists tighter. I vividly remember looking at the gold ring on my finger. It had been a gift from Uncle Edwin, from his time in Saudi Arabia. I stared at the delicate pink quartz stone and it made me angrier that he might damage this than that he might hurt me.

I somehow got free and left and didn't go back. He rang the house and asked to speak to me. Irritated, Mum made me go to the phone to deal with it even though I begged her to tell him I wasn't there.

'You always give stuff up,' she said, exasperated. I had no idea what I'd ever given up. 'Why do you want to leave, just like that?'

I couldn't answer. 'DJing isn't for me,' I lied.

After this, I was in a dark place. I felt it was my fault; after all, I'd gone there and then gone back again and again. I felt I deserved it. I still feel that way. This is how shame works. But I was angry too. Angry that a man had treated me that way. I'm sure I'd have felt this way after Peter, but I couldn't remember it, not consciously, so the rage was vaguely familiar but terrifying. I was a girl who believed her mum might be 'taken away' again if she shared her shameful secrets; I was a girl with no one to speak to if even if she dared talk; I was a girl who had buried plenty already so what was one thing more?

Claire, Grace and Colin went through their own teenage years with difficulty, even though for theirs I was coming out of the other side of mine, and probably never fully knew their experiences until now. You can live in the same house, breathe the same alcohol-heavy air, be part of the same family, and yet your private world is an entirely different place.

Grace: *As a teenager I felt I was repulsive. I remember being told that when I was at school. I knew I could never tell Mum. I felt worthless. During my tough times as a teenager, Mum was either wrecked or with violent maniacs or in an asylum. I had an eating disorder. I would diet rigidly. I dropped to eight stone, which is ridiculous. I was permanently hungry, literally eating Louise's* *left-over crusts for some meals, Diet Coke, and salad without the salad. I'd exercise every day and if I missed it, do it twice the next day. The power of that control was incredible. That's what I focused on when I felt worthless.*

I remember Grace eating my leftovers. I wrote a poem about it.

CRUSTS

When you've moved on to higher things in life,
I'll eat my toast alone, cut into triangles with a knife.
As I spread the luxury jam, quenching my lusts,
I'll eat with relish, but I'll save you the crusts.

Claire went in the RAF at the tender age of seventeen. We all left home young, by the age of twenty. Is it any surprise? Grace was particularly affected by her twin sister leaving, which is understandable.

Grace: *When Claire went away in the RAF, I found it so hard. Mum was with a new and very violent boyfriend called Des, and my first boyfriend said he didn't love me. I was heartbroken but, as always, Mum was just pissed with Des. I moved into Louise's house because Des was awful to me and Mum did nothing. I was so lonely there because Louise had a boyfriend, Claire was away, and Mum just didn't care.*

Being the youngest, Colin was the last to be at home, and lived with Mum on his own for a period. When he was sixteen and doing his GCSEs, she spent time in a mental hospital again after splitting up with boyfriend Des, and as a result having a breakdown. Des was a real delight; he was banned from most pubs, had a penchant for throwing not only meals but people around, and he once locked me in a room with him until I agreed to 'forgive him' for something I can't even recall now.

Grace had to leave home when he called her a cunt just because she politely asked them to turn the music down at 3am because she had an exam first thing the next morning. Grace hoped Mum would get rid of Des for speaking to her like that, but she did nothing. When they did finally split, and she went into the asylum, it was left to me to make sure Colin was OK. I'd pay Mum's rent and bills for her, and go to the house daily to make sure Colin had food in.

Colin: *Through my teenage years, I didn't have much in the way of available family. You had all gone, so it was just me and Mum. She was with Des a lot of the time. There were all the lies and the betrayal of that; she was with him and then she left him, she was with him and then she left him. This, of course, partnered with the drinking. I remember one night in the house, sitting on the sofa with my friend, and Mum and Des came home from the pub. He didn't like something I said, so he held my heavy guitar above my head, in front of Mum, and threatened to smash it over me. You'd expect a mum to kick such a boyfriend out for that, but no. During my GCSEs, Mum went into a mental home. I was alone. Louise was effectively my guardian, but without living there. Obviously, with an empty house, I was popular. Me and my friends got into cannabis and Ecstasy. Everyone would come over and we'd get stoned – poor old Tiggy the dog used to be stoned too because he was in the same room. Once Grace walked into the living room to this and calmly rang Louise and said, 'I'm coming to yours – there's a drug party going on here.' I remember my form tutor sitting me down and saying he'd been made aware of the situation at home, my mum being in an asylum. When we got our exam results, he looked down the list of them, found my name, and his body language changed. He was clearly shocked at me getting high grades. I pissed about at school, but I had a smile on my face doing it. I think the teachers were fond of me. My friends were my family; this is why I hold them in such high regard now.*

By the time I was sixteen, I found my voice and used it, on the page and off. I wrote a novel about a girl whose parents had split up, how she copes by building a motorbike from scratch for the boy she loves. At school, I spent more time sitting on the steps outside the English classroom than inside it. I disrupted the class, talking non-stop. In

Maths, I put my hand up and told the teacher I was bored eight times in a lesson. In Chemistry, I drew silly pictures of the teacher in my exercise book and wrote ridiculous poems about him.

I didn't want to hurt anyone or cause trouble – I was just letting off steam.

I took it too far in the first year of sixth form.

A group of us did a Ouija board on the school stage. We ended up so addicted we had to seek advice from a priest. That – and the fact that I got expelled from my theatre work experience for running up a huge phone bill and trying to break into Keith Harris's dressing room to steal Orville's eyes – meant I was instructed to leave the school and never come back.

I waited until Mum was drunk to tell her I'd been expelled. Sometimes her inebriation served a purpose.

'You'll have to get a job,' was all she said.

I did, in a care home and then a café.

It was around this time that she told me she had tried to commit suicide when I was nine and we went to live with Grandma. It was a morning after a night before; she was still drunk. I enjoyed being in her confidence, having Nice Mum. I wasn't shocked by her words. On some level, I'd probably always known. She just confirmed a feeling.

She told me she went to a deserted place, took all her pills, and 'would have died' if a homeless man hadn't found her. She said she was unconscious, so she never got to thank this charitable stranger, and was then in intensive care for twelve weeks. This was only a version.

Is it true? I don't know.

Grace got a different story.

Grace: *Mum told me she was found somewhere near Swanland, somewhere 'in the sticks', sitting up, leaning against a tree, by a homeless man. She had taken pills with vodka. She was then sick, came to. She was apparently in intensive care for about twelve weeks. Mum said Grandma 'never even visited me' which one friend 'never forgave'. No more than that was told to me.*

I'm angry and sad that Grandma was criticised for not visiting Mum. How the hell was she supposed to when she lived ninety miles away from the hospital, couldn't drive, and was caring for three children under nine, the one person who stood between us and the care system?

Claire also got a different story, though its author is a mystery.

Claire: *I don't know how I know this, because Mum never spoke to me about it, but I've been told she was in intensive care for just a week. I don't know where that came from? And also, I was told – again, I don't know who by – that she took all her pills with vodka in her car. That she was sitting in her car when a homeless man found her. On reflection, the vodka part is odd as it's not her drink – it's too expensive!*

Colin was never told any version.

The two given to my sisters differ from the one I was fed. We have worked out that the car story must have been fiction because Mum didn't get a car until 1981. This suicide attempt happened 18th March 1980. I always thought that being in intensive care for twelve weeks after taking an overdose sounded exaggerated, especially when the bridge jump only meant she spent a week there. Our care records state that by May Mum was seeing Colin at his foster home once a week. This was just seven weeks after the overdose, so it's impossible that she was in the ICU for as long as she claims.

This is another rewrite of history.

It may seem nit-picky to be bothered by it, but so much has been hidden from us or given to us in self-serving pieces over the years that when I look for the facts, they seem to warp before my eyes. It's hard to know what to trust. Mum has always rewritten the past to either cover it up or paint herself in a better light. I've been in company with her, heard her tell people some glorious tale of the marvellous things she did with us as children that are outright lies, and had to sit there and listen because I felt no one would believe me if I tried to object. Recently she told me that saying we were 'in care' painted her in a 'bad light'. Thank God for those care records. For the black-and-white proof that we *were*, or else I might just lose my mind.

My own memory often lets me down, so I hate being deceived in any way. It feels cruel. Is it any wonder that I ended up telling stories? That when I do, I strive to make them ring true. When I do, I use the truth from my own life.

On my seventeenth birthday, our father left our lives for twenty-five years. I've never really known why. Maybe everything got too much. Maybe being on the spectrum, he needed to be alone. Apart from in the street, I never saw him again until I was forty-two, when we wrote and suggested we meet up. We now see him again. During those absent years, he didn't ring or visit. But I sent him photos of my successes, of Conor when he was born, of my wedding day, then Katy. He never wrote back, but I now know he kept all these things, plus cuttings of every newspaper column I wrote. In some ways, nothing changed. You can't lose what you never had. I was my own father. I was my own mother.

And now, I was an adult.

I was sure I was going to be a writer.

The best in the world.

But the world had different plans for me.

44

Emotional distancing

*A daffodil pushing up through the dark earth to the
spring, knowing somehow deep in its roots that spring
and light and sunshine will come.* – **Madeleine L'Engle**

The world has gone silent, and we've all come inside.

We're still in lockdown and it looks set to continue. Thousands of
people have died of Covid-19. The Thursday clap for the NHS looks
like it will be a weekly tribute for those on the frontline. The Queen
spoke to the nation – only the fourth time ever amidst a crisis – saying
better days will return and that 'we'll meet again'. The adverts on TV
take me back to those during the AIDS crisis in the 80s. The key words
are Stay Home, Protect The NHS, repeated over and over, like a rap.
Children are now being home-schooled across the land and hang their
paintings of rainbows in windows to keep us positive. It's deathly quiet
at night; no one rolling home from the pub, no cars passing.

In 2007, the Hull floods drove us out of our home.

Now a virus is keeping us in.

Six months after the bridge jump, Mother was confined to hers.

The day she moved back home, I met a social worker at the
house who outlined the care package. I later described it as 'bloody
outstanding' to the others in our WhatsApp chat. It was fully
funded and involved six visits every day. Carers would help her

dress, make sure she'd eaten, empty the commode, do washing and shopping, and give Mother her medication. It was permanent unless something changed.

Mother also had a Lifeline fitted in case of emergency, which could be activated via a buzzer that she wore around her neck. 'This is only for an *absolute* emergency,' I told her. 'Not because there's a huge spider or Coronation Street isn't on.'

The social worker asked if I wanted to be informed if she rang Lifeline.

I said no. I didn't want to know something I couldn't do much about at three in the morning when I was already shattered. 'Only tell me if she's dead or dying,' I said. *Even then*, I wanted to say, *it can keep until a decent hour.*

Smoke alarms were fitted and a medical safe put on the wall so she couldn't overdose on her drugs. There was a coded key box outside so carers could get in, and anyone else in an emergency. At the social worker's request, I gave her Mother's general history. I mentioned the alcohol.

'She apparently stopped drinking at the start of last year,' I said. The word *apparently* was because we could never be sure. She has told us many times that she 'doesn't drink now' or she 'drinks less' or that she's 'going to stop'. The years and years of heavy boozing had now caught up with her, I felt, and we were left with the fallout.

'With that in mind,' said the social worker, 'do you want to be informed if the carers find evidence of drinking?'

'Absolutely. I think the whole team need to know, especially with the medication she's on. We hope it doesn't happen, but you must understand my lack of trust, given her background.'

I bought Mother some food before she arrived home and rolled up the rugs so she wouldn't trip, and put them upstairs.

Despite all these things being in place, she struggled. As previously described in one of the meetings, the house wasn't suitable. It was no quality of life, washing herself at the kitchen sink, sandwiches for most meals, hardly able to walk, unable to carry things while using her frame, and not being able to leave the house because there was no ramp. She looked frail, which was sad to see. When I was there, I had to distance myself as protection. Not the social distancing we're doing in lockdown but *emotional* distancing. That's much more difficult. I chatted and engaged and encouraged but my well was empty. I washed her hair at the sink when she couldn't – it was like the *Out Of Africa* scene between Robert Redford and Meryl Streep, except less picturesque.

Other than that, I was spent.

The last six months had almost destroyed me.

Mother's knee swelled up and looked shocking, red and angry. Physios came every other week and often cancelled. I'm no medic, but I knew she should be having physio more than twice a month. Mother, understandably, was upset.

Edwin wrote: *The orthopaedic management of that knee is deplorable. Stuff her in a car and take her straight to hospital. If it's hot and swollen, it's likely a raging infection.*

I wrote: *The doctor is coming soon and if he does nowt, I'll ring 999.*

Claire wrote: *Just spoke to the doctor and he isn't concerned. He said tomorrow's hospital appointment will suffice.*

Luckily, the following day Grace and I took Mother to the hospital for a routine leg scan. The surgeon peeled the dressing off and looked at the wound, but he didn't seem too concerned.

'I'm not worried about an infection, despite the heat and swelling,' he said. 'It's likely due to the foreign body of the frame pins in there. They can cause this kind of reaction.' He looked at Mother. 'Are you feeling unwell with regards your temperature?'

I couldn't help but laugh. 'She ate five bloody cheese-and-tomato sandwiches in the waiting room. I think she's OK.'

Grace said that she wouldn't have been eating if she had sepsis or anything.

'I'll book an urgent CT scan to get more visuals though,' concluded the surgeon. 'We do plan to take the cage entirely off and have a removable cast on instead.'

Edwin wrote: *When will this scan be?*

I wrote: *16ᵗʰ Sept. That is the definition of soon.*

Edwin wrote: *There'll be new technology by then.*

I wrote: *NASA will be doing it on Mars.*

At the end of August, Joe and I went to Miami for our twentieth wedding anniversary. It was the escape I needed: a cruise around the Caribbean, blue skies, cocktails, just the sea for miles around. I tried not to feel sad that my mother wasn't enjoying something like this. I saw many wheelchair-bound people on the ship, so I knew she'd be able to one day. While I was away, my siblings kept all news from me.

When I got back, Mother had a horrendous bed sore. The physio cancelled the visit yet again which meant nothing for another fortnight. She couldn't put her foot flat, and they insisted she should be able to. Her mental health seemed to have deteriorated, but maybe my holiday had made me forget her previous mood. The carers were lovely and came punctually and treated Mother well.

Claire wrote: *Mother's adamant she wants independence and to stay home but things are deteriorating – she had a bad fall. A carer called the crisis team a few times. They're going to review. That bed isn't suitable, so they are assessing that too.*

Edwin wrote: *Why did the carer call the crisis team?*

Claire wrote: *Mother was very low in mood.*

Edwin wrote: *Sounds like she's going downhill again. She needs to be in a care home.*

Claire wrote: *The carer told me Mother's saying she's managing fine, but it's not true.*

Grace wrote: *She's scared of getting sectioned.*

I wrote: *I'll assure her that just cos she's having hard time, she won't be sectioned.*

Claire wrote: *The leg is still oozing, and she can't bear weight.*

Edwin wrote: *What a fucking mess.*

Grace wrote: *She has a grade three bed sore. I'm horrified.*

Claire wrote: *Poor Mother.*

Grace wrote: *I'm crying.*

I wrote: *Who can we ring right now? Such a decline in just ten days.*

Edwin wrote: *Look at care homes and persuade her to do that.*

A special orthopaedic mattress arrived for the bed sore, and eventually Mother's wound began to clear up. She fell for a second time. We knew she needed to be in a home. She was telling carers she was fine, so we had to tell them it wasn't true. Mother nodded and agreed when we suggested a care home, but then told the social services team the opposite. She was scared, we understood that.

Amidst all of this, while we awaited the results of the scan, I went to London to receive my award from *Best* magazine. I had to do a terrifying impromptu speech. Then I walked home in my bare feet because my shoes were pinching; my feet hurt, and my heart, but it had been the best *career* year of my life so far.

Edwin wrote: *I tried to persuade Mother that care is the best option.*

Grace wrote: *She got upset with me and said she didn't want to. I broke down because it's heart-breaking to see her like this. She feels locked in, numb, and she's not sleeping and has no appetite. She said she's close to those ending-it-all feelings again.*

I wrote: *She can't get to the bridge or get her pills. But I guess there are other ways. God, what to do?*

Colin wrote: *She ate a massive stir fry I cooked yesterday.*

Grace wrote: *I hope she isn't playing up for me.*

* * *

I went with Mother for the results of her CT scan. I took notes while the leg specialist talked, and my scribbles once again read like a poem.

The Continuing Tale of The Leg
The leg joint has collapsed,
which we kind of expected
because it didn't look right.
Tried to fix it and that has failed.
Difficult to see where we go from here.
We did our best.
Leg function will never be the same.
Options are this:
Take frame off, see what happens.
Or more surgery including,
knee replacement and straightening of bones.
Or you should consider amputation.
Whatever choice you make,
you'll never walk the way you did
again.
Amputation is safest option,
in the hospital for a few days,
and then home for a cup of tea.

It was what we expected: amputation. The knee had collapsed. This was why Mother had been in so much pain. She seemed quite happy to get rid of it now, but they suggested she have more time to think once the frame was off. In the meantime, another meeting was arranged to discuss her decline and ideas for care. I had come to hate these gatherings, but luckily both Claire and Grace could attend.

On a September afternoon in Mother's tiny front room, we assembled, the commode cooking nearby in the heat. A member of the crisis team, a social worker, and the lovely head carer were present. Grace began by explaining that we felt Mother should go into residential care.

'I don't think that's necessary,' said the social worker.

'We're here to discuss that,' said Grace calmly.

The key word was *discuss*. We were tired of decisions being made and us not being privy to the process. The physios had insisted Mother weight-bear, ignoring her pain, and we now knew that the agony had been real because she'd basically had no knee joint. But they hadn't listened to us.

'Mother has fallen twice,' said Claire.

'Just twice?' asked the social worker. 'It needs to be three times at least.'

'Are you serious?' I asked.

She looked as though I'd asked her to empty the commode. 'Yes. More than three times and we'll consider it a risk.'

'I'm not waiting until she falls again,' said Claire, disgusted.

'Even so, she fell weeks ago. It isn't recently, and she's fine now.' The social worker glanced at Mother, on the bed, clearly not well at all, her eyes dead and skin pallid.

Yeah, she's fucking excellent, I wanted to say. *Ready to party it up.*

'She's going with an amputation now,' said Grace.

'Oh. Is she?' The social worker flapped. 'We didn't know this.'

'We're telling you now,' said Grace, 'and I know some nice homes, so let's talk about that, shall we?'

The social worker told us the ones Grace mentioned were pricey and the family would have to pay for a lot of it. Then she said she would source a respite bed for after Mother's imminent amputation, and we could ring around for a care home in the meantime. The psychiatrist would also look at Mother's medication now the depression had descended again.

Mother sent me a text that night to thank me for being at the meeting.

What else would I have done?

I'd never see any harm come to her.

We tried desperate to cheer ourselves up with silliness in the chat group.

Claire wrote: *I never liked any of you before... I do a bit now.*

I wrote: *I still don't.*

Edwin wrote: *I like Colin most.*

I wrote: *You're alone there.*

Grace wrote: *Colin looks better in Mother's underwear than us.*

I wrote: *You clearly haven't seen Edwin in it.*

At the end of September, Mother went into a care home. It would just be respite until she had the leg amputated; if she liked the place she could stay there afterwards and if not, she could go somewhere else.

Colin and I dropped her off on a beautiful day when the leaves were crisping, and the sky was hopeful blue. It was a large, old house, with pleasant grounds as these places often have. We left Mother having some lunch with the other, mostly older, residents. I glanced back as we departed; she was sitting at a table, untouched food in front of her, tiny, lost, and looking at me as though for help.

It was unbearable because I knew how she felt.

I knew that feeling of being removed from my home.

And there was nothing I could do for her.

45

Daffodils

*Daffodils that come up with foliage but no
flowers are referred to as 'blind'.*

I love daffodils.

They don't care if there's a global pandemic. They don't care
if people jump off bridges. They don't care if we can't get hold of
toilet rolls. They don't care if I'm crossing out the year ahead in my
diary, scribbling out holidays, literary festivals, hair appointments,
meetings, trips to see family, all cancelled due to a virus. They don't
care if legs stay on or come off. They don't care. They are blind.
But beautiful.

46

Bruised and battle-scarred

A daffodil bulb is so poisonous that if your tot puts one in his or her mouth, you should seek medical advice.

The world had plans of early motherhood for me.

I was well-prepped. I'd been caring for my siblings since I was four. It was still a surprise to find myself pregnant though; it's not an ideal situation when you're nineteen, belatedly sitting your A levels (I'd gone to college eight months after being expelled from school) and working all weekend in a care home.

I'd been with Gerard for two years. My ability to trust was fragile because of the vile men Mum had let into our home, and my experience at hospital radio. My first boyfriend had broken my heart when he found another girl. I'd built protective barriers and found it hard to let people in, but Gerard initially proved dependable. He was in the army so away a lot, which suited my independent nature. Neither of us were perfect; we were both unfaithful to one another one time, and I could be argumentative, testing to see if he really loved me.

But then we became serious.

I had wanted to go on the pill when we met but Mum – when she learnt we'd slept together in the house on my eighteenth birthday

– made clear we were never to do it 'under her roof' ever again. She was 'disgusted' with me. Now, I find it shocking that it was fine for a man to come into my bedroom when I was ten, yet when I invited a boyfriend there to have consensual sex, this was unacceptable. After her reaction, I didn't dare talk to my mum about contraception. Teenagers who must depend on condoms is a recipe for disaster.

I was making a pot of tea during a shift in the care home when I realised.

I *felt* different.

I can still see the view from that kitchen window as I paused there; the roses weaving around an archway, the overgrown hedge and grass, the uneven patio. I can still hear the chit-chat from the nearby lounge, feel the sun on my face. The smell of the tea made me nauseous. It occurred to me that my period was a week late. And I knew. A home test the next day only confirmed it.

I was pregnant.

Despite my age and the situation, I was excited. I carried the knowledge around for a few days, not wanting to share this delicious secret. Not because of shame, but because it was perfect, and it was all mine.

I knew once I told people, that moment would be over forever.

At first, Gerard was shocked, but then happy. He talked about marriage (which I said no to, for now) and a rosy future. Then, when I was five months pregnant, he stopped writing to me and stopped calling from his base in Northern Ireland. This was before social media and mobile phones, so I couldn't contact him. When I was seven months pregnant and still hadn't heard back, I sent a letter ending the relationship. I had to decide. I assured him that he could visit our child when it was born – just call me to sort it out.

I'll summarise Gerard's final part in this story. Only he knows it in full; only he knows his reasons for backing off and it isn't fair for me to speculate. Just as I did with my own father when he left, I sent pictures of our son to Gerard once a month for the first year of his life, saying that just because we were over, I still wanted him in his life. But, apart from a brief moment in a courtroom trying (and failing) to get maintenance, I haven't seen him since.

I wasn't afraid when I ended up alone.

I was ready for it.

I waited until Mum was drunk to tell her. I left a note on the kitchen table while she was out. When I woke in the morning, she had slipped a reply under my bedroom door, saying everything would be fine. It was the first time she had said such a thing to me, and so I really felt it would be. Though she was still drinking heavily – at this time her buddy was a nice woman called Cally who came over with her autistic son for boozy sessions – Mum was great while I was pregnant, proud and happy to tell people. She had, I suppose, been young when she had me.

Telling Grandma Roberts broke my heart. I expected her to be angry because of her devout Catholic beliefs. 'I wanted so much more in life for you, Louise,' she said, sadly. This disappointment was harder to deal with than anger.

'I'll still do things,' I said, naively. 'It won't change anything.'

I put my name on the council list for a flat because I had no money. They offered me one twelve years later just as Joe and I were buying our first house. I left the care home and finished college and got a job as a waitress, where I worked until three weeks before my son was born. I saved every penny towards what I'd need for him, and towards a deposit to get a private flat. I still lived at home when he arrived. I shared a bedroom with Mum because Colin was twelve by then, so needed his own room, and it wasn't fair for a crying baby to disturb Claire and Grace, who were doing their GCSEs.

My due date was 9th January 1991.

On the morning of the 8th, I woke up in pain, having been aching on and off all night. Claire, Grace and Colin – getting ready for school – were excited, asking if it would be born today. By lunchtime I was really hurting but when I rang the hospital, they said first labours could be lengthy, so it was best to wait at home until the contractions were four minutes apart and lasting a full sixty seconds.

'Anyway, I need to get the car,' said Mum. She had been drinking at a friend's house the night before and sensibly left the car there. We went in a taxi with Tiggy the dog because she thought it practical to walk him before coming back. Once home, she said, 'Do you fancy a vanilla slice? I'll pop to Skeltons.'

'No, I bloody don't,' I cried. 'I want to go to the hospital now.'

We arrived mid-afternoon. Upon examination, the midwife said I was only three centimetres dilated, so I had a way to go. At teatime, Mum went home to feed the gang. On her return, she said they had all asked if I was OK.

'Is she in pain?' Grace had asked, concerned.

By now, I really was. I had a bath, but they wouldn't let me have it as hot as I wanted so I got out. I walked about – back and forth, back and forth – while a storm gathered strength outside, and darkness fell. When I got to six centimetres, the contractions slowed down, and I was so tired I collapsed on the bed. I'd had no pain relief; it had been manageable until then. The doctor was concerned that things weren't proceeding as they should and suggested they speed me up with oxytocin.

'You might want to consider an epidural too,' said the midwife. 'Things can get intense with this drug.'

I took her advice. Finally, at 6.44am, bang on his due date, forceps dragged my nine-pound-nine son into the world. My mum was with me and I was grateful. I'd been in labour and awake for over thirty hours. But as the storm died with my pain, and they handed him to me, I fell completely in love. Blood and fine blond fuzz covered his head; a scar from the forceps underlined one eye;

his finger tightly held mine as though he might otherwise lose me. Bruised and battle-scarred, he was all mine.

I called him Conor (because I loved it) Martin (because Grandma was praying to St Martin to 'get me a house from the council') Roberts (because I wanted to give my son my grandma's surname).

'Bless you,' said the midwife. 'You never stopped smiling the whole time.'

Claire, Grace and Colin came to visit that night.

Claire: *We walked down a hospital corridor and the wards were off it. I looked in one room and saw this adorable baby in a plastic, see-through crib, and thought, 'Aw, how cute, I hope he's like that.' We got lost. When we came back, we realised that it was Louise's room, and that baby was Conor. He was such a gorgeous baby.*

It felt like Conor brought a lot of love to the house. He slept in a Moses basket on the landing because I was sharing with Mum and – understandably – she was up early for work and didn't want to be disturbed when he woke in the night. There was no central heating in the house, and it was January. I had a huge blanket next to his bed and I wrapped us both in it when I fed him at night. Happy though I was to have him, I did get the baby blues, and often cried, feeling alone in the dark.

But that passed.

It's a cliché to describe him as the happiest baby in the world. But he was. A friend asked if he ever cried. Of course he did, when he was hungry or tired, but he was mostly contented, thriving on simple routine. And I was never happier than when I had him snug to my chest in a baby sling, and he looked up at me with a gummy smile, or when he cooed and tried to 'talk', responding to my words. Being a mother felt natural to me, but I was barely a kid myself. I still liked to be silly with Claire and Grace. One Sunday, we fired water guns from a bedroom window at the people coming out of the church opposite. A snooty and soaking wet woman knocked on the door and asked if it was us.

'How *rude*,' said Grace, face innocent, dripping water gun still in hand. 'Of course, it wasn't us.'

I sometimes wanted to share a room with my sisters again and tell ghost stories into the night. They still had their freedom; often the house was quiet in an evening when Mum was out drinking, and they'd gone to see their friends. My own friends had gone to university or were travelling Europe. Edwin sent a beautiful walnut cot that stood in its box in the front room until I left home because there was no room for it on the landing. I wanted my son to have a proper bedroom. I didn't want rootlessness for him. I was both of his parents; I was responsible for it all.

I left home when he was eight months old.

A friend of Mum's was renting his house out, cheaply, and I had enough for the deposit. It was in a basic state of repair, with a single gas fire in the whole place, but I knew I could make it homely. I could finally build the cot and create a bedroom with bright curtains at the window and boxes of toys.

But I was lonely.

I'd grown up surrounded by noise and chaos and other people. I didn't miss the drinking or disruptive music or unwanted guests, but I missed family. I loved the simple routine Conor and I had. He was always up at five-thirty (a real killer when I was the only one) and enjoyed his Weetabix and milk and then a nap before a long walk and then play. Our simplicity was not unlike lockdown now during the Covid-19 pandemic. But it was lonely when he went to bed. You can love your child and still want more. This is human nature. My mum had sought this at the neglect of her children and making unwise choices. I didn't believe I was entitled to a life, as she always said, because Conor *was* my life. But – looking back – I was depressed, and this vulnerability meant the childhood trauma I'd buried for so long shifted about inside me like an insidious snake.

Sometimes I'd go home for the night, with Conor in a travel cot next to me, just to see Claire and Grace. They often slept over at my house and we'd talk long into the night like we had as kids. Claire went away in the RAF when Conor was almost two and Grace sought my company then as much as I sought hers. Colin was a teenager and had his own life. Being the only boy often meant he was separate to us.

I had no time to write during this period. It was the first – and *only* – time in my life when I didn't get lost in storytelling. Was it just because I was wrapped up in being a single parent or were the words too difficult to put down? Whatever the case, my dreams of being a world-famous author were briefly forgotten.

Conor was two when Mum met Des. Before he came on the scene, she would babysit now and again so I could see friends or go out. When Des showed his true colours – calling Grace a cunt and threatening to hit Colin with his guitar – I told Mum she could only look after Conor on her own. I didn't want Des near my baby when I wasn't there.

Instead, she stopped babysitting altogether.

'If you don't let Des come,' she said, 'then *I* won't either.'

I had to find a young woman to babysit occasionally.

Mum's relationship with Des was volatile. She often had black eyes that she made excuses for. They broke up and made up, over and over. Colin was the only one still at home and I felt for him, enduring that. During one of their splits, Mum ended up depressed and in the asylum again. As soon as she came out, she got back with Des.

It was a punch in the gut.

I had run her house and cared for my brother in her absence, and this was how she repaid me. She would rather be with yet another unsuitable man. My anger at her rejecting my son in favour of such a creature was rawer than at her rejecting us. This was *my* child she was affecting now.

I didn't speak to her for six months.

And I went into one of the darkest times of my adult life.

49

Like an avalanche later

Daffodils use their leaves as energy to create next year's flower. They continue to absorb nutrients for about six weeks after the blooms have died.

Mother settled into the care home. It was respite, with the option of her staying after the amputation if she so chose. The operation was set to go ahead – she had decided absolutely – we just had to wait for a slot. It felt like everything had led to this. It had just taken a hell of a long time.

Edwin wrote: *Amputation is next leg of the journey, excuse the pun.*

Claire wrote: *At least for the first time in her life she can't deny that she's legless.*

Edwin wrote: *She'll be out on a limb there.*

I wrote: *She could start dance group Leg and Co. Or join Steps tribute band, Step.*

The rest of the metal cage around the knee was removed a few weeks prior to the op. The leg with the pins out looked horrific – it was bent at an odd angle, still swollen, red and scarred. Mother was in pain. At another appointment that I attended, the surgeon said she had limited upper core strength and was too old to consider a prosthetic leg so she would be wheelchair-bound after the amputation.

'She'll be perfectly mobile though,' he said cheerfully. 'She'll be able to move from chair to bed to toilet to chair.'

Right up to the operation, it was back and forth as to whether they would actually do it. A different consultant chimed in with his thoughts, suggesting the possibility of rebuilding the leg instead. Mother panicked; said she didn't want to go through all that. We stood by her and encouraged her to insist that she was in pain all the time, that she was happy with the decision, and she definitely wanted amputation.

Grace wrote: *If she bit onto a piece of wood, we could do it with a chainsaw.*

Colin wrote: *Fuck, can you imagine?*

I wrote: *That's what they did in the war. Also last Tuesday down by us…*

Edwin wrote: *Unless a priest is available, amputations are best left to vascular surgeons.*

Claire wrote: *A ward cleaner did mine the other day.*

When Grace and I visited the care home, we had to sign in, and we wrote that we were seeing RoboTrish. No one ever questioned it in the month she was there, and during repeated uses of this nickname name. It cheered us immensely, that we got away with our devilment. We were still kids at heart.

In Mother's room, which was again high-ceilinged (a bit of a motif in my life now) and spacious, she said, 'Now the metal frame is off, I want to request ECT.'

This is electroconvulsive therapy. It's most often used to treat severe depression and psychosis that has not responded to medication. It is still done – less barbarically than back in the 40s – but has negative associations. Mother had it in 1980 after her first suicide attempt. It apparently 'did the trick'.

'If you had it with the frame *on*,' I said, thinking of the shock, 'you'd have bigger hair than mine.'

'My friend told me it's all that works for her,' said Mother.

'I don't think that's the answer,' said Grace, kindly. 'You need to look at yourself. Face your inner demons. Explore *why* you've been depressed and not just look for quick cures.'

'I'm trying, I *am*,' Mother said, voice tremulous with self-pity. 'But there's no light at the end of the tunnel. I feel so low.'

'Medication won't solve what's inside you,' I said, firmly. It was time to say what needed saying. 'You need to look at *why* you abused alcohol for almost forty years. I mean *really* look at it. Get therapy. Engage in some intense counselling.'

Grace nodded, catching my eye. 'You should be grateful so much counselling is being offered to you. Everyone is doing so much for you. You have psychiatrists, counsellors, the mental health team, the carers here. Use it.'

'You don't know how lucky you are,' I couldn't help but say. 'I went to my doctor to ask for some counselling on the NHS in 2012 and I'm still waiting. You have it all at your fingertips.'

'Jump off the bridge,' Grace said to me. 'That'll get you some.'

'I'm trying so hard,' repeated Mother. 'I just can't see the light.'

Again, I wanted to scream in her face that she drank for forty years when we all told her over and over and *over* to stop. When she knew that it didn't help depression; when it led to cruel and stupid behaviour; when it destroyed our relationships with her. And now here she was, complaining to us, after all we had done and were still doing.

But again, I didn't.

Again, I put the rage in the crowded place with the rest.

Eventually, Mother seemed to accept that it was up to her to get better and stopped arguing. No one else had the magical cure. But we felt what we had said would make zero difference, and as I complete this sentence, I don't believe she has had a single session of counselling.

Before we left, she asked if one of us would cut her toenails like I had in the hospital. Curiously this does not seem to be the job of a carer or nurse.

'No fucking way,' said Grace.

Like a fool, I agreed. 'I'm only doing one foot,' I said, grimacing at the overgrown talons.

'Why?' she asked.

'I'm not wasting my time with the one that's getting chopped off.'

'But I want it to look nice for the op,' she said.

'What do you want me to do? Paint your nails for the surgeon?'

Grace stepped back from visiting so often after this, understandably to concentrate more on her own family.

Grace wrote: *She's manipulating us. Some days I'm livid. Some I'm sad. Then I feel guilt. There is no positive emotion with Mother. Because I have stepped back a bit from the circus of it, she's now asking if I've taken the kids to Hull Fair. While this is nice, she's no longer bombarding me with her anxiety because I've dissociated from it. So, she plays the caring game instead.*

Edwin wrote: *Even if you all left her now, you'd have NOTHING to feel guilty for. You have stood beside her in spite of what she has wreaked upon you to the point of physical and mental burn out. We all have flaws. I even had a flaw once, but I think it's gone now.*

We knew this manipulation game of old. Mother drinking and saying or doing vile things and then eventually apologising when we hadn't spoken to her for months and she realised it was all that might get us back. She told us now that she had no appetite, but we watched her savage a large chicken dinner and generous dessert. She acted confused by all the information from a variety of professionals, but other people told us she seemed to be quite clear about what was going on.

Was she 'enjoying' her helpless state because she got more attention?

We are human though, and as she grew anxious about the upcoming op, we did our best to be there for her. Grace and I took her out for a day to the Old Town, wheeling her chair along cobbled streets, and responding over and over to her 'When will I get better?' question. She insisted that she would pay for lunch but put in the 'wrong' card number four times until it got blocked, and then Grace's husband Brent had to pay.

Another time, Colin and I took her to the restaurant we like near the Humber Bridge for a Sunday carvery. We saw someone he knew who, due to the blustery wind, didn't hear Mother say hello to him.

'You really get ignored in a wheelchair,' she said afterwards.

'No one would dare ignore you,' I laughed.

During October, life continued. I smiled and tried to give my sparkle to the events I did, including a talk for almost a hundred women at a lovely church group. This brought me great joy. I finished my novel and wondered what to start next. For a long time, I had mused on the idea of a memoir. Since Mother jumped from the bridge, the idea had grown, and was tugging insistently on my sleeve like a toddler wanting to share a great secret.

And then on 11th November – she always picks her moment, this time outshining the veterans – Mother's leg was removed just above the knee. I began this memoir that day.

In our WhatsApp group, I wrote: *Once the op is done, Mother needs to find a male companion with the same size shoe and the opposite leg removed and they can share shoes.*

Edwin wrote: *Any news yet?*

Colin wrote: *No. She's still in surgery.*

Grace wrote: *I'm getting worried…*

Claire wrote: *She'll be bloody fine. Don't know about you guys but I'm sick of hospitals and waiting to hear things. This is taking me back to February…*

I wrote: *I agree. Very tired today.*

Grace wrote: *I'm numb to it all. That's good now but think it will come down on me like an avalanche later.*

I wrote: *I think none of us have truly dealt with this.*

I don't know if we ever truly will.

48

Have you seen my bike?

As part of the Week Without Violence campaign, Salt Lake City community leaders plant daffodils each October to honour the victims of gun violence.

You might think my mum would have been open-minded about me experimenting with alcohol when I was a teenager/young adult; that with her abuse of it, she would see it as an understandable result and turn the other cheek, or at least have no judgement. But you'd be wrong.

The first time I came home drunk – aged eighteen, after a night at a friend's house where we foolishly mixed sherry with cider – she shamed me for it. She was smoking in the kitchen as I staggered in the back door. I hid in the nearby bathroom and tried desperately to sober up with splashes of cold water.

'Are you drunk in there?' she demanded through the closed door.

'No,' I said, knowing I sounded it.

'Come out now,' she said.

I did, trying to act like everything was fine. I could hardly see.

'You're a disgrace,' she said.

When I woke with a killer hangover the next day, I felt ashamed. I'd grown up with drinkers around me – and I'd hated it – but now

I was 'one of them'. Now *I* was the disgrace. That's how she made me feel. The hypocrisy of this didn't rear its righteous head then. Her criticism made me feel I had to hide it if I occasionally drank with my friends.

For the first three years of Conor's life, I only went out occasionally. We lived on benefits during those years because I got no money from his dad. Tax credits didn't exist to help with childcare, so I couldn't afford babysitters when Mum chose to see Des over her grandson. I briefly had a boyfriend then. He left without explanation after eight months. To be fair, I'd kept him at a distance; we never lived together or talked about a future, and to Conor he was just 'my friend'. I didn't want my son getting attached to people who might abandon us.

It seemed to be a pattern in my young life. Men suddenly left.

Or did I subconsciously pick ones who wouldn't stay?

I didn't want to live with a man. I couldn't imagine it. I was never the typical kid that dreamt of marriage. I liked the idea of family, children, but a partner somehow didn't quite factor into that. I felt a house would be safer if it was just me. Even though I missed the noise from my siblings growing up, I didn't want arguments and loud music and uncertainty for my children, or for me.

Grace moved in with me to escape from Des's violence at home. We loved living together; we laughed at *Blind Date* and *Gladiators* on a Saturday night, dieted together, exercised to the *Cher Fitness* video together, and had nights out. We laughed for hours one morning when she simply asked me, 'Have you seen my bike?' and we realised it had gone and must have been stolen. It wasn't even funny, just ridiculous. We laughed forever another time just because the man next door turned his water hose on.

During this time, she paid for us both to go out; she worked in a care home so had good cash each month, and we could pay a regular, dependable babysitter for Conor. Every other week, we dressed up and hit the local hotspots, wanting to escape the mundane. I loved being a mother, and I loved my son, but it was exhilarating to let off steam, to be a young woman on the town like others my age.

Grace: *We were rebellious, doing whatever we wanted as long as it made us laugh. We were unable to form proper relationships – connections. We thought that was normal, just part of being young. Obviously, it wasn't. We took the piss out of men but didn't want boyfriends. I loved the attention, but I was unable to emotionally connect. It was just a laugh.*

I loved the escape. That's what it was. We drank in the taxi on the way out, took cassettes for the driver to play, and then danced all night. We took our own alcohol into pubs – one time I tried to deny it was my own drink, despite the cup being a plastic Lion King beaker – and we were removed a few times. But we just went somewhere else. No matter how little sleep I'd had, I got up at six-thirty with Conor, back in Mum-mode, there for him. I was two people. A single mum during the day, but twice a month, at night, a party girl.

At times, guilt gnawed at me, like maggots on old meat.

Was I doing what my mum had done?

Was I neglecting my son?

Grace: *Nothing mattered when we went out. We'd drink as much as we could, smoke loads. Our friends often came too. We asked Louise's married neighbours once if they wanted to 'come out and score with us' but strangely they declined. We took silly poems and egg whisks and drawings out with us. We ordered ridiculous drinks – Louise asked for a quarter of cider when we ran out of money. A man at the bar once told me I was standing on his shoelace. 'Sorry,' I said, 'I thought it was your penis.' Laughing at it all afterwards got us through the entire week.*

This was when I started sleeping around. With men. Any men. Multiple men. Men whose names I didn't know. Men who I likely wouldn't have looked at twice sober, whose faces I can't even recall now. I had sex in cars, in parks, at a local country spot. Sometimes I had more than one at a time; sometimes so drunk I could barely speak. I thought I was wild, carefree.

I didn't bring them home if Conor was there though.

That was a sacred place.

Looking back from twenty-six years in the future, I'm sad for that girl. She thought that if she gave sex away, no one could take it. If it had no value, no one could ruin it. If she didn't care, she couldn't get hurt. But she buried this knowledge. Told herself she was having fun. I know now it was a delayed reaction to trauma, but she buried this dawning realisation too. Fourteen years after she kicked off the bed covers in Grandma's house to freeze her pain, it began to defrost. Thirteen years after Peter came into her bedroom, and she tried to pull those covers tighter, the rage and the shame showed itself in destructive and self-harming behaviour.

Grace: *I met the father of my first son during this time. The first time he met Mum, she set fire to herself smoking a cigar, and she stole his brandy. The next time they met, she was in the local asylum. I have no idea how any of the more decent men we met stayed with us once they were introduced to our mum. But then I have even less idea how any of us are normal. (Normal being used very sarcastically here.)*

I managed my addiction – for want of a better word – to promiscuity by keeping it separate from my motherly life. They were two worlds. Conor never saw or met any of these men. That's how I coped with the guilt that came as acutely as the raging hangover.

I was not my mum. I was not my mum.

This mantra I chanted without words. But I didn't believe it. I felt worthless. Yet I couldn't stop the behaviour. I was unable to trust men, treating them like cheap clothes you wear once and leave in a charity shop doorway. I craved the attention. The rush. The chase. The win.

Then Grace had to go to Aylesbury to do a nursing degree.

Claire had gone in the RAF three years before.

On her last day with me, Grace simply said, 'Word,' while doing a bro fist as she walked away from the house. As ever, we were unable to express our true pain and fell back on silliness. But I was heartbroken.

Mum was depressed again, so as usual, my pain was secondary.

I continued sleeping around on my two nights out a month, with a friend now instead. But it had a darker edge. If before, there was at least an element of it being fun, now I flirted with danger. Did I actually want to be hurt? To *die*? Maybe. The risks I took suggest that. I went to the homes of men I'd just met. I had sex in a night club toilet. Sometimes I went out alone, pretending to the babysitter that I was meeting friends in the town. Dangerous since no one knew where I was.

But I didn't care.

There was a man I must have liked enough to meet a few times. He asked one night if I loved him. I laughed. I didn't even love myself. Another time – when Conor was away with his paternal grandparents who had been seeing him since he turned two – I took a man back because he wasn't there; it wasn't our *home*, just a house. Halfway through sex, I changed my mind and rang him a taxi.

'You're a cold bitch,' he said.

Then I was angry. 'Get the fuck out,' I told him.

'You invited me!' he cried, hobbling out, half dressed.

I didn't know who I was. I'd violated my home by taking him there. I hadn't even asked his name. I didn't care. My home was precious. I cried. Couldn't wait for Conor to come back the next day. When he did, I hugged him and buried my face in his hair. I decided that no men were coming to our home again.

Mum got over her depression after another stint in the asylum, and started dating our family friend, Johnny, who we all liked. He's still in our lives. I hoped it would work out, but she got drunk and ruined that too eventually. I often went there for Sunday lunch with Conor, along with Johnny and his young daughter. She was Nice Mum while she was with him: on her best behaviour.

'Do you want a glass of wine?' she asked me once, as the Sunday lunch I had so often prepared in the past simmered away behind us.

'No thanks,' I said.

I never drank during the day, while I was with Conor. And I especially would not drink on a Sunday and give him the kind of day we had endured as kids.

'Why not?' she asked.

'I don't want to,' I said.

'But you drink all the time now,' she said.

'I don't. I never drink at home.'

'You can never criticise *me* again,' she said. 'You and Grace used to get paralytic when she was here. And you do now, when you go out.'

'The difference,' I said, 'is that I only drink twice a month when I'm out, and I'm there for my son the rest of the time.'

I wanted to say that I had never moved paedophiles or violent maniacs into my house. I wanted to say that I had never needed social workers to tell me that Conor needed me. That I never expected anyone else to take care of him. That I had never put a single person before him. But it would have caused a huge row. And maybe she was right. Maybe I *was* a terrible mum. I wrestled intensely with this.

An act of violence ended my dance with debauchery.

One night, while out, I had a disagreement with a man. He chatted me up in a pub but clearly had a girl with him, so I told him to leave me alone. I came around, on the floor, at the other side of the pub. He'd hit me so hard I'd been knocked out cold for two full minutes. My friend helped me up, but no one else did anything.

We went to another pub, to avoid him, and carried on drinking. Then I started to feel queasy. A woman asked what had happened to me, motioning to my face. When I looked in the mirror, it was bruised black.

'You should go to the hospital,' she said, kindly.

We did; I had an X-ray and found out that my jaw had hairline fractures.

'It should heal without any intervention,' someone medical told me.

There was little sympathy.

I felt I didn't deserve any.

I treated the experience with the usual mockery; I made light of it all by flirting with the staff at the hospital, by trying to steal my X-ray pictures to send to Grace, by seeing if my friend could have an X-ray too, and by ringing anyone who would listen to tell them where we were.

It was an all-time low; it was a wake-up call.

I didn't want this kind of life for myself, and indirectly for my son. I had kidded myself it was 'fun', an 'escape', but I knew, deep down, that it was just pain. Self-inflicted. Finally surfacing.

I stopped sleeping around. I made plans. I began writing pieces about being a mum, which I would add to years later when Katy was born, and which eventually formed my ten-year newspaper column. I went to college when Conor started school. It was good to have purpose again, something that was mine that didn't involve danger.

It was here that I met Joe.

He has since told me that I was difficult to get to know, that I had built a wall around myself. But he persevered in taking apart those bricks. We were friends first, which helped. There was a snowy night, a month after we started dating, when he biked through a blizzard to tell me he loved me. There was a first Christmas and his gift of twelve red roses and a new phone to plug in upstairs so I could talk to him until I fell asleep. Still, letting him move in when we'd been together for two years was hard. I almost thought I couldn't do it – couldn't let my guard down fully and trust him. But I did. And recently we celebrated our twentieth wedding anniversary.

He's the only man I've ever lived with.

He's the only man I've been with or loved since I was twenty-six.

49

Lockdown life

*How can you force daffodils to open? Place them
in a cool location that receives low to medium light.*

Lockdown feels like normal life now.

The daily Covid-19 news update at five feels like it has happened since the beginning of time. The many numbers of deaths are hard to take in though. Numbers like this are unreal. Impersonal. Alcohol is on the news a lot. Pubs may be closed but supermarket sales of booze are apparently going through the roof. My relationship with alcohol is so mixed. I grew up seeing the effects of its abuse, feeling the direct results. I enjoy a glass of wine as much as the next person – and love a few at events or when out – but I rarely drink at home.

Lockdown is no exception.

The intensity of being alone makes writing hard at times, liberating at others, and yet even in this darkness, the act of creating stories – even this very real and close to home tale – is my saviour.

50

A solitary red sock

To be in flower for Christmas, planting must be done ahead of time; daffodils planted in September might surprise you and flower after just ten weeks.

News finally came of Mother's amputation surgery; it had gone well, and she was recovering comfortably on the ward. I didn't sleep that night though. I tried to imagine life with one leg. A life low down, sitting, always looking up at others. A life lighter, in some ways, but heavier in others.

I still managed to joke as we shared our thoughts though.

Colin wrote: *Just spoken with Mother. Sounds relaxed. She said last night, straight after surgery, she felt as 'normal' as she's mentally been recently.*

Claire wrote: *Weird, cos last night she told me she was anxious and praying.*

I wrote: *Oscar Pistorius is alive and well and living at Hull Royal Infirmary.*

The first time I saw Mother with one leg she never stopped talking for the hour-and-a-half visit, her voice demanding attention over the cacophony of hospital noise on the ward. It was likely that morphine made her garrulous. Colin and I couldn't get a word in. She had made friends with every patient on the ward and knew everything about them, as well as about most of the staff. Joe has always said that her best trait is that she can talk to anyone. It's true. And it's a grand gift. She can engage with people from all walks of life, and this is part of the charm that others are drawn to. Edwin is the same; walking with him when he was in the UK, he'd happily chat to anyone who crossed our path.

'Take a breath, Mother,' Colin said at one point.

'I'm just happy,' she said. 'Happy to be alive; happy to say goodbye to the leg; happy to be out of that care home. I never liked it, you know. If you'd seen the things that went on there…'

And then we got the tales of everyone there. I was happy she was happy, but I was concerned that this was just the post-surgery drug rush and she would crash again. It was a rollercoaster, and part of me wanted to unclip my safety harness and get off and run and run and run. But I stayed in my seat, hoping the fairground mechanisms would fail and she would remain at the top.

I could see the outline of her stump under the thin sheet.

'You can look properly if you want,' she said.

I would have, but Colin said he'd rather not. It was surreal how fine she was about it. I wondered if this acceptance would wane when real life hit and she got sent home, wherever home ended up being. We didn't yet know where that might be. She insisted she did not want to return to the previous care home but accepted that her house would never be suitable for a wheelchair.

A solitary red sock hung on the bar of her nearby walking frame.

'You lost this,' I said.

Then I realised. She would never need it again. One sock. One shoe. One slipper. This would be her footwear.

Within two days of the surgery, they expected her to start moving with a frame.

Colin wrote: *There has been talk of her getting a prosthetic leg.*

Edwin wrote: *It's quite doable for a seventy-one-year-old who is reasonably fit. They would jump – or hop? – at the opportunity.*

I wrote: *There was a paraplegic man on the news this morning who climbed Everest. She could start there. After all, she's good with heights now.*

Edwin wrote: *I'll see if he's there next week when I go.*

I wrote: *Give him my best.*

Edwin wrote: *Best foot forward?*

Grace and I took the kids to see Mother. They were unfazed, as small ones often are, by her lack of a second leg and enjoyed pushing her up and down the hospital corridors in the chair. We all sang 'Onward Christian Soldiers' like it was a coach trip to the coast. There was a raffle to raise money for the ward. Grace and I bought twenty-two tickets each, our excitement at winning no-brand men's aftershave and past-date chocolates manic.

Mother seemed well again. Was it because the leg had gone? Perhaps the hindrance of the heavy frame and painful bones had hampered her mental recovery. Such an injury would hinder the healthiest of us. She insisted the drop in her mood had been because she hated the care home.

'I've written to my local MP,' she said as we had a latte in the hospital café and the kids ate their November-raffle Easter Eggs.

'A love letter?' I asked, smiling.

Shaking her head, she said, 'I'm applying for a council flat. I can't go back to the house, and I won't be in care forever.'

'You may not get one,' said Grace, kindly. 'You own a property that you can sell and buy a flat with the money. Council houses are for emergencies; homeless families and people with nothing.'

'My friends tell me I'll go to the top of the list with my disability,' she insisted.

We discussed this issue.

Claire wrote: *She'll have to wait for tenants to die, sadly, as there are no council flats.*

I wrote: *This is what happens when you prance up to the bridge and wreck your legs.*

Claire wrote: *I love it when you use prance.*

I wrote: *I told a friend the story with that verb and she spat her lungs out.*

Mother messaged us constantly, asking us to keep ringing the council on her behalf. She said she was calling and getting no answer. One of her friends contacted me to say that she had a lot of her own health issues to deal with, so couldn't keep calling the council when Mother asked. I insisted she ignore these requests.

At the end of November, Mother got offered a council flat just a few minutes away from her house, close to the shops and other amenities.

'It's a miracle!' she told us, delighted. 'Now... we need to get my house valued...'

I was glad she had somewhere to go that would suit her needs. She could begin to make a new life for herself. This might be a positive turning point.

Around this time, Edwin went on an epic trip to Nepal, and climbed 'the first two inches' of Everest. He sent regular pictures of the views from his accommodation and the mammoth trek. He flew from Kathmandu to Lukla in a twelve-seater plane and walked twenty kilometres, mostly uphill, which he said was a very hard climb due to low oxygen, but that it was magnificent to see; another world.

Just before his trip, Edwin sent a message to Mother saying that now she was better, she should acknowledge what her children had been put through, not just during this last nine months but since childhood. She wished him well on his trip and sent love to his family but didn't acknowledge what he had said about us. Instead, she told him he 'knew nothing of depression'. She told him that she had never had a man to support her, and that she might not always have been a good mother, but no one ever mentioned when she *had* been helpful. Her friends were apparently amazed by how much so.

We told Edwin to ignore her and enjoy his well-deserved holiday. When he did, Mother told him to 'stop sulking'.

She had plenty of physio sessions before being discharged from the hospital, some of which Colin and I attended. She had to raise the stump regularly while on her bed, which was odd to see, still wrapped in white bandages. She had to be able to confidently move from one place to another, to wheel her own chair. The idea of a prosthetic was forgotten; she seemed happy with this.

Then they let her go.

She moved to a temporary care home in a town an hour from ours, where she would reside until her council flat was made suitable, with a ramp and wider doors. It was hard for me to visit her there, not only mentally, but physically. As a non-driver, it was impossible to get there unless Colin or Joe took me, and as we went into December my shifts at the theatre tripled. We had two festive shows on at once, three times a day. I had one day off a week and was simply too exhausted to give what I had left to my mother.

'Get the bus,' she said when I told her this.

'What?' I asked.

'The one that goes to York passes here,' she said. 'I used to get it all the time.'

She expected me to sit for two hours on a bus, there and back, on my only day off, after the year we'd had and all we had done. It was another reminder that she had far less regard for our needs than her own. That she would let me sacrifice my scarce free time to devote it to her. If I knew she loved me the way a mother should, I'd have given her *all* my free time; I'd have travelled overnight to be there. I have always been expected to look after her emotional needs, but she has rarely taken care of mine.

'I'm not getting the bus,' I said.

It was quite a big thing for me to say no like that.

When I did go, I went for Colin. To support him. That protectiveness from when he was the pink-cheeked toddler still lingers. I couldn't let him deal with it alone, even though he never requested I go with him. Grace, quite understandably, began keeping her distance. Claire too had backed off now. I supported them both fully in this. I wanted them to put themselves first. We can only manage what we can manage. As the oldest sibling, I feel responsible at times for them. Other than that, I can't explain why I continued to visit my mother as frequently as I did.

When I decide I'm done with something in life, nothing changes my mind. In the past, I often put up with Mother until I thought I'd implode with rage. Then something would push me over the edge and I'd not see her for months. I didn't know if this would happen again, but the bridge jump and its aftermath had impacted me deeply. Like a rock hitting water, it had not only caused waves but revealed the true depth beneath, the sharp hidden dangers and the swirling undercurrents.

I tried to get excited about my next book coming out. An early copy arrived just before Christmas; the best gift aside from Katy coming home, and the three of us driving to see Conor and Ieva on Christmas day. I opened it, smelled the pages, and looked at the words I'd written during the hardest time of my life. So many paragraphs had been influenced by my year. So many sentences pulsated with my pain. So many words were chosen by a woman looking for some that might comfort.

Then it was New Year's Eve.

Edwin wrote: *Happy 2020 to one and all. I hope it's a better one. Here's a picture of the fireworks here.*

I wrote: *May your firework be aimed in the right direction and go off with a bang.*

Grace wrote: *I'm having a cheese board, and then bed by six.*

Claire wrote: *We're watching Jools Holland.*

I wrote: *We just came out of Star Wars. Very misty here.*

Edwin wrote: *Who's Misty?*

I wrote: *Joe's new bird.*

Colin wrote: *I may go out for beer and food. 2020 can only be better than 2019…*

51

This is from all of us

In Gucci's Spring/Summer 2019 Collection, multiple ready-to-wear pieces featured embroidery of the last lines of Wordsworth's Daffodils poem.

As I went into marriage with Joe when I was twenty-eight, and we had Katy the next year, I had the kind of life I'd never imagined I could; a nice house, a hands-on stick-around father for my kids, routine, security. I know now that I achieved this through the choices I made. I chose to marry a decent man. I chose not to drink to excess. I chose to try to be the mother I'd never had, even if I too made mistakes. I was too strict at times, because I was trying to be a father figure; I was too soft at other times because I was trying to be the kind of mother I'd seen in movies; I was difficult at times as I worked through my issues.

But I broke the cycle.

I have a good relationship with my adult children.

In our marriage, Joe and I have experienced the difficulties most people do: testing teenage years with both our kids, family bereavement, three redundancies, differences of opinion. We've also had a few challenges that not everyone faces, like the 2007 floods that destroyed everything we owned, Katy's type 1 diabetes diagnosis at the tender age of seven, and Grandam Roberts' newsworthy death.

In life, we have little control over what happens, but we can choose how we respond to these things. Through these tough times I turned to my joy once again: writing. I wrote my newspaper column, and I wrote short stories, and eventually I wrote novels. Every word I put down, I shared a true part of myself. Writing stories helped me look at things more clearly, to make sense of what had happened to me.

I wrote in the first chapter that I could trust in it. That it gave back what I put into it. It listened to me. Now I know that even my fiction was life writing. Inspired by my experiences, I could be honest with that safe literary distance. Now, finally, my own experiences are laid bare here.

I wrote an important letter, too, in 2010.

It would be impossible to address the full extent of my mother's almost forty-year drinking problem. It's a huge story. A tome. Too complex. So, I must choose the scenes that best show the effect it had on us, select the subtle moments and the major events. But which are these? They are the bits that I included in a painful and desperate letter.

In many ways, a letter is as good as a chapter.

It has a beginning and an end. It is complete. It is succinct.

Let me preface it by telling you that Mother met Andrew in 2001 and married him two years later. The ceremony – in the church opposite The Cottage – puts scattered confetti and our small children carrying flower baskets in my head. We're glowing in the photographs. Andrew was kind and decent. My children were fond of him; he read Katy bedtime stories and did great impressions of Wallace and Gromit.

We hoped this stable relationship might mean Mother stopped drinking. It didn't. Andrew asked us why we never warned him about her problem, which of course it wasn't our place to. No one had ever listened to us anyway. When he sadly died of cancer just five years after their wedding, Mother's alcohol abuse escalated. By then, my siblings and I were in our thirties and had tried speaking to her about it many, many times. We had tried harsh words; we had tried kind words. We had tried not seeing her for a while. We had tried everything.

Nothing worked.

Things came to a head at Christmas 2010.

Grace's husband Brent was away with the army in Germany, so she was alone with her teen son, Tom. Mother kept ringing her, drunk on Christmas Eve. Grace told her to stop. Because of repeated, abusive, drunken late-night calls, we had a rule that she couldn't ring us after six, but she still did. When Grace refused to speak to her that night, Mother called Tom instead.

Grace had to deal with her. 'We've grown up with this abuse,' she told her. 'But Tom isn't going to face it too.'

'Well,' said Mother, haughtily. 'Don't bother coming for Christmas dinner tomorrow then.'

Grace had no turkey prepared. No crackers. No dessert.

'Have you got room for me to eat with you?' she asked me, clearly upset.

We did. But I was more furious with Mother than I'd ever been. I rang her a few days after this and screamed at her that she was going to lose Grace, once and for all, unless she stopped the drinking and tried to make it up with her. It made no difference. Mother was drunk the next night.

It was then that I sat down and wrote a letter.

I've always loved letters. In the past – before WhatsApp and texts and DMs – if we wanted to correspond in ways other than a phone call, we had to put pen to paper. I find it a lot easier to speak through the written word. It gives time for reflection. Time to edit. Time to set it down and go back. It's then impossible for the recipient to open the envelope and *not* read the contents. They can't interrupt you or put you off. Then, when they read it, they can't ignore your words.

My siblings read the missive and gave it their full backing.

I think it shows how hard we tried.

Dear Mum,

This is from all of us. It's not an unkind letter, but the truth. You said you're tired of being 'put down' but none of us have done this. We've only tried to address the things you have done and continue to do as a result of your drinking. We have tolerated it for a long time, we've forgiven and overlooked many things, and it's got to end. If you say you didn't read this letter, that's disrespecting our right to express how we feel, and we can never move forward.

A letter is necessary since we've tried all other ways to sort out these issues. Grace and Louise sat with you last year and in a kind and non-judgemental way tried to make you see how your drinking affects everyone and has done for years. You acknowledged this and promised to try. We explained then how your drinking brings up many painful issues for us. You've every right to your life and to drink if you choose, but we have the right to not want to talk to you when you are. We don't answer the phone in an evening because of this, yet you still ring – when we don't answer, you send sarcastic texts.

To say that you're sick of being 'put down' belittles our valid reasons for responding as we do to your drinking. We've never accused you of something that isn't true or said anything for the sake of being cruel. Just because you don't like to hear it, doesn't make it a put down. Take responsibility for your actions. You say how awful it was when your dad died. It must have been terrible. But we had an awful childhood, and it's never acknowledged. All we're told is that we have 'no idea' because we've not been depressed.

Our childhood was not entirely your fault – some was Dad, and some was because of your depression and us living in homes/at Grandma's etc – but when you got better, you were neglectful, letting unstable men live in the house, going to Geraldine's and getting pissed all weekend, leaving Louise responsible, having your friends berate us if we rang, and being told we were a burden and that you were entitled to a life.

When we address this, you say, 'Oh, you're telling me I'm an awful mother.' We've never said that, but you must face that these are facts and that if that means you had failings as a parent, you must address it.

We're entitled to peace. You may have lost your father young, but you knew he loved you. Grandma may have had her flaws, but you knew she loved you, and she did anything she could for you. In her later years, you had little time for her. Yes, there are good things you've done for us at times, but those are the normal things that any parent does.

Read the following list of drinking-related occurrences and then tell us you don't have a drink problem. If you can, fair enough. If you feel this list is cruel, that's tough. We've tried more gentle approaches. When you're not drinking, you're snide and edgy and sarcastic. Drinking makes you lie, be devious. You told Claire on Saturday that you were getting into your pyjamas for a night in. Then you texted Grace to say you'd been to a barbeque sober. Which is true? We never know. You've lied so many times.
Everything listed here is absolute fact…

The night Grace gave birth to Thomas you were drunk, turned up at the hospital, tried to get in, and were understandably turned away.

When Claire arrived to stay at your house with her broken back in a splint you were drunk. Claire was in agony. The next day she moved to Grace's and stayed there until Mae was born. She could not stay at yours because of the drinking.

The night Mae was born you were drunk, asking if you could come to the hospital with us; obviously we said no.

You babysat for Grace, got utterly inebriated. When Joe walked Grace to your house to get Tom, you called her a whore, said she was sleeping with him, and did Louise know this? You then told friends Joe was having an affair with Grace, which is the most despicable lie.

Down in Plymouth for Mae's blessing, you drank all the wine belonging to the priest in the rectory where you stayed free of charge. Grace had to protect Grandma from you because you were then vile. You never replaced this wine. We had to apologise about it.

At Louise's engagement party to Joe, you were inebriated before you got there, even though you'd stressed that we should all meet up sober with Joe's mum and dad early on.

When you went to Claire and Gordon's home you got so drunk that you smashed the garden furniture, burnt the dog with a cigarette, and wouldn't go to bed. Gordon said he'd never have you there again.

You did the same in Scotland with Julian and Claire – while Claire was in hospital with her broken back you got so drunk you ranted at Julian about how wonderful a mother you are.

At Grace's barbeque you were so drunk that Colin and Andrew had to take you home in the car.

When Andrew went looking for you because you'd gone shopping and not returned, you were in the pub drunk. He asked Grace why we hadn't warned him of your drinking problem. Sadly, no one has ever listened to us. Grace took you back to the house, stopped you from hitting Andrew, and made you go to bed.

The five-year drink-driving ban – it goes without saying that you were drunk.

You had us many times ring in sick for you at work when it was a hangover, not illness.

The men you've selected through drink. The relationship with most of them was about drink. You choose friends who you can drink with. Many of these people are dead because of drink.

The night Des threw your dinners at the wall and called Grace a cunt, she had to live at Louise's. You did nothing. You let your eighteen-year-old daughter leave home. When you had a breakdown because of him Louise visited every day in the asylum, took care of your house, paid the bills, made sure Colin was OK. As soon as you got well, you were back with Des.

When Claire was home from the RAF to see you, you were with Des the whole time, not once coming home to say hello to her.

Claire's family won't stay at your house unless it's unavoidable because after Grandma died you woke them at 3am, drunk, yelling that they were selfish bastards. Andrew sat up all night with you while you ranted. We loved Grandma too but never behaved this way after she died.

After Andrew died, Claire stayed with you to make sure you were OK. You opened a bottle of wine ready to get stuck in. You only stopped because Claire told you she would leave if you drank. You told anyone who would listen the next day that **you** *had decided not to drink.*

When babysitting for Louise you drank her Jack Daniels that was a 21st birthday gift.

The champagne Edwin bought for Grace and Claire's 21st, you drank and replaced with cheap wine, giving no apology.

At Grace's party you took home loads of the alcohol and when Grace confronted you, you replaced it with cheap cider.

You had to be marched upstairs by a cousin because you were drunk at the fancy-dress party. When Louise and Grace knocked for breakfast the next morning, you were still pissed.

You stole Alex's brandy and set fire to the chair while smoking.

While Conor stayed at yours when Louise was flooded, he saw you drunk frequently, being vile to Andrew who was weak with cancer at that time. Andrew apologised to Conor for him witnessing this, but obviously Conor said it wasn't his fault.

At Claire's you drank their vodka, saying you were having orange juice. They knew you were lying because the vodka went down. This is why Claire will not allow you to drink there.

At different times we had to stop you looking after Tom/Conor because of drinking. You got drunk having Tom when Grace depended on you for care as a single parent doing a nursing course. You recently told Tom not to tell Grace when you'd had a drink, which is devious and unfair to put a child in such a situation.

Grandma Roberts often asked us why you sounded 'funny' sometimes and were unkind.

Your relationships with many friends have ended because of drinking.

We know when we talk to you exactly how much you've had. It comes from years of having to, so we'd know if we were going to get any sleep or suffer music and verbal abuse.

There have been numerous fallouts over the years because of the drinking; times we didn't speak for a while. You've said that your friends thought we were awful because of this and we've had to endure being seen as the bad ones. Fortunately, we had each other. People are beginning to realise for themselves that you have a drink problem. We're not claiming to be perfect and never have done. But we've done nothing to you except respond to what you've done to us. You're lucky we're still around. We hear what other people's mothers do for them and it makes us sad. But because of the drink, we can't depend on you and have never been able to. We've simply learnt to live with this and tried to do the best we can in our lives, and with our own kids.

You have a drink problem. Address it and get help.

52

Home

*Daffodil Blindness is when in subsequent years
flowering may be reduced or fail completely. They
need extra care and attention in this time.*

I've been locked in this book for six months; and I've been locked
in my house for six weeks. Release from my story looks like it will
come first. The deaths sadly still increase. I worry that we are
developing number blindness. That it doesn't feel real.

It's just too many – too sad.

So how should I conclude a story that's incomplete? Unlike
with fiction, a memoir goes on after the final page. Things are not
neatly tied up. Questions are left unanswered. The little girl in my
first novel said of stories that there's always the end and then what
happened *after* the end. She said stories don't stop dead, and no one
lives happily ever after. That even when we die, the things we did
live on after us, like the spray from a homeward-bound ship.

I'll go on writing, I know that.

I'll have to find another story now though.

I'll have to stop looking back and return to my imagination.

I'm looking to the future. To when we come out of our houses
and I can see my brother and sisters again. To finally seeing Conor
and Ieva's new house, and to when Katy hopefully graduates next

year. Covid-19 may forever change how we interact. Now we love from afar, hug without touch, show affection with words. I know this distance. I was forced into it. Grew up in such a place. But then, as now, I miss my loved ones. Now, as then, we'll meet again.

We've been taking care of ourselves during lockdown, and of our homes. I've never seen so many newly painted fences, sparkling windows and clean cars on my daily walk. People have been buying gloss and freshening up tired rooms while we're stuck in. I painted my bedroom walls bright, hopeful yellow.

Ever since I eventually shared my picture of those riverside daffodils online, readers send me cards and give me gifts that are related to this lovely flower. I'm deeply touched by this kindness. And that's what I want my story to do; encourage kindness; open conversation; offer hope; bring another perspective. If one person reads this and finds the strength to tell someone that they were abused after burying it for years or gets help for a lifelong addiction or goes to a family member instead of to a bridge, then every sentence will have been worth recording.

I began with a radio interview and the question, when did you start writing?

The other day I said to a local BBC news reporter before I launched my new novel online, 'We just have to do things differently during lockdown.'

Then I styled my hair and put on my red lipstick. My armour. I opened the Prosecco. Behind me, I placed rows of my new book on shelves, and flowers my publisher had sent in a vase. Then I sat in my front room – on a hazy, sunny evening – and clicked Facebook Live and let the world into my home.

At one point, a hundred and twenty people were watching. *With* me. That's how it felt. Claire, Grace and Colin were there. The time difference meant Edwin watched afterwards, as did my kids. Friends from all over the world joined me. I could see their comments as I did readings and answered questions and connected.

After two hours, I started flagging. I love to make people laugh. I always have. I like people to feel safe and comfortable in my company. But it's hard keeping people entertained alone. Being your own guest.

'I don't want to switch off.' I was close to tears. 'Because then I'm just a knobhead sitting alone in my living room. Right now, I have you all with me.'

But I had to turn the camera off.

And it was just me.

What makes a house truly home is who we let in. Who we choose to share it with. We're only locked in if we don't want to be there.

I can open the door though and not be afraid of the wolf. He is still there. He might come close to the window again, circle the garden, scratch at the door, snarl at me. But I'm bigger than he is.

Home is where I am. This is my home.

I am home.

I'm just going to look back one last time. At one last letter. One that perhaps began to work where the previous didn't. And after that, it's only going to be about future words.

53

I am

A special kind of South African daffodil could be used to
treat diseases originating in the brain, including depression.
It seems that as well as enchanting the senses, these
flowers could have an important neurological usage.

You might think the 2010 letter from the previous chapter did the
trick. That our mother read it – every word of heartfelt emotion and
honesty – and changed. Realised how much she had to lose; how
hurt we were. No. You would have to be reading a fairytale, not
this story, for that to be the case. People rarely change overnight,
and rarely at someone else's prompt. It has to come from within.

But still, we tried.

At the end of 2016, I wrote one more. It followed another
ruined Christmas. They say this can be the worst time for families,
and it's true. When I volunteered with the Samaritans, we got more
desperate calls over the festive season than at any other time. The
incident involved Grace again, curiously – the daughter Mother
said she'd have adopted but would save if there was a fire.

I've always found it easier to defend my loved ones than myself.

I wrote a second letter, again with the backing of my siblings.
Sharing these letters here is the best way to summarise something
that would otherwise take twenty more chapters. It's not intended
to be cruel. I'd never share something my mother had written to

me, because that's hers, and that's private. But my note illustrates best how desperate we were again to make our mother see how we felt. How much we wanted her to stop drinking.

Dear Mother,

I'd like you to stop, in texts, making snide remarks about 'no one' being in touch with you. If you continue, I'm not going to respond. If I want to get in touch, I will. If I don't, I won't. You won't make me feel guilty. I have nothing to feel guilty about.

Right now, Grace is understandably keeping her distance after the vile things you said to her. I have no clue how I've managed to be civil, but I try to be a kind human. Now you are beginning your game with me, and I'm not going to play.

You said to Grace that she stews in her misery, she enjoyed getting her social service records, that she's bitter and money-minded, reminded her that, 'Well, your father didn't care,' and most despicable of all, said that she clearly needs more therapy. Saying something like that to anyone is vile, but to your own daughter defies anything I can think of. A daughter who recently had therapy and saw for the first time her very difficult care records.

And all this vileness simply because when you tried to contact Tom inebriated in an evening, Grace asked you politely if you would not ring drunk, but ring during the day, and go through her. That was all.

I'm tired of overlooking snide comments. I'm tired of repeatedly giving you chances, hearing excuses. I'm tired of listening to you go on and on and on about how awful Edwin is, and other people. I'm tired of being around you when you're snappy and irritable. I'm tired of putting up with it all when deep down I'm trying to deal with all the horrendous things that happened to us as children.

You said to Claire that you don't spend time looking at the past, clearly as a criticism that we are. You don't need to. You had a secure childhood, with two parents who loved you, who were there for you. We look back at the past to try and remember, to make sense, to heal. Of course you would rather bury it and not look back. You were the perpetrator of the very things we're trying to recover from.

I recently got my care records too. I know your response to that will be, 'Oh, you're all just trying to punish me, doing it to be mean.' But this isn't about you. Our whole life has been about you. You 'wanting love', your depression, your friends, your drinking, your boyfriends, your life, you.

The facts are there in our records, in black-and-white, that you didn't want us as children. I could even try and be compassionate about this, if it were to do only with postnatal depression, but this was when you were well enough to have boyfriends, well enough to have been back home and living with Robert, NOT in the hospital for almost a year as we were led to understand. You wanted us in care. You wanted Grandma to 'give up her life and come and live permanently in Hessle to look after us'. You asked about 'boarding school, nannies', anything not to have us.

Now, if this had been a childhood where you'd tried to care for us when you were well, I would happily overlook all this. But this was a childhood of you drinking, spending whole weekends at the pub or at Geraldine's or with men, while I looked after the little ones. This was a childhood with no affection, no care, with absolute neglect. Illnesses were not taken care of – a broken arm left until the next day, asthma ignored for years, eczema too. This was a childhood of cruel words (you're gormless, selfish, moody, your dad doesn't even care) and denial. Of choosing totally inappropriate men. We hoped our records might have info about Peter, but there's nothing. We as kids must carry forever the knowledge that something terrible happened to us at his hands, and not know or remember what it is, so never be able to deal with it. Social workers told you repeatedly that we 'look to you for security' because it was clearly not something you naturally thought of. You were 'irritated that we were clingy' after having been with Grandma/in foster care for almost a year. There was no compassion at how we must have all felt going through such a trauma at so young an age. We were on the observation register for four years.

We were a burden and you showed this towards us in every action, every word, every moment of neglect.

You often say, as though it's some sort of excuse, 'Well, your dad wasn't there.' I agree. He wasn't for a time. And that's something else we four must deal with, accept, face, and cope with. But rather than be compassionate about it, rather than try and make up for this other absence in our lives, you use this fact as a cruel tool, to remind us how unworthy we are of anyone taking care of us. I have never and would never say such a thing to Conor. He must be hurting enough without me reminding him that his own father gave him up. Instead, it is up to me to be both parents. I'm nowhere near perfect, but I know I've done the best I can for him. You, however, seem to rejoice in our father's faults so that your own might be ignored.

Saying to Grace that she needs more therapy is disgusting. How you can have said that and clearly not think of saying sorry for it, I'll never understand as long as I live. You clearly think we somehow have done something to you. We have done nothing but forgive and overlook, again and again and again.

Grace has distanced from you, not as punishment to you, but for her own mental and emotional wellbeing. She does not want to hurt anyone; she simply wants peace. You do not bring us peace. You do not love us how a mother should. I am accepting of this. I have over the years come to terms with this. None of us are perfect. We're all human. I'm not a perfect mother at all. But I'm a mother. You are not, because no mother would say what you said to Grace.

I want to report that this letter had a huge impact on Mother.

But I can't.

It did make Katy cry. It made a friend cry. It made me cry. But it can't have been as powerful to our mother because she continued drinking excessively for another year or so. She 'gave it up' in 2018. I put this in speech marks because we'll never truly know. Only she knows. It took a visit from Edwin during Christmas 2017, and his very firm words, to finally do the trick.

Throughout 2018 she claimed to have stopped. My lack of faith in this as fact is only due to the last forty years, to the endless lies. If she really did stop, then it's a sad irony that by the end of the year the worst depression of her life began, and ultimately led to the bridge jump. I believe that if she had stopped ten, twenty, thirty years ago, the darkness would not have descended as heavily as it did. I believe that her shocking act in 2019 would not have destroyed us all.

I'm done with it now.

She can drink or not drink.

Either way, it's not part of my future.

I am.

54

We are written

*How To Grow Daffodils Indoors: They need a cold season
to thrive and bloom. Growing them indoors is known
as forcing bulbs. When you force daffodils, you must
replicate the conditions of the cold season they would
experience if you had planted them outdoors. You must
give them hardship to be rewarded with their colour.*

Mother has enjoyed the care home following her amputation. She
has enjoyed a day out and bartering in a shop for a discount on
designer shoes because she only needs one of them. She has enjoyed
writing some poetry and playing Scrabble with other residents.

Perhaps it was because she knew a flat was being adapted so she
could move into it, and that friends were boxing her items at the old
house. A new life was being created for her. Edwin, thousands of
miles away, barely hears from her anymore, and asks us occasionally in our chat how she is.

We joke now about lockdown life in our chat.

Edwin wrote: *I've bought 400 padlocks, 3000 boxes of drawing pins
and a box of chewing gum.*

Claire wrote: *Jules is at B&Q buying all their ceramic tiles.*

I wrote: *Let's just say there are also no tampons right now in B&Q either.*

Claire wrote: *They're essential for fighting coronavirus.*

Edwin wrote: *I only have one fold-out map of Nepal – what shall I do?*

I wrote: *If you come across any hand-drawn 1983 maps of Northern
France, for God's sake buy them. Severe shortage in Hessle.*

Edwin wrote: *And how's your mother?*

She is good. Crisis over. The leg has healed without issue. She manages her mobility well. Either the drugs have kicked in or she has clawed her way back to sanity; to mental wellbeing; to as close to the human as she ever was once again. Is she drinking? It seems not, but we will never be sure. She has dried out for twelve months with little say in the matter, a variety of wards and care rooms preventing the easy availability of cheap wine. Now, with the freedom of her in-between place, she can buy and do what she wants. Whether she sees this as the chance to start afresh is up to her.

If she drinks again, I will walk away.

I can't change what she does, but I can change a lifetime of tolerating and forgiving and not speaking and making up and forgiving and tolerating and not speaking and making up. I'm done; I'll be fifty at the end of the year, my children have grown up and gone, and it's time for me.

Colin and I visited Mother in the care home just before lockdown. She was therefore one of the last people I saw in the normal, free, old world. On our way there, we went to the drive-thru MacDonald's for coffee, but it was shut. In the nearby Greggs, we got two lattes, paying the gloved and masked staff by card as they weren't accepting cash anymore.

Mother was excited about her new flat. 'I just need curtains,' she said. 'Maybe you can get me some?'

'Bigger things are happening,' I said. 'You may not be able to move if the country goes into full lockdown, which I think it will this week. Who's going to do it all?'

'Well, you can help, can't you? I know washing powder is heavy, but if I need a shop once a week you can...'

'Mother,' I interrupted firmly. 'If we go into lockdown, we won't be able to see you. We'll all have to isolate. We'll only be able to see the people we live with.'

'You'd be better off staying here,' said Colin. 'You get meals and your washing done, and there are other residents to chat to. The new flat doesn't even have carpets, and no one will be able to fit them in the near future.'

There was no telling her.

She was moving in.

We suggested getting some sun in the care home garden and followed her there in her state-of-the-art electric wheelchair. She told us she had been painting and writing poems. She read a couple to us. Partly joking, I suggested she begin a memoir of her own.

'I think it's vain to write an autobiography,' she said.

'I've started one,' I said.

'Oh. Well, I mean, if you have something to say, I suppose it's fine.'

That last day I saw her, she never referred once to what has happened, to the previous year. She never really has. Not seriously. That's fine. It's her choice. How she deals. How we have all therefore learnt to deal. By not mentioning things. By not speaking. Silenced by shame and by example. But I've finally broken that 'rule'. I've more than mentioned it – I've written every detail here. I've written about all the things I'm not supposed to. I'm not silent now.

Edwin wrote: *Let Mother enjoy her newfound freedom and independent life and you get on with yours. I've not communicated with her since before Nepal and I like it that way, I just worry about you guys.*

Grace wrote: *I'm uneasy around her. I don't understand my emotions.*

Edwin wrote: *I can understand that.*

I sent them all a picture of Colin in Mother's wheelchair.

I wrote: *UPDATE – Colin jumped this morning and he's now in a wheelchair. But he should be up and about by teatime.*

Claire wrote: *Not seeing Mother is the best decision I've ever made.*

I wrote: *Lockdown and isolation was perfectly timed…*

Mother didn't let a world crisis stop her moving into a new flat. She found a removal company who were prepared to get her in. She's there now. I haven't seen it. I can't visit due to the rules. She sent me a picture of her fridge in a random WhatsApp message and said she is delighted with it, despite the lack of carpets and curtains.

Stupidly, I'm still sad if I think of her being alone. If I think of her feeling unhappy. I have no idea why this emotion still occurs. Is it the unbreakable mother-daughter bond people speak reverently of? No. That bond never existed to begin with. Is it my personality? A flaw. A curse. A wish for something that never was and never will be. Is it the six-year-old me still looking up at her depressed mother in the daffodil-yellow dressing gown, trying to make her happy and not succeeding?

I try to explore this sadness with a level head, but a logical approach makes it even harder to understand. It's the child inside me, and I can't change how she feels. I just have to carry it around. It passes. Anger replaces it. That's the adult me. That's an understandable emotion.

But finally, I absolutely, objectively know that my mother isn't my responsibility. Her happiness is not my responsibility. Just because I feel sad for her, I don't have to act on that. I don't have to let it guide me back into past behaviours of tolerating, forgiving, overlooking, over and over and over.

The week before she jumped off the bridge, in her deepest depression, Mother said to me during a walk, 'I've never been there for you.' Having her acknowledge that was huge. I didn't say anything. I let it be. Let the words get carried away by the wind. Then I walked away before I could cry because I just can't trust her with my vulnerability in case she crushes it all over again.

When she jumped off the bridge, we all smashed up.

But I did everything I could to help her last year, a duty I wasn't obliged to fulfil. I was her voice when she didn't have one. I fought her corner. I visited her as much as I possibly could. Other difficult things happened in my life last year, things I didn't have the room or heart to explore here, that were overshadowed by my mother's suicide attempt. But I put it all aside, for her.

She is recovered now. If she remains sober, I'll see her when I feel like it; if I don't want to, I won't. I may feel guilty if I pull away, but I won't let it drive the decisions I make. I deserve to be happy. I deserve to put myself first now.

I think about care.

I think about Grandma Roberts.

It's fifteen years since she died. Hours after she passed away, when I was alone in the house, crying in my kitchen, I heard her voice as clear as though she was in the room with me. 'It's alright, Louise,' she said. 'It will always be alright.'

She was the only adult who ever made me feel it would be.

Grace and I visited Mother's old house today – The Cottage – for what could be the last time now it's up for sale, to get her the keys from the outside safe. It was bare. Echoey. Dusty. Cobwebby. Cold. Boxes were stacked in the corner of the kitchen as though playful children had been building a castle. We looked through them. Found photographs. Not many of us when we were small; the few there, we hadn't seen for years because they had been in the loft all this time. There were staged snaps of us around Father Christmas, our smiles forced; posed ones with a professional photographer, smiles barely there; natural ones of us girls in a church garden, wearing white veils, smiles natural; cute ones of Colin being bathed in a sink.

I saw the four of us, as we used to be, long ago.

I imagined our voices.

I heard us whispering, 'We're glad someone is finally telling our story.'

I put two of the pictures in my bag to take home. They should be enjoyed, framed, not hidden away in a damp cardboard box.

Grace and I were quiet in our thoughts. I felt immense pride in her in that moment. In all of my siblings. How far they have come. How brave they have been. How much I love them.

We left The Cottage. That's what it was for a brief moment, in its emptiness, in its readiness to be home for a new family, for the first time in forty years. Would someone else find happiness here? Would they scrub the walls, gut the place, demolish and rebuild? Would the ghosts be gentle ones, or would they stagger up the stairs? Would they hear the whispers of our past, childish voices, echoes of music?

I hope not.

We're not there anymore. That time is done.

I've written our words.

We are written.

Afterword

In 2021, aged fifty, I ended my relationship with my mother.

I wish her safety, wellness and happiness.

I wish that for myself too, but it might never happen while she's in my life.

It hasn't been easy, and I'm often sad, but my mental health has improved greatly.

Acknowledgements

A huge thank you to my earliest readers who were my siblings, Grace, Claire and Colin, and Uncle Edwin. They read each chapter as I wrote it, and – as you'll have seen – they contributed invaluable memories and stories to the book. I could never have written it without them. Nor could I have written it without the support of my dear husband Joe, and my children Katy and Conor, who are quieter background characters in this story, but whose presence deeply sustained me.

Thank you also to my beta readers who gave feedback at the next stage, John Marrs, Madeleine Black, Lynda Harrison, and Susie Lynes. You were the first people outside of my family to read the things I'd never shared with anyone. I'm also grateful to Victoria Goldman for the early edit – you have such sharp and perceptive eyes. Lots of love and gratitude as well to Lesley Harcourt who narrated the audiobook version, adding nuance and lyricism to my, at times, painful words.

Big love to my extraordinary and dear agent Emily Glenister at DHH Literary who has been fighting my corner for almost two years. We knew we had a challenge with this book, for many reasons, but she never gave up.

I am indebted to the brilliant gang at Mardle for bringing my very personal and raw story to the page so beautifully, and with such a fantastic, touching cover. Thank you Jo Sollis, Mel Sambells, Kaz Harrison, and Duncan Proudfoot for your passion, for the belief in my story, and for giving me a physical legacy I can keep on my shelf forever.

During the period that I wrote this memoir, and shared the journey on social media, I received the most wonderful messages and support from followers and friends. I was inundated with daffodil inspired gifts and cards, which has continued ever since. Thank you to all those kind people.

Books need readers, and I'm eternally grateful to all the wonderful bibliophiles out there who have read my previous novels and who may hopefully now read this memoir. I place myself in your hands again, and I thank you in advance for giving my own story your time too.